122

D0397874

THE

LUNAR

HOUSEWIFE

❖ ❖ ❖
❖ ❖
❖
❖

ALSO BY CAROLINE WOODS

Fräulein M.

THE

LUNAR
HOUSEWIFE

A NOVEL

CAROLINE
WOODS

❖ ❖ ❖
❖ ❖
❖

DOUBLEDAY

NEW YORK

www.doubleday.com

DOUBLEDAY and the portrayal of an anchor with a dolphin are
registered trademarks of Penguin Random House LLC.

*Jacket images: woman © RetroAtelier/E+/Getty Images;
stars © Erick Ventura/EyeEm/Getty Images
Jacket design by Michael J. Windsor
Book design by Pei Loi Koay*

LIBRARY OF CONGRESS CATALOGING-IN-PUBLICATION DATA
Names: Woods, Caroline (Caroline Courtney), author.
Title: The lunar housewife : a novel / by Caroline Woods.
Description: First edition. | New York : Doubleday, [2022]
Identifiers: LCCN 2021030507 (print) |
LCCN 2021030508 (ebook) |
ISBN 9780385547833 (hardcover) |
ISBN 9780385547840 (ebook)
Classification: LCC PS3623.O6752 L86 2022 (print) |
LCC PS3623.O6752 (ebook) | DDC 813/.6—dc23
LC record available at https://lccn.loc.gov/2021030507
LC ebook record available at https://lccn.loc.gov/2021030508

MANUFACTURED IN THE UNITED STATES OF AMERICA
1 3 5 7 9 10 8 6 4 2
First Edition

For my daughters,

with a wink

PART I

SUMMER

1953

✦ ✦ ✦

✦ ✦

✦

✦

◦ | ◦

In a room packed to the gills with New York mucky-mucks—
Truman Capote was tucked into a corner of the couch; Arthur
Miller, sans Marilyn, stood smoking by the window—I had
my attention fixed on a waitress.

I hadn't noticed her peeping at me until Joe and I went to
stand at the fireplace beside Harry and Glenys. Scanning the
party guests, I landed on her and froze, the champagne glass
cold in my clammy palm. Harry began delivering his toast
beside me, but I didn't hear a word. Joe's hand rested, warm
and firm, at the small of my back.

The waitress stood apart from the crowd, tall and slim,
holding her empty tray against her thighs. She wore the
typical uniform: black blouse, black pencil skirt, tawny hair
pulled into a chignon. Her eyes were narrowed in my direction. I knew her name: Beverly.

I prayed she didn't remember mine.

". . . the more anyone said, 'Hell, you can get sports on the
radio, you can get politics from the *Times* or the *Journal*,' the
more we'd pack it in!" Harry crowed to resounding laughter. "How many times did I ask you, Joe—'How much will it
cost to add another teensy four-hundred-word feature? Just
another column?'"

"Every damn day," Joe replied, to more laughter.

I tore my gaze from Beverly and smiled stiffly at our audience. Damn it to hell. This was supposed to be a hotshot moment for me. Sure, most of these people probably saw me simply as Joe Martin's girl, the armpiece of one of *Downtown* magazine's founders. Little did they know I had written a feature for this issue, right after the short story from Flannery O'Connor.

"Anyway, thank you for believing in us sons of bitches," Harry continued.

Everyone cheered, lifting little bowls of champagne like sparkling breasts. We'd gathered to celebrate the launch of *Downtown*'s second issue in Harry and Glenys's apartment, a sprawling classic six on the Upper East Side. There'd been a more formal party for the first issue, which had been a smashing success largely thanks to Harry's popular article about the storied Harvard-Yale football contest, "The Oldest Man at the Game." This should've been a more intimate bash, but the living room was crammed with people, three-quarters of them male. The attractiveness of the remaining quarter, the female guests, far outperformed the national average.

Joe took a step forward. "If I can add a few words," he addressed the room in a voice that wasn't quite his own. I could smell his sweat and the metallic tang of the Saint Christopher medal he tucked under his collar. "Harry and I—well, especially Harry—were confident we'd make it to a second issue, but we appreciate your faith in us. Thank you for spreading the word among writers, for bringing investors. . . ."

Harry lifted his foggy champagne glass. "And if Nelson

Rockefeller were here, we'd say, 'Thanks a heap for the interview, old man!'"

"To Rocky!" shouted a guy on the couch, lifting up his joint. Coils of smoke ribboned around him. Everyone laughed again, everyone but me.

I cleared my throat and waited for the noise to die down before delivering my planned line. Unconsciously, I glanced toward Beverly, who, thank goodness, was being led into the kitchen by the bartender. I tucked a tendril of red hair behind my ear. "Oh, boys," I said loudly, and the din died down, a hundred eyes on me, everyone waiting to hear what this dish had to add to the speech. "You forgot to thank Miss Newmar for bringing the cheesecake!"

The room erupted in applause as a plush-lipped young actress named Julie Newmar, her mile-long legs sheathed in fishnet stockings, stood and genuflected. I, like everyone else in the room, could picture just what was under her velvet blouse; Miss Newmar had appeared topless on the inside back cover of *Downtown* No. 2. Harry whistled and clapped. Beside me, I sensed Glenys clenching her teeth.

The toast over, Joe and I turned to each other and clinked glasses of Veuve Clicquot. There was still a bit of bashfulness between us, a little electricity crackling in our brief kiss. We'd been inseparable for a year and a half, ever since we met at a *New Yorker* party while Joe was still working there.

I turned around to see that Glenys and Harry stood slightly apart from each other, both of them blitzed. A rowdy group of men were already calling him from across the room, while his wife hung back, her face grayish. Here was the tragic difference between the two of them: as they drank, she grew more limp, he the opposite. And women adored him. Harry had been first baseman at Yale and grew up sailing off Martha's Vineyard. He made a good public face for *Downtown:* he was the blueblood talent, the boyish philosopher, while Joe drew the plans and raised the money.

"Where're the kids tonight, doll?" I whispered to Glenys, squeezing her elbow as she watched her husband walk away.

"Mmph, don't remind me I've got kids," she slurred, then, after a beat, added, "They're at the nanny's." She looked as if she needed a bubble bath and a long night's sleep. Fortunately, Joe came up behind me then and rested his warm lips against my ear.

"Louise," he said, "there's someone I'd like you to meet."

"Oh, darling. You're finally introducing me to your mother," I joked, but my heart began beating very quickly.

"My mother's not allowed within fifty miles of this place." He gestured to a couple getting frisky on the sofa, the man's hand traveling past the girl's garters. "No, it's even better than that. This could be a big night for you, too, Lou."

I licked my lips and took his hand. As we crossed the room, I hated that I had to worry about Beverly, to look for her tall frame among the crowd, but she was nowhere to be seen. Joe led me past men whose importance oozed from the leather patches on their elbows, past waiters with trays of canapés. Beside the bookcases, a group of guys were trying to pour champagne into a pyramid of glasses, even though everyone knows that never works, and I caught a glimpse of Glenys nervously eyeing her Oriental rug.

"Is that . . ." I said as a dashing, suntanned man brushed past me, flanked by two girls. He looked just like the actor

Rory Calhoun, whom we'd seen a few weeks ago in the Western *The Silver Whip*.

"It is." Joe's grin stretched from ear to ear. Harry might've been the more obviously handsome of the two of them, with his blond hair and big shoulders, but he was a bit too buggy-eyed for me. Plus, I didn't do the married-man thing. Joe had caught my eye the minute I saw him, setting off a hunger like I'd never known, and I'd been hungry in one way or another for much of my life. At twenty-eight, he was a few years my senior. His roots were nearly as humble as mine—Italian red sauce, tenement life—but that didn't show in his exterior. He had a shock of black hair combed carefully with pomade, a wiry, strong build, and intense dark eyes that looked through you and past you and beyond, laser-pointed on the future.

I didn't realize until we were toe to toe that Joe had brought me to the feet of Mortimer Clifton, the new publisher at Clifton & Sons now that his father had finally retired. I recognized him from pictures in the society pages: thick white hair, tufty black eyebrows. Towering over everyone at nearly seven feet tall, Mr. Clifton was a physical reminder of the famous old men he published—Hemingway, Fitzgerald, that ilk.

"Mort," Joe said, his voice nearly squeaking in excitement to use the man's nickname, "I'd like you to meet my friend Louise Leithauser."

I grasped the man's dry hand. "Mr. Clifton, it's an honor."

"Oh. A pleasure to meet you, too," he replied. He'd been in the middle of a point, it seemed; the two smaller men who'd been lapping up his words glanced at us in irritation.

"Louise is an aspiring novelist," Joe yelled over the music.

"Are you?" Clifton spoke in a somewhat unnatural-sounding accent, formal and vaguely English. "What do you write?"

"I'm writing a romance," I replied, and the sycophants around him snickered.

Clifton raised his eyebrows politely. I had the sense he was abiding me at this point, waiting for me to leave. "We've done a few of those. Don't laugh, gentlemen," he said to his audience, even as a note of amusement lifted one of his wolfish eyebrows an inch higher. "They sell like hotcakes, especially in England, but here, too. The girls can't get enough of them."

I made myself smile warmly. "It's not all that I do. I've also written a few political pieces for *Downtown*. Under my pen name, Alfred King. I wrote the last issue's story about the unrest in Iran."

The smirks on the two lackeys' faces were gone, replaced by uncomfortable stares. They looked pained. Clifton inspected me as if I were something he'd discovered on a flower petal, a curious little bug. "Well!" he said, after a beat. "Mr. King, we meet at last. I read that Iran story. I found it very interesting. But if I'd known the author was a gorgeous redhead, I'd have read more closely!"

The other men laughed now, happy to be in familiar territory. Reluctantly, I tittered along with them. If it hadn't been crass to discuss money, I'd have told them just what Joe had paid me for the article, down to the penny—probably more than either of these guys had made for a single piece in his entire career.

"Louise is one of our best writers." Joe paused. "And certainly the most beautiful."

Clifton laughed again, then reached out to chuck my chin, as if I were a five-year-old. I took it with my teeth set. "You should send me your book when it's done," he said easily, "and I'll pass it along to our paperback team." With that he went back to his conversation.

Joe and I drifted away, in the direction of one of the waiters. My head spun. *Send me your book when it's done*—he'd said it to me as if it were not at all unusual, as if I were one of the boys. I felt the urge to bolt, to run home to my typewriter.

No, no, I needed to throw my manuscript away, to start anew; I suddenly realized my novel-in-the-works was shit and should be tossed into my furnace. What did I think I was doing, putting my heroine on the moon, for Pete's sake! Was I crazy?

I had other ideas, didn't I? Or were they all shit, too?

I needed a drink.

"Okay," I said to Joe as I took a Manhattan, served up and filled to the brim, off the waiter's tray. "I'm impressed."

Joe's face broke open in mock offense. "I knew it. You've been using me all this time to get your novel published."

"How dare you even suggest it, my love," I said, pulling him in for a kiss so that he wouldn't see how I was blushing. I kept my eyes open, looking around for Beverly.

For the rest of the evening, I tried worming my way back into conversation with Mort Clifton, but the pack of eager dogs who followed him about the party (all with the bad haircuts and shiny elbows of aspiring writers) was difficult to penetrate. Clifton left early; I'd hoped to corner him in the bedroom where they kept our wraps and coats, but it seemed he hadn't brought one. Dejected, I returned to the party. I watched Joe play host, hobnobbing with other writers and edging his way toward Rory Calhoun, who looked bored as he leaned away from the young women caging him in. In general, Joe seemed ecstatic. I decided not to bother him.

I flopped down on the sofa and took out my compact, slicked my pet shade of Revlon onto my lips. Glenys sat on the opposite side of the couch. I noticed her silk scarf starting to dip into her whiskey sour. "Dear." I reached for her knee. "Are you all right?"

Behind her, in the kitchenette, Harry already had his hand resting at the base of a young woman's back, a girl with a stunning figure.

"Mmm, fine." Glenys tried to slap my hand away. I knew she assumed I'd gone to bed with Harry. Everyone else had. She may not have been able to imagine it, but Joe and I were loyal to each other.

I waved, now, to Harry, and the girl he was with turned around. My skin froze when I saw that it was Beverly. She'd even removed her apron. Ignoring her, Harry came around the kitchen island and into the living room, where he slapped Glenys's thigh as if she were a horse.

"Evening, Louise," he addressed me, smiling with red, moistened eyes. Bourbon wafted my way. "Tell me, what's the latest on your brother?"

I felt my face grow hot. My twin brother, Paul, had last been seen on a hill near Pyongyang. No one outside my family, aside from Joe, knew he had been declared missing in action. I feared saying it aloud would make it more real.

"Still in Korea." I flicked my cigarette at the little tray on the coffee table. "Last I heard from him, he was doing all right."

Last I'd heard from him was in April. This was July.

Harry nodded thoughtfully as Glenys, whose eyes had closed shut, tipped toward him. He brushed his blond hair from his forehead and offered me a dazzling smile. For a total cad, he was a brilliant writer. In "The Oldest Man at the Game," he'd managed to sound square and glamorous at the same time. The life of enthusiasm, which he claimed the kids currently at Harvard and Yale were lacking, was one of fine whiskey, finer women, and all the spoils of postwar American capitalism. He claimed half of the Harvard kids had still been in bed at kickoff, then roused themselves only by halftime to linger in Harvard Stadium's student sections in neither Crimson red nor Bulldog blue but disappointing black. "Dare I say it's time," Harry had trumpeted, "for us who came of age during the war to tell these damned kids to get *excited* about *something*?"

Joe teased me for how I'd fawned over Harry's article, but I'd gobbled it up. The boys had met in the Ivy League, but I was a product of the SUNY system and took some pleasure in hearing Harry scold those indolent prep-school graduates. For my part, I'd worked hard and hadn't had anything handed to me on a silver platter, and to me, that was the epitome of the American Dream.

"Peace talks continue, you know," Harry said now, referring to Korea.

I took in a deep breath, letting my rib cage expand. Peace talks had been going on for two years. "Armistice any day now," I said, willing it to be true.

Harry craned his neck; someone had called him from the kitchen. "Your brother will be out in six months," he said. "Mark my words." At that, Glenys plopped facedown in his lap. There was a sprinkling of laughter as he lifted her back onto the cushions, then stood up.

"Harry," I called after him, glancing nervously at the crowd in the kitchen. I couldn't tell if Beverly was still among them. "Can't you just"—I gestured toward Glenys, sleeping on the couch—"keep your wife company, for once."

"Oh, Louise. Don't be a party pooper." He slithered away.

I spent a few seconds chewing my nail, then went to find my purse and Joe. "Time for me to make like a banana," I whispered into his ear, visibly irritating the chubby-faced writer who'd been deep in conversation with him about how to punctuate poetry properly in print.

"That's a lotta 'p' words." My comment produced a sour-puss look from the hanger-on.

Joe took my hand. "Just one more minute, and I'll get you a taxi."

I stood beside him with my arms crossed as they blathered about margins. I understood if Joe couldn't come home with me tonight, but he'd damned better give me a proper goodbye and put me in a taxi. The magazine's sponsors were paying for this party; I figured they could also foot the bill for my cab.

People were leaving now in twos and threes, citing the various bars and lounges where they could be found. On the sofa, Glenys began to snore. Two stoned young men managed to unlatch strands of crystals from the chandelier in the foyer and drape them around her sleeping body as if she were Bathsheba. "For the love of . . ." I said to Joe and the poet, who glanced over for a second. "Would you look at what's happening over here? Does no one care?"

Glenys didn't even stir when Harry came stumbling past her. My heart leapt to my throat when I saw he had his fingers intertwined with Beverly's as she dragged him to the bedroom. She gave me a meaningful look as she passed.

"Can't go in there . . ." Harry said, slurring his words. His blue eyes fluttered; his sandy hair was matted with sweat. He stopped at the door of the bedroom. "Can't go in, they're listening. They're listening."

Beverly giggled. I could tell she'd helped herself to several cocktails on the job. "Who's listening?"

Harry steadied himself with a hand on the wall. "The FBI, darling, the FBI. The CIA. All of them. They're watching. . . . They're listening, they have bugs everywhere—"

In a rush, Joe came alive. He was there with his arms under Harry's before I'd even realized he'd left my side. I followed him. "What are you on about, old chum," Joe said, out of breath, "little green men?"

"The little green men," Harry mumbled, nodding. "Them, too . . ."

"Come on," Joe said in a lower tone, "at least have the decency to take this bird into the guest bedroom. Let your wife have her own pillow."

Joe's suggestion seemed gentlemanly, in a way, and I heard someone applaud, but the whole scene was nauseating. I took this as my cue to take Glenys, stumbling, to her room and lock the door. People's damned wraps and hats were all over the bed. I took the pile and dumped it in the hallway.

"Hey!" someone yelled. I shut the door.

There were brightly painted toys scattered on her bedroom rug, a baby bottle half full of milk leaking a small puddle on her carpet. "Come on, Glenys," I said in a gentle voice. I took off her shoes when she curled atop the blanket, and I stared at the four bulbous bedposts, considering what Harry had said about bugs.

"Louise."

Her voice stopped me just as I reached the door. I felt depressed to think she knew more of what was going on than I'd realized. "Glenys?"

"Thank you." I could hear tears in her voice.

I inhaled. "Get some sleep, darling." After closing the door, I stepped over the pile of coats in the hallway. A few stragglers with red eyes and sweaty hair huddled on the sofas and armchairs. One couple argued. Another were passed out, arms around each other. The carpets reeked of spilled liquor. Joe and Harry were nowhere to be seen. I found Beverly slumped against the wall beside the spare bedroom. Her eyelids had fallen shut.

After glancing around to make sure no one could hear us, I toed her thigh with my shoe. "Go home."

She opened one eye. "Louise Leithauser," she said. "Didn't you and I work a party together one time? The *New Yorker* Christmas party, right?"

Shit. She did remember me. "Sorry, sweetheart, you have me confused with someone else," I said, even though she'd gotten my name spot-on. "Go home. You're in another woman's apartment. Her children will be back in the morning." I stood over Beverly for a minute, until, finally, she flung the chain of her pocketbook over her shoulder and got up to leave.

The door to the spare bedroom was open a crack. I put

my hand on it, ready to step inside, but what I saw through the gap stopped me. Joe had Harry by the lapels of his jacket. Harry's head lolled. He was bigger than Joe, but Joe held him upright. I strained to hear what he was saying over the dregs of the music.

". . . dangerous, you hear me? You can't go around saying things like that, you could get us in a lot of trouble."

A long, low laugh rolled up from Harry's throat. "Dangerous, you're telling me it's dangerous? You're the one got us all mixed up in this horseshit. . . . Told you it was dangerous—"

Joe cut him off. "Didn't hear you complain when he gave us the bread. And you sure as hell don't mind . . ." His voice lowered, and I missed the rest of his sentence.

"Didn't need him," Harry mumbled. "I coulda done . . ."

"He's here now," Joe said. "So shut up."

"Or else what?"

"Or you'll get us . . . I don't know . . . killed."

My breath caught in my throat. I put my hand over my mouth to keep myself from letting out a little shriek.

There was a pause. "Well!" Harry said, sounding much sharper than he should have been. "Even I think you're being just a bit dramatic."

Someone came behind me and shoved open the door; damned Beverly had come back, announcing loudly that she was looking for her wrap. Joe sprang backward from Harry, stumbling into the nightstand. Harry just turned and gave me a murky, sheepish look. Then he pulled Beverly onto the bed.

I watched them, alarmed, wondering if she'd say anything to Harry about me, wondering what Joe had meant when he threatened Harry.

Joe came quickly to me and cupped my elbows in his palms. "Are you ready to leave?" he said with a false attempt at cheer, trying to steer me toward the front door of the apartment. "Let's find your things."

"Joe," I whispered. "What was that about? You said you might be killed."

"It's a figure of speech," he said at the coat closet. "Here, your gloves."

I stood with my arms crossed. I'd almost have believed him if I hadn't seen the look on his face when he caught me listening. He'd sent a little tray on the nightstand crashing onto the floor, coins and buttons flying this way and that. We stared at each other a moment, Joe's dark eyes boring holes into my head.

In a sense, it was a relief to discover that he might have some secrets of his own.

"I just hope you aren't mixed up in anything unsavory," I said, shoving one arm into my cardigan.

"Unsavory? Me?" He laughed lightly as he reached around me to open the door. "What could be unsavory about editing a little old magazine for men?"

2

The apartment I rode home to that night was no palace. I lived up in Yorkville, at Ninetieth and Second, above an Italian restaurant that reeked of garlic and sent at least one stray mouse a day up the pipes and into my kitchen. More than once, I'd enlisted the waiters downstairs to kill one of the little bastards, which they did, horribly, with the help of my long-bristled broom and a heavy stomp. I had only a refrigerator and a hot plate, a bathtub in the kitchen, and a bedroom so small that my bed touched three walls. Once, I'd noticed a footprint on the wall at the foot of the bed. Joe's—it was too large to be mine. I'd had to scrub it off right before my mother arrived for a last-minute visit.

My mother had never met Joe, knew nothing about him, in fact, and that was all right by me. He might've come from humble stock himself, but I worried that, if he met my mother and saw her missing tooth, her hands chapped from scrubbing the houses of the richer set in Ossining, New York, he'd look back at me and finally realize I'd been working as a waitress when we met at the *New Yorker* party.

Shortly after I met Joe I'd stopped waitressing, when I found a job at a law office on the Upper West Side, doing the typing and filing for an old, kindly divorce lawyer. The money wasn't bad, but I wanted more out of life. I wasn't writing a romance by coincidence. I was writing one because the things sold. If my mother had taught me anything, it was that we girls couldn't rely on men to take care of us forever. Any of them could become drunks, like my father, or be called to war, like my brother. I planned to be able to support myself. Hell, more than that—I planned to buy myself a fur and real silk stockings. I wanted it to be my smug, smiling face on the back jacket of a best-seller, and since my name wasn't Jerome or Norman, I'd have to write something for the girls.

The *Downtown* No. 2 party had been on a Sunday evening, and for the next few nights I didn't see Joe. I went to bed alone in my cold cream and rag rollers, unable to sleep, wondering if Beverly had said anything to Harry about me, replaying what I'd heard Joe say to Harry that night. It had sounded as if they were beholden to someone who'd given them money. Joe was Italian, but the likelihood of them going to the Mafia for magazine funding seemed far-fetched to me, and the idea of rich-boy Harry running to a moneylender was something out of science fiction.

Joe finally phoned me on Tuesday evening.

"Hello, handsome," I said. "Interesting party the other night." I'd been thinking about how to press him on what he'd said to Harry. "If I didn't know better, I'd have thought you and Harry were in trouble with a loan shark."

"What? Sorry, I'm calling from a pay phone on Fifth. Just had a meeting . . ." Car horns honked behind him, right on cue. "Listen, I've got a proposition for you. How would you like to go with me to Rome?"

"Rome!" My desire to probe him vanished. "As in Italy?"

Joe laughed. "Yes, as in Italy. Not Rome, Georgia. Are you in?"

"Rome!" I'd been trying to peel an orange in one go, but the rind ripped and dropped to the floor. I sucked my fingers. "When do we leave?"

"Next Monday."

"Oh . . ." My mind scrambled. I'd have to ask my boss at the law office, and I wasn't sure how much vacation Mr. Franklin would allow me. "You don't give a girl much notice, do you?"

"Listen, Lou, it's a trip to meet with some investors, and I had to twist their arm to throw in another ticket on the jet."

"The jet," I repeated, breathlessly. I'd never flown before, never gone any farther from New York than Chicago. "Just think. Next Monday, we'll be orbiting the Earth."

A sound whooshed into the receiver, like rain on a tin roof, and Joe cursed. "Damned truck—now my pants are all wet. We won't be orbiting exactly, Lou. We're not going all the way around."

"No need to pack my space helmet, then."

A burst of laughter. "I love you, Lou."

I felt my cheeks turn crimson, a silly grin spread across my face. We'd only said it to each other a handful of times. "I love you, too."

Joe and I did it all wrong upon arrival at Ciampino Airport—slept off our jet lag when we got to our hotel, an oleander-shaded yellow building near the Colosseum, just after ten in the morning Italian time. Then we woke at 6:00 p.m., with ravenous appetites. I stepped into patent heels and threw on black sunglasses, even though the light was beginning to wane. I already felt like a woman of mystery; we'd checked in, blushing and smirking, as "Mr. and Mrs. Samuel Clemens" so that they wouldn't give us a hard time about sharing a *camera matrimoniale*.

"So, Mr. Clemens, what's on our agenda?" I asked Joe after we found a spaghetteria around the corner and tucked in. The spaghetti with cream, salmon, and capers was the best thing I'd ever eaten.

"This takes me right back to my grandmother's house," Joe said as he cut his pasta. He'd ordered *amatriciana*, which turned out to be red sauce with what looked like bacon and seemed more at home in a Jersey kitchen than at a Roman table, at least to me.

"Oh Lord, Lou," he said, watching me lift a huge ball of spaghetti to my mouth and bite it, a few leftover strands dangling. "If anything could make me lose my appetite right now . . ."

"I know, I know," I said, mouth full of pasta. "Real Italians don't twirl. You forget I'm not a real Italian."

"You're not even a faux Italian," he replied, grinning. The humidity brought a curl to his combed hair. He seemed more Italian to me here in Italy, and even more desirable. I'd already known he spoke the language with his parents, but he never did it for me. I'd loved hearing him converse with the driver, concierge, waiter, though he seemed to feel the opposite; his cheeks flushed as the words tripped off his tongue, and when we checked in he'd told me to stop staring at him.

"Our agenda, Mrs. Clemens," he said now, "is as follows: Tomorrow I have meetings in the morning with potential investors in the magazine. Then, tomorrow night, we shall have dinner with a mystery guest."

I raised my eyebrows. "A mystery guest! Am I allowed to ask for clues?"

Joe thought for a bit, a dimple showing in his cheek. A breeze caught the flowered tree above his chair, dappling his face with setting sunlight. "Clue number one: he's American."

"Jack Kennedy."

He laughed into his napkin. "You think I'd be this calm if that were the case? No, he's a writer. Clue number two: you've read his book."

"That isn't much of a hint," I scoffed. "Could be anybody." I blotted my lips, inspecting my napkin. "Say, what was that with the driver this morning?"

His forehead wrinkled. "The driver?"

"When you tried to tip him. He wouldn't take payment."

To my surprise, we'd been greeted on the tarmac by a driver in crisp uniform, holding a sign that read MR. JOSEPH MARTINO. Joe had tried to pay him when we reached our hotel, but the man smiled, said something in Italian that Joe could understand but I could not, and drove off.

Joe shrugged. "Maybe they don't tip here." He continued shoveling pasta into his mouth.

"But who paid him to begin with? Had you arranged it in advance?" I asked, and when he didn't answer, I giggled. "And he wrote 'Martino' instead of 'Martin.'"

"My family's name probably *was* Martino, before Ellis Island," he said.

"Oh, but you should change it back! Martino is so much more interesting than Martin."

"Martin sounds more American," he said firmly, as though this explained itself. He took a healthy sip of red wine. "You should know that, with a name like Leithauser. That can't have been easy during the wars."

I considered this. I'd always blamed my father's drinking for his auto upholstery shop having gone out of business, but perhaps the name "Leithauser Custom Interiors" had something to do with it. He'd had Hummel figurines perched on the dusty windowsills: a boy fishing, a little girl with the Big Bad Wolf.

Joe was waiting for me to respond, but we'd veered dangerously close to questions regarding my family. "What's in a name, anyway," I said, and I reached to offer Joe a forkful of my pasta.

"Let's just go in for a quick dip," Joe murmured.

By two in the morning, after wine had loosened our joints and tongues and set us laughing again as we explored the city on foot, we'd returned to the hotel to find we were not at all tired. I liked Joe when he was three sheets to the wind. He grew bolder, sillier, more likely to take charge. He'd led us to the white wrought-iron railing of our hotel pool, the two of us trying not to make noise and having a bad time of it. The courtyard had a view of the illuminated, fortresslike Castel Sant'Angelo, but by now the pool was locked up, dark, the lounge chairs piled atop one another, the water as smooth as glass. Behind the pool, the city glittered and hummed. The traffic never seemed to stop.

"We don't even have our bathing suits," I hissed, but before I knew it Joe had hoisted me up, his warm, sweaty hands under my foot, and I placed the other atop a curlicue in the gate.

"Shh, shh," he said as I yelped. He hopped over behind me, to land lightly on his hands and the balls of his feet.

We plunged into the pool in our underwear, breaking the still surface into choppy waves. The water felt different, somehow, from American pool water—slicker and softer, as if we were wading through oil.

"Let's go up on one of those lounge chairs," Joe whispered into my wet hair, giggling like a schoolboy. I could feel him grow hard against my leg. He may have been a gentleman, the boy in the library rather than on the football field, but put a drop of blood in the water and all sharks act the same.

We kissed deeply, hands cradling each other's faces. With every kiss my resolve crumbled. I thought about the diaphragm I'd packed, which remained in its case in the hotel above. "Joe, we can't. Not right now."

Joe responded with a lingering kiss. "Please," he whispered against my mouth. "Please."

I tasted wine and cigarettes and his own particular sweetness. His skin felt slippery and firm, warm in the chilly pool. *Ding-ding* rang the warning bells in my brain, and yet I could not tear myself away from him.

We began to make love right there in the pool, engulfed in the delicious fear that someone would come shine a flashlight on us at any moment. Soon we moved to a lounge chair, bodies intertwined, blissfully unaware of how uncomfortable the positions of our elbows and knees would normally feel. I burrowed my face in Joe's wet hair, which still smelled of pomade.

Afterward, we found white towels in a bin near the shuttered bar. We lay on the same lounge chair, breathing, watching clouds illuminated by streetlights. It had to be at least three in the morning by now, maybe even four. The clouds parted, and the moon appeared, so full and white that it made me gasp. The Italians called her *la luna*, one of the few words I knew in the language. It may have been the wine, or the magic of the place, but for the first time I thought of her as "she." "I'd like to go up there," I murmured.

"Castel Sant'Angelo?"

"No. The moon." I rolled onto my side. "What if you looked up there and saw . . . writing, in the dust?"

"Ha! What would it say?"

"Send help! SOS!"

Joe laughed a little, closing his eyes. I shimmied onto my back. "I'd like to be an astronaut," I said. "Can you imagine the view of the Earth? The way you'd bounce? There's very little gravity."

He sighed. "That sounds nice. To be weightless."

I rolled over, thinking of what he'd said to Harry at the party, the anxiety that had been in his voice. "What do you mean?" I asked. "Have you been feeling heavy?"

He hesitated. From somewhere behind the hotel walls came a shout, followed by a sprinkling of youthful Italian voices. A light went on inside one of the rooms.

"Come on," Joe said, taking my hand. "We need to find a way back over the fence."

The next morning, he came out of the bedroom with his tie untied, holding a copy of *Popular Science*. "How'd this get in here?"

I'd been drinking peach nectar from a champagne flute, my freckled legs extended into the balcony's sun. My hair was still in rollers. I reached over to fix his tie, but first, I took my magazine. An illustration of the planet Saturn decorated its cover. "It's mine. I brought it from home."

"You read *Popular Science* now?"

I knotted the tie tightly. "A girl can only take so much *Glamour*."

"What's the matter with *Glamour*?"

I sighed. "*Glamour*—the magazine 'for the girl with a job'—is mostly made up of ads for silver patterns. Doesn't seem like they expect the girls to keep the jobs for long."

"You have to admit, most girls don't."

"I guess." I reached up to kiss him. "Good luck. Who are you meeting with again?"

"Some people from an outfit called the Congress for Cultural Freedom."

"The what?" The name struck an odd chord. It sounded more like a government agency than a donor. "Congress like U.S. Congress?"

"No, nothing like that." He took control of his own tie, messing up what I'd fixed. "It's an independent organization formed in Western Europe for funding the arts abroad."

"All right, say no more." I pointed to a spot on his chin. "You missed some whiskers." He disappeared back into the bathroom, and a second later I heard the buzz of his electric razor.

When, at last, he was gone, I let my hair down and styled it in loose waves, a brushed-under bob like Grace Kelly's. I pulled another silk scarf out of my suitcase, which I'd spread open on the bed. I'd maybe gone overboard in my preparations, splurging on a new wardrobe in a black-and-white scheme, red for accents: full skirts, Juliet hats and matching gloves, a see-through robe to wear for Joe, a quilted dressing gown for room service.

I put on a snug cardigan and white linen trousers, the sunglasses and scarf, and went out. Part of me wanted to explore the city by myself on foot and eat gelato out of a tall paper cone, but I'd been longing to write for days. I posted myself near the open front window of the first café I found. Stainless-steel espresso pots gleamed on the stove, and the air smelled of flaky pastry.

The waiter didn't even bother with Italian. "Good day, madame. What can I serve you?"

"Umm." All my Berlitz went out the window. "A pastry, please, and *un cappuccino*."

His eyes rolled. "*Un cappuccino*, coming right up."

A man in short sleeves and dark sunglasses had come in and taken a seat a few tables away from me, newspaper opened in front of his face. Something about him seemed American, though I couldn't say what. Maybe his full face and puffy, whitish hair; the Italians seemed to wear theirs shorter. But his newspaper was in Italian. When I got up to fetch an extra napkin from the counter, I noticed that he had an English-language book hidden behind the Italian newspaper. I tapped it and he looked up, startled.

"Shh," I said. "Your secret is safe with me."

"I—oh." He closed the book sheepishly. "*Grazie*."

"*De nada*," I said. "I only speak Spanish." We both laughed. I caught the waiter's grimace as he frothed milk behind the bar. Without a doubt, we were confirming every unflattering preconception he had about Americans.

I went back to my table, pulled the cap off a brand-new pen, and began to write.

THE LUNAR HOUSEWIFE

The Traveler

A little starship, no bigger than a Volkswagen bug, shot through Earth's atmosphere and into the starry beyond. Its target: our rocky satellite.

There were three men inside, but they would not stay long. Their purpose was to transport a young traveler to her temporary place of residence, then return to Earth to report back to the press.

As the craft approached the moon, it slowed. Its pointed cone of a nose dipped up in the air, and the rockets in back shut off. Two robotic feet emerged from the bottom, and slowly, with a few puffs of steam, the ship landed with a gentle bounce. Several yards from where it touched down sat a sealed glass dome, inside it a ranch-style moon station, comfortingly similar to the kinds of kit homes available for purchase from Earthly catalogues. In fact, perhaps it *was* one of those kit homes.

At the top of the dome and above the glass door, red flags flew, adorned with the hammer and sickle.

The men disembarked gracelessly, dressed in protective suits with oxygen tanks, carrying a fourth person: our heroine, drugged and blindfolded for the journey. The men in charge claimed this was to ensure she could not steal any state secrets or technology, in case she was a double agent with plans to return to her mother country. For, as much as the men seemed ecstatic to have recruited an American defector, they despised her for her treachery. They treated her, our heroine observed privately, the way she imagined many men treat whores: with both gratitude and disgust.

After the men slowly walked her to the station—more of a swim than a walk—they pressed a series of buttons and carried her inside. Someone else waited there for her. He watched as they removed her oxygen and protective suit—inside the dome, oxygen flowed freely—and strapped her to one of the two captain's chairs on the observation deck. Through the glass, Earth was a swirled crescent, Europe and Africa bathed in daylight.

The three men left. The rocket ship pushed through the moon's thin atmosphere with little resistance and disappeared in an arc of white smoke. A half hour went by, until the man in the space station began to see movement: first the girl's eyelids fluttered, then her fingers clenched and unclenched, reaching out in front of her, grasping at nothing.

There was a weight on Katherine's chest, on her arms. Someone was holding her down. Her heart picked up a staccato pace. When her eyes opened, they were foggy, unable to focus. Bright lights overhead. A medicinal smell.

"Hello?" she called in a panic. "Hello?"

They had said she wouldn't wake up alone. Where in God's name was her cohort? Why was she strapped down? She tugged at her restraints. Under her scalp, her skull throbbed. Something was not right about the gravity in here; her stomach felt as if it was in free fall inside her body.

"Help!" she called again, breathing hard, and then he was there. He held a little metal cup with a straw inside.

"Drink," he told her.

She wished she could get a handle on his face. The light played tricks here on the moon; she could already see that. Somehow the two of them were in full sun and a nighttime darkness at the same time. His face was harshly shadowed, but she had the sense that he was close to her own age, possibly a few years younger. He had dark hair and a long Slavic nose, the slope of which invoked memories of Russian prowess in winter sports.

"What is it?" she said, indicating the cup.

He uttered a low chuckle, more of a growl. "Water," he said in his thick Russian accent. She still had not gotten used to those accents. She took a sip. It was cold and tasted wonderful.

"Thank you," she said. "Now will you undo me?" She tugged at her wrist cuffs.

"Not yet," he said, to her surprise. He leaned forward, toward the panel of gizmos in front of them, a sea of buttons and levers and blinking lights. One of his arms lifted stiffly—his broad shoulders were encased in a hard-shell uniform that looked primed for walking in space—to point at a shiny black eye embedded in a round white orb. A green light blinked beneath the glass lens.

"Say hello," he said pleasantly. He enjoyed this, she could tell. Her being tied down, while he was free, holding the cup.

"What in the world is that?" she asked, indicating the green light.

"It's a visio-telespeaker," he replied, as if she should have known this. "Say hello."

"A camera?" She kept her eye trained on the lens. "Say hello to whom?"

The man didn't answer right away. Instead, he waved at the camera and put his arm firmly around her shoulders. This was all supposed to be voluntary—her idea, even—her defection, her choice to join the Soviet space program. But right now, it did not feel so voluntary. Right now, she felt like a hostage.

Especially when he replied, "Say hello to *everyone*."

3

"And you, Louise?" the man asked me, tapping his cigarette on the table. He was slim and stylishly dressed in a pale suit, and he possessed a confident gaze that was now trained on me. "What do you write?"

I took a drag of my cigarette to kill time. What was a former waitress to do when she found herself in Rome, the Eternal City, with her fella and the likes of James Baldwin? Throw out her elbows, that's what, smoke languidly, take up as much room at the table as her little body allowed, and hope that they wouldn't notice her tremble.

"I've done some political pieces," I said at last, even though I'd written exactly one, for *Downtown*. Sweat dripped from the back of my neck into the collar of my new red blouse. Rome was rippling with heat that evening, like the air escaping from an oven. Scooters and small cars kicked up exhaust beyond the patio where we sat. I could see the lights of the Colosseum, and a naked column lit up in the Forum, standing with nothing to support.

"And I write fiction," I added, a bit shyly.

"What kind of fiction?" asked Baldwin. Baldwin! I understood now why Joe had seemed so nervous in the hotel, tying and retying his tie, chain-smoking on the balcony as he waited for me to get ready. The anxiety was catching; I had it now, like a coughing bug. I'd read *Go Tell It on the Mountain* the minute it hit the shelves, and, in my youthful upstart way, I'd wanted to assign the book to every old white person I knew. But in the end, I'd had the guts to recommend it only to a few friends who I knew would be receptive.

We'd spent the early part of our meal discussing writers whom both Joe and Baldwin knew, what they were working on these days, their whereabouts and states of mind; that is to say, I'd been silent for the most part. This guy had decided to try his hand at poetry; this other fellow was following Hemingway around Havana, even though Hemingway couldn't stand him. Joe and Baldwin seemed to have known each other for a while, and spoke with some camaraderie, but I noticed a sort of veil between them. They would chuckle together, but their laughter would end too soon. To me, Baldwin appeared a bit guarded, Joe tense. Both seemed relieved to turn their attention to me.

"I'd like to hear this, too," Joe said, smiling, as he reached for his wine. "Louise is quite private when it comes to her work."

I cleared my throat. "I'm writing a novel about a girl who moves to the moon."

Both men made sounds of surprise. "A girl who moves to the moon," Baldwin said. "Science fiction?"

"In a sense. It's also a romance." I waited for the requisite masculine eye-roll, but Baldwin's expression did not change. I couldn't read Joe's. "She accepts a mission to the moon because she can't stand where she is anymore. The girl was a pilot during the war, when there were no men to dust crops. Now that the boys are back, she's expected to keep house. But she'd rather be sent into space."

Baldwin tilted his head. "Who sends her?"

I hadn't expected him to ask. Joe lifted his chin, watching me. I paused to take a bite of grilled octopus and took my time to chew.

"The Soviets."

"The *what*?" said Joe.

"The Soviets," I repeated, watching Baldwin react. He nodded slowly, a hint of a smile on his lips.

Joe raked a hand through his hair. "But that'll outrage your readers. They'll be clutching their apron strings."

I let out a throaty laugh, even though my fingertips tingled in irritation. "Joe, dear, don't make me wrap an apron string around your neck. The American heroine gets the better of the Soviet spaceman in the end. You'll see."

"Is it a rape fantasy?" Baldwin asked.

"Oh, goodness, no," I said. The idea of writing a rape fantasy, though I knew it was the convention, made me feel sick to my stomach.

Baldwin raised his eyebrows. "Premarital relations, but not rape? That's even more scandalous. You know they're strict about who can have relations with whom, how it all goes down in fiction."

"Good luck finding a publisher in that case," Joe added.

I was fully ticked off at Joe now. I'd never heard him speak this way to me, so mocking, so disdainful. "Again, fellas, you're assuming I haven't worked all this out for myself. My hero and heroine are on the moon, remember? Marriage isn't an option."

Baldwin laughed. "Good girl."

I beamed at him, ignoring Joe's scowl. "I will say, it has something in common with rape fantasies. The male is always dangerous—an outlaw, a Greek god, some sort of rogue. I'm simply giving my reader the ultimate in forbidden men."

"A romance with a Russian space captain." Baldwin exhaled a laugh through his nostrils. "Might be just what the doctor ordered."

Luckily, our dinners arrived before Joe could add anything. A waiter refilled our wineglasses, and Joe asked for a martini. When it arrived, he took a sip and opened his mouth to speak. I was halfway through my sea bass with lemon sauce, and Baldwin had tucked into his *frutti di mare*. Joe had barely eaten a bite.

"And you, old boy," Joe said, and winced. In turn I winced for him, and for Baldwin. *Old boy?* Baldwin regarded him evenly. "What is it you're working on these days?"

Baldwin wiped his mouth with a napkin. "Essays, mostly. I have one coming in *Harper's*."

"Really?" Joe asked, leaning forward. "What about?"

"A little town in Switzerland, of all things. I went there to recuperate, after having had some troubles. To 'take the cure,' as people say. Lucien brought me there, to stay in his parents' chalet."

Joe nodded. I felt myself flush. I'd never heard a man speak so frankly of his male partner before. Baldwin's face remained admirably cool.

"The white people, in this isolated Swiss village," Baldwin continued. "I was a stranger to them in the purest sense of the word: they had never seen a Black man before. There was a naïveté to their brand of racism. The children smiled as they called me the devil. The adults boasted of having 'purchased' heathen Africans and brought them to Christianity, as if this were a good thing. As though they had no idea there were echoes of the slave trade in their language, their 'buying' of Africans." He took a drag. "It was the kind of innocence that American whites act as if they have, regarding racism. White Americans pretend to have no racist past, even though it is absolutely embedded in our history." He regarded Joe for a long moment, without blinking. "That's what the essay is about."

I noticed then that Joe's left hand, its fingers splayed on the table, trembled a little. "Racism . . ." he began. "Embedded in American society." His voice sounded artificial, to me, anyway; I wondered if someone who didn't know him well would be able to tell he was nervous. I supposed it was only natural, a white man feeling strange asking a Black man about race. But why was he pushing the issue? "What do you mean by that?"

"What do I *mean* by that?" For the first time, Baldwin, too, seemed ruffled. "Oh, Joe." He slid his fingers into his jacket pocket, searching for another cigarette. "There you go, proving my point."

My heart beat violently. I couldn't look Baldwin in the eye. When he spoke of "American whites," he wasn't counting us as exceptions. We were part of the problem. And why wouldn't Joe just shut up, already? Instead, he attempted a laugh. "I just mean . . . can you tell us any specifics, old—" He stopped himself. "Any other specifics, from the article?"

A waiter appeared and lit Baldwin's cigarette. He gave the man a nod. "There's a specific for you." He gestured in a coil of smoke. "That man right there, lighting my cigarette. In the U.S., right now, there would be no white waiter offering me a light. I wouldn't even be allowed to sit at this table."

"It isn't right," I said, feebly.

Baldwin didn't acknowledge me. "You can't expect us to be silent," he said to Joe, pointing his lit cigarette at him.

I looked from him to Joe. I had a sense they'd had a conversation like this one before. Joe was licking his lips, seeming to search for something to say. He took a long drink of ice water as Baldwin smoked.

I laid my hand on top of Joe's. "Darling," I said, "you can always read the essay when it comes out."

Finally, Baldwin laughed. "That he can," he said, and returned to his meal.

Joe smiled, but it was more of a grimace. He waited a second, then withdrew his hand from mine.

"Hey," I said later as we walked toward the hotel, "I wanted to shoot the breeze for a while; let's go back to the fountain." We'd just stumbled through the little square that held the outsized Trevi Fountain, or at least I thought that was what it was, tucked among throngs of young people eating gelato and smoking. At well past midnight, the crowd seemed only to be getting started, and I had no desire to return home to bed.

"The food was tops, don't you think? Just amazing," I said when Joe didn't answer. I hobbled along with him, the backs of my heels shredded to lunch meat by the new pumps I hadn't bothered to break in. "And what Baldwin said about McCarthy losing power—I hope he's right. Can't you slow down a bit?"

Joe kept looking forward, ignoring me. He'd said very little after we left the restaurant. I assumed he felt embarrassed by the gaffes he'd made and ruffled by what Baldwin had to say about race. In the green light cast by a neon pharmacy sign, I saw a muscle clench in Joe's jaw.

At last, I kicked off both shoes and scooped them up, leaving my bare soles to the grimy paving stones. "Ouch. Much better." Joe walked a bit ahead of me, hands in his pockets, and I had to skip to catch up with him. "You haven't said a word in five minutes. What's on your mind?"

He paused for a while, pursing his lips. "If you must know, it's you."

"Me?" You could've knocked me over with a feather. "Me?!"

"Yes, you. Going on about your novel, about a girl defecting to the Soviets. What in the hell would make you think that was a good idea?"

My face felt very hot. "I thought it wouldn't matter, since—what was it?—the average apron-wearer reading my work probably wouldn't know anything about politics."

He raised both clenched hands in front of him, as if he were crushing an imaginary beach ball. "You're an American writer," he began, as if I didn't know this already. "You write things that are critical of America, you're doing exactly what the Soviets are doing to us *deliberately* and effectively at this very moment. Haven't you noticed how rude they are to Americans here?"

"Not really," I muttered, even though I had felt snubbed in a few places.

"Well, they are, because the Kremlin wants them to be. There's propaganda all around us, floating in the airwaves, over the wires: Americans are illiterate cowboys who eat cheeseburgers and drive Chevrolets. Americans have no culture. Baldwin may be right about those Swiss treating him badly, but he missed the bigger picture: we're *all* strangers in Europe, because we're Americans. White or Black."

"I don't know that our experience really compares."

Joe ignored me. "We're going to lose this war if at the very least we don't put our best faces forward and get some of Europe's elites on our side. You can't aid the Soviets in producing anti-American propaganda."

I watched him wipe a bit of spittle from his lower lip. Were we still talking about me, or was this really about Baldwin? Was I the easier target? "My book isn't Soviet propaganda," I replied. "A woman defects to the Soviets, yes, but that doesn't mean I'm pro-Soviet." I was on a roll now, my voice gaining volume. "I already told you, the girl gets the better of the Russian guy in the end. My book will be critical of the Soviets *and* the Americans. Weren't you listening?"

We'd passed yet another apothecary, and in the sickly greenish glow I'd seen someone I knew. But that was impossible. We were in Rome, not New York. I craned my neck, peering over Joe's shoulder.

"Wait a minute," I said. "We just passed someone I've seen before."

"That's impossible, Lou, we're nowhere near home," Joe replied. He'd just begun to walk faster, it seemed, and I strained to focus on the man in the hat huddled in the doorway.

"Oh!" A memory fired in my brain. "I know where I saw him. He was the man in the café this morning. You would've laughed—this guy had an American book tucked into an Italian newspaper. I told him I wouldn't spill. Wait. . . ." It looked as if he'd left the pharmacy's stoop and joined the people strolling behind us. "Is he following us?"

"I doubt it," Joe said, but then his hand was firm at my elbow. We were taking a sudden left, him steering me, even though I was sure we needed to go right to get to our hotel.

"Joe," I hissed, looking backward, "Jesus Christ! The guy *is* following us. Aren't you worried? I see him this morning, and now again—"

Joe grabbed me by the wrists and slammed me against the wall of the alley. His eyes, close to mine, were dark and hooded and barely recognizable.

"Stop. It." His breath smelled both sweet and foul, like red wine. "Your voice is too loud. You're talking nonsense. Understand?"

We were alone in the narrow passage, an ancient drainage path between two stone buildings. Sluice channels, probably laid in Caesar Augustus's day, felt slimy and wet under my bare feet. I thought of what Joe had said to Harry, the way he'd held him, just as he was holding me.

"Why do I need to be quiet, Joe?" I whispered.

Joe held my gaze for another minute; then, slowly, he let me go. He looked up and down the alley—no one there. His shoulders fell a bit. "I'm sorry," he muttered, half in a daze. "I don't know what came over me."

"Joe." Tears had sprung to my eyes, even though I felt more angry than sad. "What in the world? You've never done something like this to me before."

"I'm just . . ." He wiped his hand across his brow. "Had too much to drink. I—I'm sorry."

We did not touch the rest of the way home, but I could still feel the imprint of his fingers on my wrists. My mouth opened several times; each time, it closed.

We did not speak once we returned to our room, either,

but brushed our teeth beside each other with all the intimacy of strangers on a subway, then curled up on opposite corners of the bed.

When I woke up at two in the morning, head pounding and mouth dry, Joe's side of the bed was empty. I came through the double French doors into the main part of the room, squinting. Joe stood in his loafers by the little closet, quietly getting into his jacket.

"Joe," I croaked, "come on now. What's going on?"

"Nothing," he whispered. "I have to go out for a bit. Go back to bed."

He turned his back on me. I had the sense that I was bothering him, that I'd become an unwelcome guest in my own hotel room. It made my stomach ache. I did as he said and returned to bed. But I did not sleep, not until he came in, at near five in the morning, and slid back under the covers beside me, in silence.

· 4 ·

On the Thursday after we returned from Italy, Joe called me at work.

I didn't have my own telephone—not even my own desk, really. Since I spent most of my time filing, Mr. Franklin had only given me a little chair at the far wall of his secretary's office, and a side table smaller than the desk I'd had in grammar school. Still, it wasn't a bad job. Mr. Franklin treated me respectfully, and though Mrs. Whitacre, the secretary, appraised my outfits in disapproval every day, she kept her comments nonverbal—grunts and nods.

After she answered the phone, Mrs. Whitacre ambled around her desk, holding the receiver and handset. She passed these off to me with a sneer. "You have two minutes, Louise."

"Yes, ma'am." I swung my knees toward the wall, as though that offered any privacy. "Hello?"

"Tell me, what's it going to take for a fellow to take his girl to dinner tonight? Do I have to climb your fire escape with a dozen roses?" Joe's voice was airy and upbeat, and despite myself I swooned to hear it. "Because I'll do it, Louise, don't dare me."

"Two dozen might suffice," I replied. "Roses, that is." We'd been home for four nights, none of which I'd spent with him. He knew he was in the doghouse, after the way he'd treated me on that walk back to our hotel. Each day since our return, he'd called to see if he could come by for a nightcap, and each time I'd refused. I'd wanted him to know he couldn't rough me up that way.

"You sly dog," I whispered, glancing toward Mrs. Whitacre. "You rang me at the office because you knew I'd have to say yes, didn't you?"

"Catching you off guard," he said. "Is it working?"

I exhaled, smiling. "It's working."

"Good. How would you like dinner at Minetta Tavern? Harry's asked if we'd tag along, a double date. He wants to spitball some ideas for a new feature he's working on."

"A double date," I repeated. A reason to get dressed up, and possibly to contribute something, even if it was just brainstorming, to the magazine. "What time can you pick me up?"

"I'll be there at seven."

"Don't forget the roses."

He laughed. "I won't forget the roses."

Dinner in the Village called for an exciting new getup. That evening I slid into black cigarette pants with side zippers—these were a bit snug, but I did some deep knee bends to break them into shape—pony flats, and a Swiss-dot blouse. I was just finishing poking pearl studs through my earlobes when the telephone rang, in my code for the party line. I ran for it, hoping it wasn't Joe saying he'd be late.

A frantic voice greeted me. "Louise? Louise, I need your help."

"Mother." My breathing quickened. "Can't speak right now. I'm about to go to dinner with a friend."

"Dinner out? How much does that cost?" I could picture her seated at the kitchen table with a cup of tea steaming before her, despite the summer heat. Her hair, dyed mahogany, would be up in curlers or a shower cap. Her hands would be dry, skin flaking and white from constant contact with bleach. "It's this money your brother sent home; I can't figure out how to spend it. You have to help me."

Instantly quivery, I pressed my palm to the wall. "You've heard from Paul? He sent you more MPCs?"

"No, no, I haven't heard from Paul since March. I thought you might have gotten word from him?"

I deflated. "Last he wrote to me was in April. You know that."

"Well, why did he write to you in April, and not me?"

I pressed my fingertip to the bridge of my nose. "Mother, how many times are we going to have this—" I glanced at the clock. "I really do have to go. Why do you still have military payment certificates? Didn't you convert them to dollars already?"

"I didn't convert them all at once. I saved some."

"That doesn't make any sense."

Through the line I heard her sniffle. "I wanted to keep a few things he touched."

"Oh." I didn't know what to say. Tears threatened my mascara. Images of my brother flashed through my mind: six-year-old Paul grinning at me behind our birthday cake, skinny teenage Paul holding up a smallmouth bass. "Oh, Mother."

A polite knock sounded at my door. Joe—but I hadn't

heard the buzzer. Someone must have let him in downstairs. "I have to go," I whispered.

"You most certainly do not! Don't hang up on me, I'm your mother. Louise!"

"I'll call tomorrow." I laid the phone on the receiver gently, as if to soften the blow of hanging up on her.

"Lou?" came Joe's muffled voice from the other side of the door.

"Coming!" I called as I grabbed my leather clutch. I grasped the knob and found him standing on my mat, beaming, two dozen blood-red roses clutched in his arms.

He started to say something, then exhaled sharply, as if he'd gotten the wind knocked out of him. "You're stunning."

I pulled him in for a kiss. It felt good just to be near him, to smell the scent of his soap and feel his lips curve into a smile against mine. I pulled back to take in the tall drink of him. He seemed relieved to see me as well, and, clearly, he'd dressed up on my behalf. He wore a tie I'd given him the summer before, a pale-blue paisley.

Thank God my mother hadn't called just a few minutes later, I thought as we put the flowers in a vase. How embarrassing—this man had been to Harvard, and here was my mother scrabbling over what likely amounted to a dollar and a half in military certificates.

I'd been to Minetta Tavern, tucked away on a corner of Mac-Dougal Street, once, with a few girlfriends, and we'd stuffed ourselves full of lasagna and Bloody Marys. But as Joe and I crossed the threshold together, I thought I'd place my usual demure dinner-date order: cold chicken, or just a green salad.

Italy had been an exception; in general, I wanted Joe to consider me delicate, not ravenous, as well as practical.

That changed when we got to the booth, and I saw Harry and his companion merrily slurping their bowls of red chowder, a pound of mussels splayed on a platter before them, most of the shells shining purple and empty. Harry's martini glass was already drained, as was the drink belonging to his date. His date who was most definitely not Glenys, whom I'd been anticipating.

It was Beverly.

Joe, to his credit, seemed just as stunned as I was as he and I took the two chairs on the opposite side of the booth table. He at least had the decency to blush a deep crimson. Predictably, Harry didn't seem to notice anything uncomfortable going on. He signaled the waiter to bring us drinks as Beverly appraised me. She sat comfortably against the leather bench, wearing a lavender halter dress that left her sharp shoulders exposed.

"I didn't know," Joe whispered to me as our cocktails arrived. He must have noticed I could barely speak. If Harry and Beverly were this serious, what might she have told him about me? And what did it mean that I was here, on a double date with not the wife but the mistress?

Harry introduced Beverly and me, and, mercifully, she didn't let on that she'd met me before. I had just relaxed one iota when Harry added, "You know Joe, of course." She offered him her delicate hand as a zing of fear shot down my back.

"I haven't been to this place in ages," Joe said, looking up at the tin ceiling.

"Oh, I hang out here all the time," Beverly said. "I live

just a few blocks away." Her eyelids were shaded pale purple to match her outfit, her eyeliner catlike. "What about you, Louise? Where do you live?"

"The Upper East Side," I muttered, feeling stodgy.

"Speaking of uptown," Harry said, gesturing with a mussel shell in his hand, "I was just telling Beverly about this new story I'm concocting."

"Ah, yes," said Joe, putting his arm across the back of my chair. "The legend of Frank's."

"Frank's," Harry held forth, placing the shell in his empty soup bowl, "is one of the few integrated joints in Harlem. Most of the restaurants there are staffed by locals, but won't serve them. Can you imagine? Frank's was the same way. Then Joe Louis started going there and changed all that."

I took a deep breath through my nose. I'd recovered somewhat, probably thanks to the martini. I glanced around Minetta's; everyone in view was white. I wondered what Baldwin would think of Harry's idea. "What's your working title?" I asked Harry.

"I'm thinking 'One Night in Harlem.' Show Harlem's good side. White and Black faces in the same dining room. It's not the Cotton Club."

"Maybe you should call it 'Two Nights in Harlem,' instead," I offered.

Joe stabbed out his cigarette in the ashtray and blew a jet of smoke out of the corner of his mouth. "Two nights? Doesn't have the same ring to it."

"Two nights, to show the two sides. So you get the whole picture. Write about Frank's, then write about the Cotton Club."

Harry frowned and tilted his head as if he'd consider it.

Joe coughed and lit another cigarette. Only Beverly looked me in the eye and gave me a little nod.

"Frank's." Harry tapped the tabletop impatiently. "Frank's is the place we should write about. Profile Joe Louis, get the cool fight angle, talk about the writers who go there. It's one of Langston Hughes's favorite restaurants, did you know that? Baldwin, too, when he's in town."

"You could have Hughes write your article," Beverly chimed in.

We all stared at her. I realized I'd been assuming she should know her place—her role as Harry's side dish was to remain silent and just remember she was lucky to be included. Instead, she had the nerve to make editorial suggestions.

"Hughes is a writer, and you say it's his favorite restaurant," she continued. "What if you asked him to write about it, give his perspective? Or Baldwin—Joe, didn't you just meet with him in Rome?"

I looked from her to Joe. How well did she know him? What else had they discussed? Joe ate his clams casino calmly, his face revealing nothing. Queasily, I realized they all must have gone out together sometime in the past couple of days, when I'd been giving him the cold shoulder.

I glanced at Harry, whose face had turned an oxygen-deprived shade of purple after Beverly's suggestion that he hand over his essay to someone else. Fortunately for him, Joe took a sip of his drink, cleared his throat, and smoothed things over.

"Hughes is a bit untouchable right now, my dear," he told Beverly, "what with his testimony before the Senate a few months ago. And, besides, Harry's a stellar writer. Surely you agree he's up to the task, Beverly?"

"Of course," she said, trying to take Harry's arm, which at the moment appeared to be made of lead.

"Why did Hughes appear before the Senate?" I asked.

Harry answered. "It was the Subcommittee for, er . . ." He waved his hand about, searching for the words. "Anti-government activities. That stuff."

"Think HUAC, but in the Senate," Joe added.

Beverly opened her mouth, but I beat her to the punch. "You don't think Langston Hughes is actually a Communist, do you?" I said.

"Most poetry sounds a bit pinko, if you think about it," Beverly added.

Our eyes met again, as if we were in league with each other. I didn't like it. I couldn't let the fellows think of us as cut from the same cloth. She was a waitress who'd slept with the host of the party. I was the writer girlfriend, the serious prospect.

Neither Joe nor Harry answered right away, just gave each other a look as if to ask what to do with these two broads and all their questions. "I don't believe that's up to us to decide, ladies," Joe said finally.

By the time the waiter arrived, Harry seemed to have forgiven Beverly. He turned his chair toward her and gazed as she ordered stuffed calamari, one of the most expensive items on the menu. I remembered Glenys at home with a knot in my stomach.

"I'll have the baked Delaware shad," I said, matching the price of Beverly's order even though I wasn't hungry anymore. "The special. And I'm headed to the ladies' to freshen up."

"I'll join you," Beverly said. She shot out of her seat.

"Enjoy," said Joe, looking at me warily.

The bathroom was tiled in deep forest green, with a row of brass lights above the sinks. It seemed we were alone. I'd hoped to touch up my lipstick and gather my thoughts in peace, and now here was Beverly beside me, dabbing bits of rouge onto her fingertips and rubbing them into her cheeks. After a few seconds, I snapped my compact closed and turned to go, but she stopped me.

"I want to get something out in the open, Louise. I know you don't want Joe to know you were a waitress at that party last year. You don't even want him to know you know me. I don't understand why, but listen: the cat isn't out of the bag."

I felt the blood vessels in my face expand in embarrassment. Surely Beverly understood that, the longer a lie went on, the harder it became to tell the truth.

The night Joe and I met, at that Christmas party for *New Yorker* staff when Beverly and I had been working as waitresses, I'd watched him all evening, captivated by his intense stare, his hearty laugh. I could sense he was the kind of man who really listened to people, who didn't just like to hear himself talk, and I liked that about him instantly. By the end of the night, there were so many gate-crashers it was hard to tell who was who, and at midnight I ditched my apron, let down my hair, and shimmied into the little crowd gathered around him, drawn into his orbit. When he turned to me and asked, "What do you do, miss?" I'd simply said: "I write."

Granted, all I'd been invited to publish by that point were a boysenberry-jam recipe and a featurette on hoteliers' tricks to keep your linens white.

"I suppose you expect me to thank you," I said to Beverly. "For not telling on me."

She stepped back, lifting her head high. "You could start

by acknowledging we're not so different, you and I, and stop treating me as if I'm invisible."

"But we are different," I said, perhaps to convince myself more than her. "For starters, Joe isn't married. We are an actual item." I made for the exit.

Beverly watched me go. "An item, eh?" she said as I yanked open the door. "You know that means at some point you'll have to come clean."

The plan after dinner was to go dancing on Fifty-second Street. Gleefully, Harry informed us that, since it was Thursday night, the maids from all over Manhattan would have the evening off and be eager to dance. Beverly held his hand, seemingly undaunted by the idea of Harry's ogling maids at a dance club. She and I had avoided speaking directly to each other for the remainder of dinner.

"I don't think I'm dressed to go dancing," I said when they asked if we'd join them, and everyone nodded as if this were the correct response.

After we said goodbye to Harry and Beverly, I found I was walking quickly, a few steps ahead of Joe, toward the Houston Street subway stop.

"Ah, Lou—Lou, wait." He caught up to me and grabbed my arm. "Why are you skipping off so fast—what's wrong?" His brown eyes searched my face. "Come on, honey, I'll get us a taxi."

"That's all right," I said. My voice wobbled a bit. So many worries tugged at me: the weight of the lie I'd told, the way I'd treated Beverly. "I thought I'd just take the train home."

"The subway, at this hour?" He put his hands under my hair, lifting it off my neck gently. It felt good in the heat. For a minute, we stood in the harsh light of a shoe store emblazoned with neon starbursts, until he guided me around the corner to the façade of a darkened bar. I leaned with my elbows against the brick wall, studying the ground.

"I'm so sorry," Joe said. "I never should have brought you out with Harry and his . . . with her. That was completely inappropriate. We don't ever have do it again."

But you will see her again, I thought. *Just without me.* The spheres women had permission to occupy felt so tiny compared with those of men. Men were allotted the whole world, we our narrow parcels. What would happen if Joe came to decide I belonged in a different role?

"It's . . ." I looked up as the moon, a swollen gibbous, ducked behind a veil of cloud. "It's sad," I said at last. "Seeing Harry out with Beverly while Glenys stays back with the children."

"It is." Joe stood with his hands folded humbly in front of his belt. He took a deep breath, and when he finally spoke, his voice came out slightly nervous. "I would never go behind your back like that, Louise. Do you understand? I'd never do that to you."

For a while, we just looked at each other. We hadn't discussed marriage before. This felt like the closest thing so far to a hint at our future. I'd never heard a man make a promise along these lines, and I'd wondered if I could even dream of asking for fidelity, having witnessed so much flamboyant cheating. I searched Joe's face for any signs of insincerity and found none, only a pair of earnest dark eyes that expressed desperation to make things better. I reached out to touch the smooth skin along his jawline, and he closed his eyes and kissed my hand.

He said it again: "I wouldn't go behind your back like that, Lou. You're all I want and all I can think about. It's just us."

"Just us." My face went warm with pleasure. We leaned into each other and kissed, long and languorous, until someone driving past us beeped and hollered. Through my closed eyelids, I sensed the moon emerge from behind the cloud, bathing us in her white-blue light.

· 5 ·

THE LUNAR HOUSEWIFE

A Pilot and a Waitress

The man she shared the lunar colony with had a name: Sergey. He slept in a bunk identical to Katherine's at the far end of the habitat, as she'd come to think of it, because it was easy to feel like hamsters in this big glass dome with all its little gadgets and supplies arranged just so. The gadgets and supplies didn't float around, and neither did Katherine and Sergey, because of some crackerjack Soviet invention that simulated gravity inside the prefab home.

Sergey didn't say "crackerjack," though; he said, "Brilliant technology, which Americans have been smashing their brains out trying to replicate. It is called a gravital capacitator." He spoke fluent English, which was convenient. It made it possible, right away, for the two of them to argue.

"You cannot refer to a 'day,'" he complained the first morning she woke up on the moon, "and expect me to know whether you mean a terrestrial day or a lunar day."

"Well, what shall we call it, then?" she asked, slightly annoyed.

He opened his big hands and explained, as if he were teaching physics to a cat: "We speak in hours. If you mean Earth day, say twenty-four hours. If you mean lunar day, twenty-seven terrestrial days. Simple."

Amused, she leaned back in her sitting module and attempted to cross her arms over her chest. The Soviets had provided her with a wardrobe of silver tunics with matching filmy trousers, plus an array of bullet brassieres. "Twenty-four hours is easier to say than 'Earth day'?" Her voice felt tinny in the enclosed space. She had to speak above the light hiss of borrowed oxygen constantly filtering in from a giant tank outside. Every week—if it could be considered a week; Sergey would probably take issue with that, too—a robot-manned rocket came from Earth to replenish the oxygen tank.

"Not easier," he corrected. "More accurate."

"Aye, aye, comrade."

She'd been told to call him comrade, which she did only on occasion and not without mockery. At first, the correspondence that came from Central Command was all in Russian. The typed letters curled down on ticker tape from a slot in one of the walls. She got to the first message that came after her arrival before he did. *Morse code,* she thought, *simple,* but when she began translating it, the letters made no sense.

She felt, more than heard, a rumbling laugh behind

her left shoulder. "It's the Russian Morse code. We use the Cyrillic alphabet," he'd informed her, as though she didn't know. "Here. Let me translate."

Impatiently, she tapped her foot on the ground as he jotted down the message. He made a show of holding the paper out in front of him with straight arms as he read.

"Aha! It is for you."

"So?" She waited. "What does it say?"

He grinned. "'Welcome, American defector. The bonus payment you requested for your service has already been transferred to . . .'" He indicated the ever-blinking light of the visio-telespeaker. "You don't want me to read the information for your bank account aloud, correct?"

She shook her head. "How do I know that thingama-jig even works? Let alone has the capability to broadcast our lives all over the USSR?"

He looked back at the lens. "Don't listen to her," he said in a stage whisper. In English, thus for her benefit. "I'll continue. 'Miss Livingston, a reminder to begin each day promptly at seven hundred hours on the atomic clock. Day begins with salute of Soviet flag'— they do very much want to see you do this—'and vigorous salute of Captain Kuznetsov.'" He shrugged and smiled, showing white teeth. "Those are the orders."

She clucked her tongue. "I have to salute you? I think not."

"Those are the orders," he repeated. There was still a smile curling the corner of his lips. He had his sinewy arms crossed over his chest. For a moment, she felt distracted.

Finally, she shook her head. "How do I know what it really says? I have you translating for me." She bent down in front of the camera, so all that would be visible was her mouth. "From now on," she said loudly, "I shall receive separate correspondence. In English."

In the end she got her way. Separate bulletins began arriving, written in mostly competent English. They reiterated their request for salutes, which she had no intention of fulfilling, and added more commands: "Your duty is to assist Captain Kuznetsov in his scouting tasks as discussed pre-mission: 1. Sustenance. 2. Cleanliness of lunar habitat. 3. Sterilization of equipment, especially uniform."

"Meaning, I'm to do your cooking, cleaning, and laundry," she said, brandishing the latest report. She let it fall to the floor, which it did, just as it would have done on Earth. The simulated gravity was remarkably realistic. Yet, whenever Sergey left the airtight antechamber, he bounced and bounced on the horizon, measuring craters, his boots seven feet in the air between steps. How she longed to be out there on a real lunar mission. "I'm no more than a housewife."

Sergey shrugged. He was eating slices of dehydrated apple, his feet on the cushion of the sitting module that was supposed to be hers. "You want to go back to Earth, ask for a return of your shuttle." At that point he winked at the lens—she was sure of it.

She stomped off to her bunk, making as much noise as she could in her capacitator-compliant slippers. For a while, she sulked by herself, watching him fiddle with a set of strange, S-shaped metal tools, his chest moving up and down as he guzzled the precious oxygen available in their cramped quarters.

How could he be so cruel to her, knowing as he must that she could not simply teleport back to her old life? A return to Earth would mean Russia. It was the only place that would take her now. The Soviets, or one of their territories. Both the Soviet and the American presses had made such a big deal of her defection; for a moment she'd been one of the most famous women on Earth. Now she was allegedly broadcast live on Programme One several times a day, although she had her doubts this was really true.

On Earth, she'd been a pilot. Well, a waitress. That was what she'd been when they found her. She'd learned to fly planes during the war, when any man who could handle a throttle and knew yaw from pitch had been sent to bomb Italy. A man had come into her school looking for farm girls, specifically a farm girl with steady hands and a solid temper, and her teacher had pointed Katherine out, saying she at least had the former. Within a week, she was dusting crops. She learned to love the wind blasting her face in the open cockpit, turning her lips dry and her throat parched. She loved the smell of oil and fuel, the feel of the engine buzzing her skeleton. Over time, she grew daring, allowing the nose to pitch upward so that she could imagine flying all the way up to where the sky turned dark. She'd been working on a barrel roll when the war ended.

After the boys came back, she had nothing else she could do. She had quit her little country school at sixteen to dust crops. Waitressing, then, was her best option. Men came into the dented aluminum diner and offered to marry her. She said no. She sent away an application to the new space program they'd been talking about on the news. No answer. More men came in and ordered coffee, steak and eggs, asked her to marry them. Then, one day, two men came in wearing rumpled suits. They smelled stale, as if they'd been traveling. She poured their coffee.

"That you?" one of the men asked, pointing at a framed newspaper clipping, yellowed now, on the wall. She was wearing her flight goggles in the photo and smiling ear to ear. A medal dangled from her neck. Now the same medal hung around her bedpost in her parents' house.

"Oh," she said. "Sure. That's me, all right." It was embarrassing now, looking at how proud she was in that photo. An all-women air show and flight contest. These days, people marveled at how quaint it was in wartime, when girls were allowed a crack at such things. Not anymore—the boys were back.

She went to fetch the men a cold pitcher of cream. "That was a long time ago," she said.

"Would you want to fly again?" The man smiled slyly at her. Behind him, sunshine lit up the flat yellow fields. He wasn't from around here, she thought. She couldn't yet identify the accent.

She took a deep breath. "Of course I would," she said all at once, then excused herself to grab a tray of malts and hamburgers.

The two foreign men paid and left. She watched them go outside, then stand by the road for a while and talk. When she finished her shift an hour and a half later, they were waiting for her behind the diner.

· 6 ·

I had always assumed that the end of the war in Korea might feel something like the indelible finale of World War II. I'd been only seventeen on V-J Day, nearly a senior in high school. Everyone in my little town poured out of their houses, like hibernating animals who hadn't seen the sun in quite a while. Neighbors who we knew had lost someone in battle, who'd been isolated in their grief for months or even years, came streaming outside, their faces soaked with happy tears. I'd gotten drunk, truly drunk, for the first time in my life, when Paul and I stole a bottle of our father's favorite cheap whiskey to bring to our cousin Jimmy's house. At the time, I thought Paul held his liquor better than I did because he was a boy, but now I know he must have stayed fairly sober so that he could watch out for me. Throngs of people stumbled through the streets of Ossining that night and gathered near the river, to set off homemade fireworks close enough to singe your hair, to grab strangers and shake them, hug them in a cathartic frenzy. Paul ended up half carrying me home as we sang "Boogie Woogie Bugle Boy" at the top of our lungs. Even as I stumbled going up the back steps, with Paul's sturdy hand on my elbow, we couldn't stop laughing, intoxicated by the feeling of excitement, of possibility, of the weight of that capital "V" for "Victory": we had won.

The conclusion, if you could call it that, of the war in Korea was an entirely different matter. The news came over the radio as I prepared for work on a Monday morning, bringing me to my knees on the floor of my apartment. A cease-fire agreement had been signed. Three thousand prisoners were going to be released, though no one knew when. I clutched my scarf against my face and sat there, not breathing, for what felt like a full minute. When the phone rang and I opened my eyes to get it, the scarf was all wet.

It was Joe. He sounded breathless. "Did you hear?"

"Oh, yes, darling. Yes, yes." Tears streamed down my cheeks. "It's the best news I could have gotten today. I feel like throwing a parade."

"I'm relieved for you, Lou. I hope now you'll finally get news about your brother."

I sniffed. I didn't like how he'd phrased it—I'd have preferred "Now your brother will come home." Paul had been taken prisoner, of course he had. He'd have been too smart to get himself killed. His superiors would've looked out for him.

"Yes," I said pointedly, "I suppose it's only a matter of time before we get the news he's on a ship home."

Joe paused. "Of course."

An uncomfortable silence followed, as I waited for him to say more. We at last agreed to meet at the Biltmore at six-thirty, and I hung up with the funny feeling that I wasn't as happy or relieved right then as I should have been.

That evening, I arrived at the Palm Court at half past six with some pep in my step once again. I had an idea.

It was easy to spot Joe at one of the little round tables

among the ferns and miniature palm trees. The place was half empty as my heels *click-clack*ed across the marble floor. He looked up, his face alight with affection when he saw me coming. He stood and kissed me, his hands on my shoulder blades.

"Boy, this place is dead," I mused. I took a seat, looking around. Typically, we saved the Palm Court, the lounge at Grand Central Station's tower hotel, the Biltmore, for Fridays, when the hustle and bustle of the train station seemed to usher in the weekend. Today, despite the news, the crowd felt subdued. A single saxophonist played Dixieland in the corner. Under the glass skylight, two quiet young couples pulled their cane-backed chairs together to share a cocktail menu. A handful of men in their thirties waited for a friend by the famed gold clock, heading to catch a train back to Westchester.

"I'd say you brighten up the joint," said Joe, taking a sip from the rim of a very full cocktail. "Hope you don't mind I guessed on your drink. Manhattan?"

"Peachy," I said, but I didn't take a sip. I splayed my hands on the table, fingers spread. He took hold of one, the left, touching my ring finger, and I got a little flutter in my chest. I blinked to focus. "I've got an idea, Joe."

"So do I," he said, folding his hand atop mine, like birds' wings. "You first."

I took a deep breath. "I could write an article about the end of the war, for *Downtown*. This could be my first one under my real name, because I'd talk about Paul." He started to reply, but I put my hand up to stop him. "Hear me out— I'd offer total transparency. It would be a piece written by the sister of a soldier, about the relief and, all right, the bitterness the cease-fire brings. The dissatisfaction. No parades, no unilateral excitement, not for our generation. We're in a new, cold world, and I'm just the girl to write about it."

He frowned a little and took his hand back, then fetched a matchbook from his jacket pocket and lit a cigarette. "Are we so sure the war's over?"

I felt an itch of irritation at the base of my neck. My fingers fumbled to scratch it as I leaned forward to take a sip. "Of course it's over. There's a cease-fire."

"But what's been resolved? Korea will probably be split into two states. The northern half will remain Communist. We didn't use all our might to stop that from happening, as we should have."

I had a headache coming on now. "Are you saying we should have kept fighting?"

"Louise, honey. Your brother may be coming home as we speak! Let's talk about something else. As a matter of fact, I—"

The saxophonist had finished his solo; I clapped loudly to cut Joe off. I wasn't going to let him derail me. "I'm sure you're going to print something about the end of the war, aren't you? Why shouldn't I write it?"

Joe took his time in replying, his lips pulled shut. As he lowered his drink, a glug of it sloshed on the table. "We will," he said. "But we'll probably find someone who can write with more . . ." Carefully, without looking at me, he cleaned up his spill with a square cocktail napkin. "More rational detachment."

I fell back against the cushion on my chair. My mouth hung open. "You mean someone . . ." *You mean a man*, I thought. "You mean someone who agrees with you."

He tried to make a joke of it. "It is my magazine, isn't it? Oh, don't give me that look, Lou. You haven't heard my news yet! I do have an assignment for you, and it's what you've been after all this time. You can use your own byline, none of this 'Alfred King' bullshit. It'll be an interview by Louise Leithauser."

I still had my body twisted away from him, arms crossed, my fingernails digging into my upper arms. "Who am I interviewing? The cheesecake girl?"

"No, not the cheesecake girl. It's a good thing you're sitting down." He looked around, leaned close to me, and blew the final exhale from his cigarette in one sharp stream toward the band. "Hemingway," he said, his lips pursed in a sideways grin.

At first I thought he had to be pulling my leg, but then I saw his face. "Hemingway?" My blood began pulsing rapidly, in my chest and ears. "What in the world—why would you give me Hemingway?"

He shrugged. "It's what the man himself wants—a girl. A writer, but a girl. He's on his way to New York from Cuba next week, only doing a handful of interviews, wouldn't grant one to Harry or me. At least, that's what his wife said."

"His wife said he wants to be interviewed by a girl?" I tried to imagine being that wife—Hemingway's fourth, I was pretty certain—requesting a young woman to interview my husband. It was all too bizarre. But still. Hemingway. An interview by Louise Leithauser.

It was plain Joe could see the stars in my eyes. He looked mighty pleased with himself, the cat that ate the canary. He leaned in for a kiss, and I let him take it. As much as I wanted to stay cross with Joe, I felt my heart swell. An interview with Ernest Hemingway, published in *Downtown*. My own byline. "This could be a big break for me," I admitted, more to myself than to him.

Joe smiled wide. "Huge."

"Next question?" Joe asked wearily.

I crossed my arms and glared at the boys. We'd been smoking cigarettes all morning—Joe, Harry, me, lighting the next with the butt of the last—and I wondered if Glenys worried we'd stain her walls with nicotine. Joe sat on the arm of one of the sofas; Harry slumped in among the cushions with his wife. I stood in front of them, a little girl whose parents have forced her to sing for company.

Cigarette mashed in my tight, grim mouth, I read the next item on my list. " 'Mr. Hemingway. How do you do your best writing—longhand, or do you use a—' "

The men had begun shaking their heads the moment I started talking, and I groaned. Harry put out his Pall Mall in the overflowing ashtray. "This is Ernest Hemingway we're talking about, Louise. There's no time for sophomoric questions like that."

"Damn it!" I threw my notebook onto the floor and stomped on it with my right foot. "Why don't you do it yourself?"

"Lou, honey," Joe said, rising to his feet. He was in shirt-sleeves, cuffs rolled back, neck pocked with shaving marks. "You're going to be swell. It's just not every day that someone gets to sit down with this guy."

"All right, how's this for a question nobody's asked our friend Hemingway?" I cleared my throat. "'As a resident of Cuba, what's your reaction to the unfolding attack on the Moncada Barracks? What's the mood like on the ground?'"

My question was met with cold silence. Joe fumbled his glass. Harry, who'd been pressing the icy bottom of his drink to the bridge of his nose, sat up straighter. "Well," he said, nudging Joe, "that's one way to get some attention."

"Lou," Joe said warily, "we can't invite our best writer to say something he'd regret. Not about a failed coup. Ask Hemingway the mood on the ground, you invite him to criticize Batista and help make Castro into a martyr. Better to ask Hem something along the lines of . . ." Joe drummed his fingers on his chin. "How serious he thinks the threat of Communism is there, and how likely it is to spread to the U.S."

"Should we just let the man talk?" Harry said. He'd put his arm around Glenys, the two of them sipping their cocktails on the sofa. She looked happy. "This is, purportedly, an interview, is that the case? Not a multiple-choice?"

Joe looked pained. "Not you, too. The Soviets have Trotsky, and Diego Rivera, and Frida Kahlo. Who do we have? Roy Rogers? We have Hemingway. Don't let him wade into red waters, Louise."

I'd just about had it with them. I needed to lie down for a minute, get my bearings. I headed to Glenys's bedroom to touch up my makeup and have a moment alone.

"Louise."

Joe tapped me on the shoulder in the darkened hallway. I turned, relieved to have a chance to connect with him alone, to see the concerned wrinkle between his eyes. A slanted yellow parallelogram of light, pouring from the open door of one of the children's bedrooms, glowed on the parquet floor behind him. I reached up to smooth one of his sideburns.

His hand wrapped around mine. It was cold. "We just can't afford to mess this up, Louise." He said it quickly, his words coming out in a huff.

My head snapped back, as if I'd been slapped. So it wasn't me he was worried about. It was how I'd perform. A little squeak gurgled from my throat, in place of a retort.

Glenys whisked by us then, taking me by the arm. "Come on, dear, I'll help you spruce for the interview." Still dumbfounded, I allowed her to usher me into her bedroom and shut the door with a gentle click.

"Sometimes they just make me want to scream," I muttered.

Glenys grunted in what I assumed was agreement. "Let me see your blouse." She reached out, tapping just between my bosoms. "You've popped a button."

I looked down; my shirt gaped in the middle, revealing my white Maidenform bra. "Oh, damn it. Would you go out and find the button for me?"

She'd already gone to her closet and pulled out another blouse, peach-colored. "Why don't you try this one?"

I hesitated, ready to say that it wouldn't fit—Glenys most certainly didn't buy juniors—but that would be insulting. The pure silk poured down like cool water over my shoulders. To my surprise, it fit perfectly. "Thank you," I said, smiling. "That's such a relief."

She hesitated, holding my hand. "Is there anything . . . Are you all right?"

"Of course I am. What do you mean?"

"Oh, you just seem . . . peaky. Pale and . . . and that with your blouse . . ."

"I'm fine," I said in a regrettably snappish tone, lifting my skirt so I could tug the tails of her shirt down over my hips. "It's almost my time of the month." I smoothed my skirt down, pushing it so that it wouldn't bunch around my thighs.

I had my own plan for my interview with Mr. Hemingway. Over dinner, I was going to fill him in on my missing brother, get him talking about Korea. I wanted to see what a veteran of the Great War thought of the way we'd ended things. Perhaps it was petty, but I hoped Hemingway would agree with me, and openly contradict what Joe had said about how we should have stayed in Korea longer. That would show him.

Oddly, Hemingway had asked to meet me at the Bronx Zoo. By the time I shuffled all the way from the subway, past the balloon vendors and the reeking rhinos rolling in dust, I was drenched in sweat and breathing hard. I found him leaning on a fence outside the African Enclosure, staring at the hoof stock.

There was no mistaking him: a bearded bear of a man, hunched in a scally cap and too-small jacket with his elbows on the split-rail fence. His interlocked hands were as large as catcher's mitts. Everyone around him, miraculously, ignored him, tending to their prams or disentangling cotton candy from children's hair. The afternoon sun illuminated all of us in an egg-yolk glow. Before I approached him, I chewed an aspirin from inside my purse.

"Mr. Hemingway!"

He turned, small dark eyes on me, his nose sunburned: a

ship's captain a bit bewildered and irritated to find himself on land. He was holding a piece of wood about the circumference of my arm, carved like one of those totem poles in the Pacific Northwest. Too late, I realized that I should never have shouted his name out loud, but no one turned around.

He waited until I stood just beneath his chin to speak. "It's in heat."

"I'm— Pardon?" The sun felt hot on my cheeks.

He nodded. "I can sniff out this sort of thing. You have to, if you hunt. Take it from me, she's in heat." His voice was surprisingly smooth and eloquent, not the grunt I'd expected. He lifted one of his huge hands and wafted the stench from the animal pen toward my nose, as if inviting me to inhale steam off a bowl of soup. "Smell that."

I drew in a rank odor, like stale urine and rotten fruit. I was hit by a sudden urge to vomit. "Ugh," I said, making a face.

Hemingway smiled approvingly. "It's why they've got the male cordoned off over there. Can't give the children too much of a show." He rolled his eyes. "Hear him? In agony."

I looked where he pointed, to a zebra trotting nervous circles in a pen by himself. A lone fiberglass baobab tree was planted in the middle, to make him feel at home. The hoarse cry he produced sounded like that of a drunken donkey.

"Zebras," I said. So that's what we were talking about. Already I felt I was failing here. My armpits seeped, soaking Glenys's shirt. I tried again to offer him my hand. "Mr. Hemingway, I'm—"

He waved his arms, stopping me. "Everyone calls me Papa."

"—Louise Leithauser—"

"Know who you are." He twitched a finger in front of my face, and apropos of nothing, began speaking in some kind of foreign accent. "Don't forget name like that. Louise eh-Light-hau-sah. Sound like girl journalist in comic book."

"Thank you," I said, unsure whether this was in fact a compliment.

"Those boys, Harry and the other one, Eager Eddie. They tell me you cub writer."

"Eager Eddie," I repeated, having just realized whom he was talking about, and laughed out loud.

Hemingway shrugged. He had a faded bandanna tied around his neck, which looked to be limiting his circulation. "You know which one I mean."

"I do," I said. "He and I are an item."

"Is that so!" Hemingway's beard puckered around his mouth. For a second, I thought he might apologize, but no. "Those boys. American Harry, Eager Eddie. The 'oldest men at the game,'" he scoffed. "Ever think you'd like to see the two of them duke it out? They need some blood on their collars, I tell you what. They're soft—like shucked shellfish. Ivy League boys." He shook his head. I wondered if he had a chip on his shoulder regarding education, since he hadn't been to college in his youth. He scratched his chin. "Always whining about how they never got their war. Am I right?"

I bit my lip. I had heard Joe say that. "You are right," I said.

"I'm sorry to say it, but your Joe would go down in the third."

"I'd be there with the popcorn," I said.

This got a laugh out of Hemingway. He slapped my upper arm, hard, with one of his giant hands. "He'd go down by the third, I'd wager you that. No worry. I give you all the writing tips you need, cub reporter. In festive mood today."

There was that voice again. It put me off my guard. Who was he pretending to be? "Uh, thank you, sir. Shall we go—"

"I know what you want me to say, you know." He fixed me with a stern eye.

I felt my face flush. "What I want you to say?"

He came close to my ear, mustache bristles tickling the lobe. "About Fidel. You get down my thoughts on that crazy Commie bastard, you get big placement for your article. Louise Leithauser, household name! Daughter, I do you one better than that."

I swallowed and nodded, trying to think of what to say next. Something clever. The nausea hadn't totally subsided; between this conversation and the smell, I needed to sit down.

"Now try it," he said, reaching for his leather backpack, which had been sitting on the ground against the fence. He stuffed the wooden idol inside.

"Try what?"

He put the backpack on. The straps looked absurdly small against his chest. "I told you, everyone calls me Papa. Try it."

"Papa," I said slowly, the word sticking on the roof of my mouth. "Should we head to the Oak Leaf?" Joe had had to bribe the hostess to get us a dinner reservation for five-thirty.

Hemingway grunted. "The Oak Leaf has become a dump," he said, already walking. The odd totem pole poked from the zipper of the backpack, its topmost face grimacing at me. "I may not live in the U.S. of A. anymore, but I know bits and pieces. We go where the action is. Daughter, you follow me."

· 8 ·

Papa, as I was somewhat disconcertingly beginning to think of him, took me where any large bear might lead his inexperienced cub: to a boxing match.

"Nowhere good to see a prizefight anymore," he'd said from the front seat of the Yellow Cab. We'd found a couple of drivers hanging out by a taxi stand, and they'd tripped over themselves trying to be the one who took Hemingway for a ride. I'd have been in awe of the man's celebrity if I hadn't suddenly been feeling so lousy.

He'd insisted on riding in the front seat, after opening the door to put me in the back, behind the driver. He rode with one large paw steadying the dash, as if he were helping to steer. I had my eyes closed, trying to ride out the sudden turns and shifts, but I could tell by the bridge we took that we were headed to Queens. I tried to focus on the taximeter as it ticked, ticked, ticked up our fare.

"That's part of what's wrong with this crummy town," Hemingway was saying. "Hafta go to the boroughs. Hafta travel miles to see a decent fight."

"I've never seen a fight," I admitted, teeth clenched.

"Don't get your hopes up," Hemingway called back to me, his eyes on the road. He clutched his little backpack with the arm that wasn't pinned to the dash. "At best, we'll see some palooka knock the stuffing out of another. None of them'll be good enough to get to the real Garden."

I was half listening. I ran through my questions in my mind. How in the hell would I interview him at a boxing match? I couldn't help feeling that Joe and Harry were in the back seat with me, pumping me full of advice, already shaking their heads in disapproval at my performance. I sneaked another aspirin out of my purse.

The arena was quieter than I expected it to be, which in hindsight made sense for a Thursday, late afternoon. The farther back in the theater you looked, the more bored people appeared to be. Down in front, clusters of men in porkpie hats who appeared to be affiliated with the boxers jabbed left and right along with the two in the ring, shouting and jeering and tearing up their little betting tickets. Hemingway led us all the way down the aisle, to a few empty seats just a couple of rows from the front. I could see and smell the sweat glistening on the faces of the two ragged-looking, skinny men punching at each other with their lips hanging open.

We hadn't placed bets—"Not what I come for," Hemingway had told me—but he had paid for my ticket, and I would have felt as if we two were on a date had he not given his backpack the seat in between us, the miniature totem's grimace facing the fight.

"What's in the backpack?" I asked soon after we sat down.

He looked at me, dark eyes glistening. "The new book. The manuscript. It's why I'm in town. To show it to my editor. Not for any hokeypokey award ceremony."

"You mean for your Pulitzer?"

He snorted. "That. They didn't give it to my best work, so what the hell's it supposed to mean to me?"

I realized I should be writing this down. When I pulled out my little notepad and pen, he rolled his eyes.

"Oh, yes. All right, have to watch what I say now," he commented in that affected accent, which part of me wished he'd stop doing. "Ears of eh-Light-hau-sah, always listening. Pen of eh-Light-hau-sah, always clicking." He stood suddenly. "Are you blind? Have you gone *blind*?" he screamed—at the referee, I presumed. Reluctantly, I looked toward the ring; one of the two fighters had both eyes so swollen and plummy at this point that I thought Hemingway could be talking to him.

I shuddered. "What's the draw, for you? This, the bullfights . . . Why watch people suffer?" I took a sip of the gin fizz he'd bought me. Maybe it was the liquor, but I was feeling a little bold. "You were in the war, you suffered, you saw suffering. Why do you want to see it now that you have the option to turn away?"

"Only a girl would ask me that question," Hemingway replied. I had the sense that if I saw this statement written, I'd believe it an insult to my sex. But hearing it in conversation, I didn't think so.

I waited. He didn't say anything, just turned his eyes back to the fight and drank his gin. The wiry hairs on his huge tanned fingers were bright white.

"Mr. Hemingway . . ."

"Papa."

"Papa. You didn't answer my question."

"Don't have to. If you'd read my books, you'd already know

the answer. Daughter, if you could read what's in here . . ." A gesture toward the backpack. "It's the best one yet. They won't give me the Pulitzer for this one, though; they have to make it fair, have to distribute. But it is the best yet."

I scribbled all this down. Hemingway claiming he had his best novel yet inside a leather backpack at the Sunnyside Garden Arena constituted big news. Still, I wanted him to answer the damn question.

"I *have* read your books. I understand what the bullfight means to Jake. I know what he feels when he looks at the steers and all that. *The Sun Also Rises*, by the way—I think that's your best work."

He grunted, as if I'd given the wrong answer, and crossed his arms.

"But I still don't understand the impulse to see other people in pain." I took a deep breath. "My twin brother is a prisoner in Korea."

Hemingway's eyes shot toward me. "Then he'll be released soon."

"Will he?" I said, and cleared my throat. I didn't want to mention that I wasn't exactly sure Paul had been taken prisoner. "What do you think about the cease-fire? Was it right to leave Korea when we did?"

Hemingway's mouth closed, then opened again, and then we heard someone yell, "Papa!"

He looked up with eyes squinted. "Moe. You rascal son of a bitch."

A man in a straw fedora rushed forward to shake his hand, and I felt a prickle of irritation at having been interrupted. Hemingway had been about to say something good, I could feel it—something about Korea. The man glanced at me, a solid gold toothpick poking from the side of his grin. He was probably wondering what there was between Hemingway and me.

Fortunately, Hemingway cleared the air almost immediately. "Mr. Moe England, this redhead is Miss Louise Leithauser. Louise is a writer. She's interviewing me for a magazine." He threw a few jabs at Moe. "Louise, Moe's one of the owners of this dump."

Evidently, Moe decided to take that as a joke, and let out a laugh that strained the buttons on his shirt. He invited us to drinks in his private office, and that's when I noticed that the fight had ended; the two poor bums, as Hemingway called them, were in their respective corners with towels around their shoulders. Neither looked happy, so it was impossible for me to say who had won. Hemingway and Moe were discussing it: the one had a glass jaw, the other had a nice long reach but was 165, though you wouldn't know it looking at him.

When I stood up, gray and blue clouds drifted in front of my eyes. I blinked a few times, clutching my purse to steady myself. My next drink would have to be my last.

Moe's office smelled as bad as I had imagined it would, like burnt coffee and socks, but the two orange tweed couches were comfortable enough. I sank into one, Hemingway into the other, and Moe left to fetch a girl to mix drinks.

"Papa," I began.

Hemingway silenced me with a raised hand. Inexplicably, he took the little totem from his backpack and cradled it against one armpit, as if it were a child. "The simple answer to all your questions: Suffering, violence, they're part of life. Boxing, there are rules. There's a form. Man blows a whistle, stops one man from killing the other. Even though we all know he wants to. The best boxer, the Jack Dempsey, he wants to kill the opponent. Whistle stops him. But the instinct is there. The killer instinct—that's all of us, Miss Leithauser, and especially all of us men."

My voice began to squeak in protest, but he stopped me. "Even your fella, that Eager—that Joe. He has the killer instinct, too, don't forget it. Don't fool yourself for a minute. He's a killer, too. He'd agree with me, if you asked him. Boxing matches, bullfights. They make it make sense, that death instinct inside us."

"I wasn't going to mention Joe," I said, trying to keep the quiver out of my voice. "I was thinking of my brother, Paul. Paul isn't a killer."

Hemingway let out a long sigh, as if it wasn't worth arguing with me. "Paul's the twin brother? Prisoner of the North Ko-reans?"

I nodded.

He sighed again. "Daughter, you wonder if we should have pulled out of the war? No. We should've stayed and finished off that damned Kim fellow. If you'd seen what I've seen in Spain, you'd know."

I felt my forehead wrinkle as tears jumped to my eyes. *Et tu, Ernest?*

He didn't seem to notice my reaction. With his left hand he began digging fistfuls of candied nuts out of a little bowl on the table in front of him. Moe returned, a tired-faced girl following him, holding a pitcher of something reddish with a few sad little melted ice cubes and sunken cherries inside. She handed me one, served up. I took a sip, to be polite. It nearly set my tongue on fire.

"Whoo-wee!" Hemingway cried after downing his drink. "Now, let's get on with the interview."

I tried to get my head in order, which was difficult. Especially with Moe the interloper sitting there listening, clucking his tongue, and offering an occasional "You don't say!" or "I'll be damned!" at Hemingway's answers. I was aware Joe and Harry didn't want the usual fodder—everyone already knew Hemingway wrote standing up—but I soon managed to wring out of him a few decent droplets of advice.

"If you want to take a day off writing, you finish the words in advance," he told me when he was on his third cocktail. "Get ahead in the count. Never behind. You get behind, you're screwed. Screwed for the rest of the book, sometimes."

"You don't say," replied Moe. He had begun, to my extreme annoyance, to ask his own questions. "Has that ever happened to you?"

"Yes," Hemingway replied.

"Really?" Moe continued. "Tell us about it."

Hemingway held up a finger as he drank. *God damn it*, I thought. That was a good question. Could I pass it off as my own in the article? The girl had come over to freshen my drink, and before I could say no, my glass was filled to the rim. I was so thirsty, I took a sip to wet my whistle.

"The last book I tried before this one," Hemingway said, holding up the backpack, "was another Nick Adams story, all Nick, one long hunting story with Nick in the wilderness, but I took too many days off and got underwater."

Moe's eyes got wide. "Papa, that's a new book in there?"

It was more than a bit odd to see another gray-haired man referring to Hemingway as Papa. I leaned forward. "Can you tell us what that one's about?"

Hemingway nodded. He seemed proud of himself, almost bursting with the desire to share his pet project. "It's about a young fisherman who joins the revolution in Cuba. Not finished, but now I know how it ends: he loses his leg storming the barracks at Moncada."

An electric current shot up my spine. *Moncada*. Just what Joe hadn't wanted me to mention. My pen couldn't fly fast enough.

"A reluctant guerrilla, you could say," Hemingway continued. "It's criminal, really; I had a young man live with me for a few months in '50, his name was Alvaro. The other day I learned Alvaro lost his leg storming the barracks." He shook his head at himself. "All I'll do is change the name, really. But Alvaro was a wonderful houseguest, and I can't imagine he'd mind."

"Whatcha doing living there anyway, Pop?" asked Moe. "National hero like you, I'd think you'd prefer to stay here in the good old U.S. of A."

"Mr. England," I said, bitterly sweet, "you're stealing all my questions."

"Sorry, doll," said Moe, and he made an attempt to commiserate with Hemingway.

Hemingway didn't look at him. He began pontificating to someone else, an imaginary person in the distance. "Could go on about the food and weather, but it's plain and simple: I'm there because they can't listen to me in Cuba."

I nearly gasped, but held it together. Moe just looked puzzled; it hadn't dawned on him who "they" were. I had a notion. Hemingway was reminding me of Harry, with his paranoia about eavesdroppers, his fear of the little green men. "They?" I said lightly, hoping he'd continue.

"They," continued Hemingway. He spoke in a serious tone now, the phony accent gone, his brow furrowed. "The FBI, government types, fill in the blank. The dullest men alive, they listen in on the rest of us because they can't stand thinking they're missing out on anything. Trouble is, when you're that sort of fellow, when you can't even see that a coin has two sides, you're always going to be missing out."

I scribbled everything down as close to verbatim as I could, even the parts that didn't quite make sense to me yet. This was pure gold. An American icon, speaking out against the government! My conviction strengthened when I noticed Moe had recoiled in horror; it was something to see.

"Say, Papa . . ." Moe rubbed the back of his neck. "Your new book . . . it ain't on their side, is it? Castro's side?"

Hemingway held up a meaty finger. "Writer does not judge. Writer does not think in terms of sides." The affectation was back again. He waggled the finger at Moe. "Try to find the truth, only truth."

All along, I'd been writing as quickly as my cramped hand would allow, my words as slurred as my thoughts. My article would be the talk of the town. God willing. I wondered if Hemingway had told anyone else about this new book. I slid the notepad over my knees, which were trembling. I couldn't ask him what he thought of Castro—that would be too direct. I bit my lip hard. "What do you expect Mr. Castro will think of the book, Papa? Will *he* mind?"

Hemingway laughed again. "Mind? I'm his pet Yanqui, don't you know. I doubt he'll mind. Not that I make the man out to be the saint the people in the countryside—the countryside of Cuba," he added for Moe's benefit, "believe him to be. I tell the truth. I have two FBI agents in the story. One's a decent sort. The other's a bona-fide American Franco, like ninety-nine percent of them actually are. But those FBI men, they're only there in cameo."

This was incredible. I was sure the ecstasy on my face matched the horror on Moe's in intensity. My hand was flying, getting everything down in shorthand and yet trying not to be too conspicuous in my notetaking.

"Get that all down, eh-Light-hau-sah," Hemingway said with a deep-throated laugh. "Might not do you much good."

I wasn't sure exactly what he meant by that, and so I chose to ignore it. I felt euphoric, ready to draw out of him as much as he'd say about the new novel.

I . . . I felt nauseated.

"What would you say about, um . . ." I lifted a fist to my mouth. I looked weakly at Moe, who now seemed ready for both of us to leave. "Where's the restroom, please?"

"Linda, show 'er the can," he directed the girl, and she led me lazily into the hall. Behind me, I could hear Moe, in a strained voice, telling Hemingway where he'd been stationed in the Great War.

I nearly had to push the girl aside, she was walking so slowly, the seams on the backs of her stockings annoyingly crooked. She held open the restroom door, and I barged into the first stall. Everything came up, the sandwich I'd had for lunch, the cocktails, the cherries I'd chewed nervously to bits.

When I came out, Linda was still there waiting for me. Impassively, she offered a towel.

Hemingway insisted on taking me home. He rode in the front seat of the taxi again, all the way to my apartment on the Upper East Side. By now, the sky was beginning to darken, with evening and rain clouds approaching. I half listened as Hemingway chatted with the driver, a woman, which I'd have marveled at were there not a jackhammer working away inside my skull. I leaned my forehead against the cool glass and shut my eyes, feeling every inch a disaster. I'd had Ernest Hemingway to myself for more than four hours, and I'd spent almost a quarter of that time mopping sick off my shirt.

"So long," I heard Hemingway say, and I realized the cab had stopped. "And good luck. I hope he shows up when you have to move your mother."

"Thank you," the taxi driver said, astonishment showing in her raspy voice.

He came around and opened my door, the little backpack tucked inside his jacket to protect it from the spitting rain. The cab sped off. "I can get rid of him, if you like," Hemingway said with a twinkle in his eye, and when I looked, Joe was sitting on the front steps to my apartment building.

He stood as we approached, nearly tumbling down the stairs. His eyes were wide, white showing all around the pupils. "Uh—wow," he said, stretching his hand toward Hemingway. "Mr. Hemingway. I hadn't expected to see you. How was your flight?"

Hemingway shook his hand. "Already gave the answers to your girl here. You can check her notes. She's a bright girl, probably wrote it all down in detail."

Joe glanced at me and gave me a quick nod, then looked back at Hemingway. "If we can get you anything: Dinner? Cocktails? Louise can mix up—"

"Louise is tired," Hemingway grunted. "Needs rest. I'm

going to see her upstairs and then we're both going to leave, you and I."

Joe nodded eagerly. "Dinner, then? I can take you—"

Hemingway patted him on the shoulder, already pushing past him toward the door to the vestibule. "Have dinner plans already. Read the notes."

All this struck me as unnecessarily rude, and also kind of humorous. I knew I should have done something more to reassure Joe, who stood there bewildered, miserable, in the rain. But my head throbbed, my stomach churned. The idea of my bed, the fresh sheets I'd put on that morning, beckoned strongly.

"I really am not feeling well, darling," I told him with a faint kiss. "I'll call you in the morning. Papa can see me upstairs."

Papa? Joe mouthed.

I made a sheepish face. It looked bad. I knew it. But I went inside, Hemingway followed me, and we left Joe standing all alone on the sidewalk.

Once Hemingway was in my apartment, I wasn't sure what the heck I'd done by letting him inside, or why he'd wanted to be here in the first place. He looked so strange, a larger-than-life figure, vigorous and elderly at the same time, clutching that overstuffed backpack and the bizarre totem pole. He took an inventory of the place, nodding slightly, and then he said, "Tea? I'll make you a cup, and then I'll be on my way. You have tea?"

"There's Lipton in the cabinet."

He gestured toward the bedroom. "You get yourself settled, and I'll make you tea."

"Thank you, Papa." In my room, I stared at my dresser

for a minute, as if I'd never seen it before. Then I got under the covers fully dressed and pulled them to my chin. For five minutes, I lay there marveling at the absurdity of Ernest Hemingway fixing tea in my little kitchen. The man had a certain magnetism about him, that was for sure. He spake, and the people obeyed.

He came in with the mug. He set it on the bedside table and then stopped to lean over me.

"Daughter," he said, "you have a good doctor? One you like, one you can trust?"

"Sure," I said. My eyes were beginning to droop.

He frowned. "Or your friends—they may know a good doctor."

"My friends?" I yawned. "What do you mean, Papa?"

"You're in trouble, see."

I chuckled. "That's for sure. Joe did not look happy with me."

He shook his head, beginning to lose his patience. "No. You're in trouble, a different kind of trouble." He gestured to the lower half of my quilt, toward my midsection. "You're in a family way."

The bottom of my stomach fell out. "What?" I gasped. "No. I couldn't be."

Hemingway nodded. "Could tell the moment you arrived at the African Enclosure. I told you, I hunt."

"That's ridiculous," I spat, before I remembered who I was talking to. I was counting in my head. Counting weeks back, to the last time I'd . . . in July, it was only a few weeks ago, I . . .

Hemingway made for the door. "Now I really should be going. I wish you luck. What's the over-under on your man watching from around the corner, waiting to see how long I stay?"

I was sitting up now, my breath coming in gasps. No way I was getting any sleep now. Not a chance.

"I tell you what, though, daughter."

"What?" I said, my voice high-pitched. Panic was setting in.

Hemingway puffed up his chest, taking up the doorway. "That was chickenshit, letting another man take his girl upstairs. Not something I'd ever do in my life."

And with that, he was gone.

9

THE LUNAR HOUSEWIFE

The Locked Door

Sergey spent his days exploring the lunar surface, collecting soil samples. All Katherine could do was watch. All day he bounced and floated, bounced and floated, fumbled with the soil canisters between his big gloves, and ultimately would return with what seemed to Katherine like nothing. Was it so hard, what he did, or was he just terribly inefficient? In any case, it was her job to seal, label, and store the samples, which would be sent back to Earth in the unmanned spacecraft that delivered their oxygen.

"What'll they do with the soil, once they get it?" she asked over their desiccated dinner.

"Test for water, gas, and minerals. See what kind of resources we have here, to set up the colony." His hooded eyes turned back toward his plate. His lips were shiny with grease from the meat jerky they'd been consuming. "We inspect for other curiosities as well. Asteroid-borne fungus. Amoebic life."

"Found anything interesting so far?"

He shrugged. "If they have, they do not tell me."

She studied his sloping nose, dark soft hair, big shoulders. There wasn't much scenery up here, but there was Sergey. Good grief, Katherine thought, I'm starting to find this bastard attractive. It was true what they said about people and their captors.

Not that Sergey was her captor—she had to remind herself she'd signed up for this—but she was beginning to feel resentful of him as she cleaned the same surfaces and garments and tubes and vials over and over again. They'd sent more detailed instructions after she settled in—no one was sure if viruses or bacteria could survive on the moon's surface, pathogens that might be unknown to humans and thus result in a brutal end for herself and Sergey up here—and so she had to sterilize everything three times a day, including his protective suit, helmet, oxygen tank, and tether. Fortunately, the habitat was not large; unfortunately, it did not take long to become mundanely familiar. It was situated on what felt like a small bluff overlooking Earth when it was visible, a far-off blue marble swirled with white. Behind them, on the dark side, there must have been some sort of cliff, for all she could see were stars. So many stars, the sky was near white with them, hills of salt poured across a dark table.

"We should chart them," she'd told Sergey. She had never seen so many stars, even in the remote farm town where she'd grown up. "We should look for constellations." She only knew a few—Cassiopeia, the big

W; the two bears, Ursas Major and Minor; Orion's belt. "Maybe Central Command will send us star maps."

"Pfft." Sergey had scoffed at her. "This is not our job, tracking stars. Besides, there are too many to see. No way of picking out constellations or anything familiar to us. On Earth, we see a tiny fraction of these. Up here, it is just noise."

He'd walked away from her then, to signal finality, but he couldn't go far. Inside the habitat were their two small sleeping modules on either side of the common area, a pantry stocked with tanks of water and massive quantities of dried food, and dozens of empty soil canisters. They each had a small closet for their limited wardrobes, and in the back wall, on the dark side of the habitat, was a door that was always locked.

"What's in there?" she'd asked Sergey on the third day.

"Always with the questions."

She'd crossed her arms. "It's strange, that's all. We're the only ones here." She recalled a lake house she'd stayed in, in what felt like a different lifetime. The owners had a locked closet where, presumably, they hid the good china and bottles of liquor from renters. The presence of this closet in her surreal lunar home made her feel even more that she was merely a guest here, even an unwanted one, rather than a vital part of this mission. "Why would they lock a door to keep us out?"

Sergey's face twitched. He didn't seem to know what to say.

"You have the key, don't you?"

He held up his hands. "Who, me?" His face broke into an uneven smile. "I say that in jest. I do not have the key. Just forget about it, okay, comrade?"

But there was very little to think about here, and she didn't forget anything. At night, she couldn't help thinking about the time she spent each day in the vestibule, helping him out of his Exo-Shell. She wore a respirator and impermeable gloves for the task, and he kept his helmet on until he came inside, but for a moment, while they were together, he would be undressed from the waist up. He had a scattering of little scars along the side of his ribs that looked to her untrained eye like shrapnel. Once, when she was feeling bold, she'd let a finger pass over one of these crags in his skin, which felt warm even through her gloves. He'd flinched and jerked away.

If she really were the sort of girl who asked too many questions, she'd ask about those scars.

She'd ask who Lizabeta was as well.

Neither Katherine nor Sergey slept well in the lunar habitat. There were nights—"rest periods," they called them, since it was not always technically night-time on the moon—when she felt sure that they were both awake, lying in silence on either side of the bubble, both staring at the myriad stars while unpleasant thoughts ran through their heads. She could tell when he couldn't sleep, because then she could not hear him breathing.

Other times, he drew in breaths raggedly, tossing and turning inside the thin silver material of his hibernation sack. He murmured words she usually couldn't understand, because they were either too garbled or in Russian, but once in a while a name rang out clearly:

"*Lizabeta!*"

Katherine hated hearing him call out for Lizabeta. She figured it might have something to do with the fact that they were all alone, she and Sergey, with no one to touch and no one else to keep them company. To witness him crying for someone else, someone he undoubtedly would rather be isolated with for this interminable period, made her feel terribly embarrassed.

"*Lizabeta, Lizabeta,*" he panted one rest period. "*Izvini.*"

That was one of the few Russian phrases he'd taught her: "I'm sorry."

To wake him, she lobbed one of her slippers in his direction. The gravital capacitator did its work. The shoe connected, satisfactorily, with his head.

10

A few nights after my interview with Hemingway, Harry came over to pick up the draft of my article. Thank goodness, he, Joe, and I had decided in advance that he'd take the lead in editing my Hemingway piece. I'd been avoiding Joe since I'd seen him outside my apartment. I'd confirmed it with my physician: I was expecting a baby. The news had totally rattled my cage. My face in the mirror looked wan and worried, and I felt sure Joe would guess what was up the minute he saw me.

And I wasn't sure yet just what I planned to tell him. We'd skirted the topic of marriage but never children. I wasn't sure how he felt about them. Plus, telling him we were having a baby was tantamount to begging the man to marry me. Where was the romance, or the spontaneity, in that? I hated to think that he'd see me as a burden, that he'd propose out of duty and nothing else.

All that aside—was *I* ready for a baby? Could I write with one underfoot, or would I wind up a full-time housekeeper?

It all made me want to weep.

Lucky for me, Harry didn't seem to notice anything was amiss. I opened the door to find his rangy figure splayed from edge to edge of the threshold, dangling what looked like a bottle of Scotch between two fingers of his left hand. He cocked one eyebrow. "Evening, Louise. Mind if I come in for a nightcap?"

I tried not to groan. I had the typed pages ready to hand over, hoping I'd be able to get rid of him quickly. "Actually, I have quite a headache. I'm not in the mood to drink."

His thick blond eyebrows leapt in mock offense. "Come on, Louise, we have to celebrate your first interview for *Downtown*! Your big break! I thought some thanks were in order." He rubbed his thumb and forefinger together, like a bellhop expecting a tip. He meant that I should be thanking him.

I attempted a weary smile. "Of course. Please do come in."

He plunged past me, into my apartment. I had my radio on, tuned to a news broadcast about the crisis in Iran. The voice was droning about throngs of loyalists to the exiled Shah taking to the streets. "The mob has ousted the embattled premier, Mohammad Mossadegh, and now are demanding the Shah's return . . ."

Harry went to the set and switched it off. "The people will have their way," he said cheerily.

"Hmm. I would've thought the people preferred having Iranian oil in Iranian hands."

"Oh, Louise," he replied with an arch smile.

I cleared some laundry from the edge of my fading floral sofa, and we sat side by side in front of the fireplace that didn't work. All of the windows were open, letting in hot exhaust and traffic sounds. Harry let his gaze travel over my tiny quarters: living room barely bigger than the couch, shoes kicked under the coffee table, piles of magazines and books stacked willy-nilly. He smirked at me in my blue summer-weight Lanz nightgown, probably thinking his maid had a better apartment. Clutching my robe around my chest, I reached for something atop the mantel.

"Looky here," I said to Harry, holding out a plain woolen scally cap.

He looked reluctant to touch it. "What's that?"

"It's Hemingway's." The morning after our interview, I'd woken up feeling as if all of it had been a dream. I'd stumbled out of my bedroom, hair a mess and mouth tasting sour, half hoping I'd imagined everything—the boxing match, the cup of tea, the pregnancy. Then I'd seen Papa's hat dangling from the knob of my radiator, like Cinderella's shoe, from the night before.

Harry's mouth fell open. "You have Hemingway's hat?" He took it from me gingerly, then, laughing, lifted it to his nose and smelled it. "Brylcreem," he said, and I nodded.

"I'll admit I gave it a whiff, too. I don't know why."

"I don't know why I did it, either," Harry said as he handed it back to me. "Maybe I hoped I'd inhale a bit of greatness."

We laughed. It felt as if we'd shared something funny and strange, both of us sniffing Ernest Hemingway's hat, and I remembered then how much I sometimes liked Harry. "You know," he told me, "you should hold on to this. You could use it to get an audience with him again."

I shrugged. I'd thought of that, though I doubted a man like Hemingway cared about some old hat. "He probably has hundreds."

"Well, keep it as a souvenir," said Harry. His eyes took on a bit of a glaze, the pupils dilated. His hips shifted over so that he sat very close to me, the knee of his wispy linen trouser touching my leg. With that move, he ruptured the happy balloon of camaraderie that had been floating between us, and I sat back on the cushions. He moved even closer. "Were you getting ready for bed?" he asked breathily.

"As a matter of fact, I was," I said, rubbing my eyes. "What's the matter, Beverly's got you in the doghouse?"

He shrugged, gave me a devilish grin. "Beverly's working tonight."

The nerve of this guy. I should have clocked him with the baseball bat I kept under my bed for burglars. Or shut him up with the news that I was carrying a little baby inside me, one who belonged to his partner. But then Joe would know. "And I'd like to go there alone, thank you very much."

The tip of one of his fingers went to my knee. "Are you sure you owe it to Joe?"

I sighed. He did this sometimes, implied that Joe hadn't been faithful to me (and he'd tried to convince me many times Glenys had stepped out on him, which I didn't buy for a second). But now that Joe and I had had our little heart-to-heart on that street corner in the Village, I knew in my bones that he wasn't fooling around with other girls. Still, I wondered if he had other secrets.

I crossed my arms. "Do I not owe it to Joe?"

Harry must have seen something shift in my face, some signal that I was done playing. "Oh, don't get like that. Sure, you do, Joe's a good fella. You know I'm only kidding with you." He put his feet on the floor and shifted forward, preparing to go, and as he got up he stumbled a little, bumping the coffee table.

"Watch yourself," he said, blushing, rubbing his shin. "That table is dangerous."

Something alighted in my mind just then, a memory:

Harry stumbling in his spare bedroom, Joe grasping his lapels. There was a question I'd been longing to ask ever since that party in July. I decided to go for it.

"What did Joe mean by 'You'll get us killed'?"

Harry's knees seemed to buckle. Quickly, he sat back down on the sofa. I thought I saw a twitch appear at his temple. "I haven't a clue what you mean," he said. His aristocratic New England accent became stronger, almost British, when he was nervous.

"At the party. I was watching, you know, when the two of you were alone in your guest bedroom. He said something to imply you were in danger, and you told him he was being dramatic."

Little beads of perspiration clung to Harry's hairline, like a tiara. I had the sense it had nothing to do with the heat. "I just remembered," he said suddenly, brightening up. "Joe said you landed quite a scoop on Hemingway. He's got a new novel in the pipeline, eh?"

"Yes." I took the bait and let him change the subject, at least for now. Despite myself, I enjoyed being the one in the know, the source of some information Joe and Harry weren't privy to. "It's about Cuba, and I daresay he seems a little more sympathetic to what went on at Moncada than I think a lot of Americans would be comfortable with." I handed him the draft of my article, typed and bound with a shiny paper clip.

Harry's buggy eyes blinked a few times, at me and then down at the article. "Well. I'll have a lot to work with, then."

I felt nervous prickles under my arms at the thought of him tampering with my painstakingly crafted work. "Don't cut it down for Hemingway's sake. Frankly, he seemed proud to tell us about it."

Harry had been perusing my first page; now his face shot up. A few fine wrinkles appeared on his forehead. "'Us'? Who's us? He told someone else about this new book?"

"Oh . . ." My cheeks went warm. It hadn't occurred to me that the boys might not want anyone else listening in on my interview. "We went to see a fight, and there was a guy hanging around. Moe something. Just one of the owners of the Garden, in Queens."

"Louise." Harry waggled his finger in front of my face. "If you want to work for us again, you can't be sloppy. Don't risk having someone else scoop you."

"The guy runs a boxing arena. I hardly think he's going to write this up in the *Times*."

"You'd better hope." Harry patted his breast pocket. "We should celebrate in any case. I've got a joint if you think that would . . . loosen you up. Ease your headache."

My spine tensed. He really had come over for his reward in return for giving me this opportunity, an opportunity he was now implying I might have blown. I'd have to get him on the defensive again, scare him out of here. I remembered his rant the evening of the launch party, about the place being bugged. "You sure we won't get in trouble?" I teased.

He laughed. "What do you mean?"

"What if my place is bugged? What if there's someone watching us?"

His face fell apart, reassembled itself into a mask of panic. And then the alarm went off.

I had no idea what it was at first; I assumed a fire truck or ambulance, but the sound started at level ten and did not die down the way a speeding vehicle would. We were both covering our ears, shouting God knows what at each other; then

Harry finally mouthed *Nuclear siren* with animal terror in his eyes, and my nerves went haywire.

Both Harry and I jumped up as if we were being jolted with electricity. Siren blaring, we ran around the room, screaming, me looking for my shoes, Harry panicking, hands over his ears, his body rocking forward and back, forward and back. Reading his lips, I saw the words *Korea, Iran, bomb.*

What do I do, what do I do? my mind asked over and over as I fumbled with my bedroom slippers, all other shoes seemingly vanished. The nuclear siren had gotten into my skin, in my bones, and what did bedroom slippers matter, who cared if they got dirty on the bottoms, they would be dust in a matter of minutes. If we weren't crushed by the building, we'd inhale the poisonous cloud, we'd be singed, screaming, burned, the planes were on their way. . . .

Breathing hard, I tried to pull myself together. Harry was kneeling on the floor, his crouched body rocking against my legs. But I was back in tenth grade, and my teacher, kind, calm Mrs. Holton, was directing us under our desks for an air-raid drill. "If there isn't time, duck and cover. If there is time, you go to a bomb shelter."

Opening my eyes, I grasped Harry under the armpits. "Come on!" I tried to tug at his great solid weight. "Come on, you bastard, there's a shelter in the basement next door."

We stayed in the nuclear shelter for thirty-five agonizing minutes, crouched and shaking and sweaty. Harry, who'd turned into a sniveling mess, turned out to have claustrophobia among many other varied and surprising phobias, and he counted out the minutes on his wristwatch for the rest of us until the firemen arrived and led us, sheepishly, out into the night.

"Us" were only me, Harry, my loony upstairs neighbor, Lena, with two of her dogs, and one of the cooks from the Italian restaurant downstairs. The rest of his co-workers had assumed, rightfully, that this was a false alarm. They'd noticed that only the one siren on our street had gone off. The cook returned to the restaurant to a cacophony of cheers and jeers from the kitchen staff.

"But it was so *loud*," shouted Lena, who was hard of hearing (a good quality in a neighbor). She was seventy-two and operated an illegal kennel in her apartment; she now wore the shortest bathrobe I had ever seen and held a blind cairn terrier in her arms. "Shouldn't we get some compensation from the city?"

"Quite right, we should." Somehow Harry had recovered after we emerged back into civilization, and had adopted all his previous airs and then some. He cracked his neck, re-adjusted the cuffs of his shirtsleeves. "This is no way to treat citizens."

The fireman looked bored. "Don't look like nobody got hurt here."

Harry sniffed, his face reddened by the flashing lights of the fire truck. "I disagree with you there, sir. I shall take it up with the mayor personally."

Lena batted her eyes at him. "You know the mayor?"

"Why, yes, ma'am," he replied, voice once again oozing charm. "I've interviewed him myself."

My ears were still ringing. Without saying goodbye, I made my way back to the glass entryway of my tenement building. Harry caught up to me. "Ah—say, Louise. This is quite the story we've gotten ourselves wrapped up in." Nervously, he shuffled the pages of my article against his chest.

"Quite the story? It's New York, Harry. It won't even make the evening news."

"I mean, I'd rather you not mention it to anyone, not even Joe. If you don't mind, that is."

I tapped my nose. "You were never here."

His blue eyes crinkled in relief. "I was never here."

"Like a spy," I said, and watched him flinch.

I went inside and climbed the flight of stairs to my apartment. Then I chained, locked, and bolted my door.

11

"So," Glenys asked quietly, looking around, "you haven't told Joe?"

I managed a sip of my drink, a Negroni, which I'd ordered to be social. It didn't taste right to me. Nothing did.

"No," I replied, my knees bouncing nervously under the table. "I have not told Joe."

I'd asked Glenys to meet me for lunch, and since she'd planned to shop all morning while her kids were sailing with her in-laws, we met in an old steakhouse near Macy's. Celebrities' designated tobacco pipes lined the walls. The scent of charred beef and buttered spuds thickened the air around us. Already that morning, I'd been sick at home, into a planter of impatiens on Fifth Avenue, and into a gutter just up the stairs from the subway.

"Louise, dear." Glenys reached across the table to take my hand. She'd always looked tired to me, overrun by her children, her frosted blond hair puffed into an Italian cut that usually looked too shaggy. But today she appeared thin, unburdened, comfortably alone in her own body. Mine felt as if it had been broken into. "I know a doctor. He's discreet. Takes cash. Let me know if you'd like me to give you his name."

My eyes squeezed shut. Yes, I wanted to know his name. Yes, I'd thought this was what I had in mind when I invited her here. But I couldn't make my lips and tongue come together to form the words "Tell me his address." I opened my mouth, which was dry; my tongue stuck to the back of my throat.

"More bread for you girls?" The waiter began shelling warm rolls into our basket with a pair of tongs. I couldn't even look at them—the spongy, yeasty blobs of dough, the slimy pad of butter melting in its ramekin.

When he was gone, Glenys sighed. "I know I shouldn't eat another smidge of bread, but I probably will." She was always dieting, probably thinking of the lithe coeds and waitresses who caught Harry's eye. "Let's talk about something else, take your mind off things. What was it like, meeting Hemingway? What I'd give to breathe the same air as that guy."

"It's not all it's cracked up to be," I said. "You end up feeling like his wayward granddaughter."

Glenys and I both laughed. We were sitting next to a table full of big men in suits and ties, with a haze of cigar smoke over their heads. Real fat-cat types. They'd been here long before we were, and the liquor of a heavy-duty working lunch had begun to raise the red in their cheeks. When another boisterous roar came from their table, Glenys leaned forward.

"Did you ask him about Castro?" she whispered.

"Indeed. Tell the truth, I get the impression he likes the guy."

"Wow," she said. "Makes you wonder how he felt about Stalin. I'd have asked him that. Force him to draw a line somewhere. I wonder who he favors to end up with ultimate power in the USSR, Khrushchev or Malenkov. That'd tell you a lot about Mr. Hemingway's leanings."

I felt a bit dumbfounded, watching Glenys calmly break apart her roll. I'd known she went to Vassar, but I'd dismissed it as just something girls of her social class were allowed to do. I'd been jealous of her, I had to admit. I hadn't wanted to consider that sad Glenys, swimming in small children, had brains.

I cleared my throat and changed the subject. "You should hear Hemingway go on about the FBI—he sounds like Harry. He says they listen in on him. And he never told me any of this was off the record."

Glenys sat back, arms crossed. "What did Joe think of it all?"

"I don't know. I haven't really spoken with him lately." I looked down at my plate. "I've been telling him I have the flu."

The pleasant expression on Glenys's face collapsed, just as the bigwigs at the table beside us began standing and slapping their used napkins onto their seats.

"Oh, Louise," Glenys said. "Why do you think that is? You're not sure about him?"

I wiped the corner of my eye. "No, that's not it, I just—I didn't want it to happen like this. I'm not anybody's burden. If I go to him and say I'm expecting, he'll feel he has to ask me to marry him."

What I didn't add was that I knew, if he asked me to marry him, if we had a child together, sooner rather than later he'd have to meet my parents. The lid would come off, and my lies would come bursting forth like trapped steam.

I wanted to stop the presses. Reset everything. Go back to where we were before.

"If I have a child now, what will become of me?" I wondered aloud to Glenys. "Will I still be able to write, I mean. Before you had children, did you think they'd be different? Less irritating, less demanding than children typically are? Did you fool yourself about it?"

A little smirk appeared at the corners of Glenys's mouth. She'd taken a leather-bound notebook out of her purse and was scribbling something in it. "Are you implying they *aren't* different from all the others, Louise?"

"Ah—sorry."

"I'm only teasing you. Yes, I suppose I thought that. My kids would be cool cats, they'd sit through meals in fine-dining establishments like German dogs. You know, the kind that go to restaurants? Most dogs aren't like that. Most children aren't, either."

I managed a laugh. "This baby *would* be half Joe. I suppose that would make up for some of my genetic shortcomings."

"Don't even joke like that, Louise. You're sensational. Any kid'd be lucky to have you for a mother."

Such praise, coming from someone whose husband had routinely tried to get me to sleep with him, made me feel terribly guilty. I felt my face flush, and I turned away to watch the busboys load up our neighbors' dishes.

"Darling," I said after a minute, "we've gone on and on about me, as usual. What about you? Are things any better with Harry?"

Glenys's face turned funny, as if there were a fly on her nose that she had to twitch off. "I'm afraid it's the same. He's got a girlfriend downtown, some waitress. He's likely with her right now. Or—who knows?—a whole flock of them. A harem. With himself in the middle, the Maharajah. In a sea of waitresses."

A nervous tingle rushed over my scalp. "He's still seeing Beverly?"

Glenys froze in the act of tapping a new cigarette pack against her hand. "You know her name?" She narrowed her eyes and leaned forward. "What else do you know about her that you haven't bothered to tell me?"

I broke into a cold sweat. How stupid of me, and how cruel, to reveal casually that I'd met Harry's girlfriend. It wasn't as if Glenys and I were close friends, but we were close enough that she'd come here today to listen to my problems and offer help. "I've heard Joe mention her, that's all," I said quietly. I avoided looking directly at her, so she wouldn't figure out that I knew more than that and had, in fact, dined with the enemy. "All I heard was that she was a waitress named Beverly. I don't know any more than you do."

I felt her watching me for a minute, and then she slumped back in her chair. "Hmph."

"I'm so sorry, Glenys." I reached across the table for her hand, leaning so far forward I worried my blouse might get grease on it. A few seconds passed, and then she squeezed my fingers.

Oddly, a faraway look came into her eyes, almost a romantic one. "Oh well. It all goes with being married to a brilliant man. Someday I'll be happy I had a part in his story."

I let go of her hand. Was this what women had to settle for, to be side characters in the biographies of "brilliant men," to be taken for granted until history rendered us footnotes? "You're better than that, dear," I said. "I say tell this homewrecker to shove off."

"That doesn't sound like something I'd do," Glenys admitted. "But I'll think about it." She fiddled with the clicker on the top of her pen. "Louise." She seemed to be choosing her words carefully. "I may be stuck, but you still have time to avoid all this. Don't feel you absolutely must marry Joe. You can . . . consider your options. You two are young. Still getting to know each other."

"I think I know Joe fairly well."

Glenys's lip came out in a sad pout. "Do we really know anybody?"

I thought of his hands clamping down on my arms in that alley in Rome. I thought of him holding Harry by the lapels. Goosebumps raised the hairs on my arms. Having a baby together would mean peeling back some of Joe's layers as well. I considered what Glenys had asked me earlier. Was I holding back from telling him about the baby because I wasn't quite sure who he was?

Glenys tore the page out of her notebook, folded it once, and handed it to me. "That's the name of the doctor. He's on West Eighty-first, near the museum."

"Thank you," I said quietly.

She stood then, gathering her pocketbook and wrap. As I collected my things, she opened her mouth and closed it a few times, like a goldfish. Finally, she added, "If you're curious, get in touch with Eli Cohn sometime. What I've heard might only be rumor, and Harry and I certainly have never discussed it, but who knows. Maybe it'll help you make up your mind."

I fiddled with one of my gloves, puzzled. Eli Cohn—I knew the name; he was a magazine editor I'd met at one of Harry's parties. "Ask Eli about what? The doctor?"

"No," Glenys said, taking my elbow and looking around. She lowered her voice to a whisper. "About Joe."

· 12 ·

THE LUNAR HOUSEWIFE

News from Earth

One day, when Sergey came in from scouting for soil, Katherine didn't dally in helping him out of his suit. "There's a dispatch," she said as soon as they were inside and unmasked, and the two of them made straight for the facsimile machine, for the long sheaf of paper that had curled up on the countertop.

"You've read these already?" he asked, picking it up.

She shook her head. "I was waiting for you."

"Aww," he said, his hand over his heart. "I am touched."

"Just read, will you? Aloud this time."

They were copies of newspaper articles from Russia, big newspapers, Sergey told her, the biggest in Moscow and two in Leningrad. He held up one of them, a front-page headline:

Пионеры!

"That means 'Pioneers!'" He skimmed a little farther. "It seems we have become the national darlings
of Russia. They tune in every evening after work to
see what we are doing. Ha! We are television stars."

She couldn't fathom it. They did nothing interesting
up here, and surely there were times when they were
asleep, or just eating dinner, while people watched
them on their little screens. "Even if they edit the film
and broadcast only our best," she said, "I can't for the
life of me imagine anyone caring about this."

He wasn't listening. He was gazing at his own face,
his head shot in his space uniform. There might have
been tears in his eyes.

"Oh, brother," said Katherine. She looked up
through the glass, at the black sky with its millions
upon billions of stars. A shooting star blazed by, which
didn't even strike her as remarkable anymore. "Let's
see what else they sent."

Sergey scrolled farther down the sheaf of paper. "Just
one more thing," he said. "An American newspaper."

He let her take it from him. It was an article from
one of the bigger newspapers in the United States, not
the best, but a good one, photos of Sergey and her, side
by side, unflattering ones in this case: herself with her
hair blown back, eyes closed, a grainy image cut from
a group photo; Sergey stone-faced, dead eyes staring
straight at the camera.

"Is that a mug shot?" she asked him.

He didn't look at her. "What's this word?"

He was pointing at *"Jezebel."* "Jezebel in Space" was the article's title. It was the subtitle that caught her breath in her throat: *"Defector's Mother Claims Daughter Was Mentally Unfit for Life on Earth."* In the article, there was a quote from her mother:

According to Mrs. Livingston, Miss Livingston's pattern of delinquency and rebellious behavior began long before her current act of treason. "First it was coming home late, drinking too much, and running with a fast crowd. Then the airplane flying. Then there's the principal of her high school. Man with a wife and six kids, and she had to lead him down a road of temptation. The family wants him and his wife to know for good we did not condone her behavior."

When asked if she'll welcome her daughter back with open arms if she in fact returns to Earth, Mrs. Livingston had this to say: "As far as I'm concerned she's good as dead. She should be behind bars." Indeed, a locked cell could be what awaits Miss K. Livingston should she survive her time in space, and make her way back to this country.

"Is this what passes for maternal affection in U.S. of A.?" Sergey muttered over Katherine's shoulder. "What kind of parent wants her own daughter in a cage?"

Hot tears were streaming down Katherine's cheeks. The principal of her high school—that part stung. How many times had she explained to her parents what really happened?

She wiped her nose on the palm of her hand and turned away from Sergey. "I suppose this is funny to you?"

"No, it's downright terrifying. The ice princess, with heart melting? Please, don't go soft, we'll never survive if you do."

"Stop it!" she shouted, wheeling around. "Stop pretending that I have anything important to do here!" She crumpled the paper, all of it, into one large ball. As she did it, Sergey winced. "Why did they choose me for this?" she cried. She threw the balled-up paper at him, hitting him right in the middle of his broad chest. "Why me, why choose a pilot? I didn't fly the spacecraft here. I could have been anybody."

Sergey nodded slowly, his mocking smile gone. His hands were slightly flexed at his sides, as though he might have to grab and restrain her. She pulled herself up to her full height. "Yes," he said slowly, "you could have been anybody. Any pretty girl, any American. It's just about the story."

"The story. I'm a storybook character." She clenched her fists and began hitting him, her hands bouncing off his chest like rubber balls on a brick wall. She was sobbing, tearing at him, all because he was the only man here and he could stand in for so many. She'd begun shoving him when he caught her hands.

"Stop," he said quietly. "Just stop. Wait."

Panting, she watched him walk over to the camera, which stuck out of one of the walls on its little white arm. He moved behind the machine, a finger to his lips. Then he reached under it and flicked a switch, at the same time holding the green light with the opposite thumb. The light went out.

"You can turn it off?" Her fingernails began to curl into her palms again. "You could've turned it off this whole time?"

"You forget I spent three weeks here without you at first. They did not explain to me how to do this. I figured it out for myself."

"How do I know it's really off?"

"Here's how." He took a deep breath, his brown eyes sad, the corners of his mouth turned downward. "I will tell you a secret. You may be here as a tool for the state, a mannequin of sorts. Who cleans. But I am here as a punishment."

A horrible thought came to Katherine then: What if Sergey were a murderer? A rapist? What if she had been sharing a tiny glass home, with no exits, with a violent criminal this entire time?

"What did you do?" she asked, backing up a bit.

Only the dark side of his face was visible to her now. He looked down as he spoke. "I was a deserter. After Stalingrad, I slipped away from my squadron and hid in a stable until a blind old lady brought me into her house. I was only seventeen. I had no shoes, no food. I was skin and bone. I did not want to kill any more Germans."

"The war ended eight years ago. What have you been doing since?"

"I took care of the old woman's farm for a while. She was good to me, better than my own parents."

"What was her name?" Katherine felt bold asking,

but the question burst from her lips as though it had a mind of its own.

"Her name was Lizabeta," Sergey replied, his face riddled with grief, and she hoped he didn't notice that her posture relaxed a bit as something unclenched within her. "I was with her when she died. She had no family." He sniffed loudly. "After that, I attempted to stay on. But the people in her village found out who I was and called the police. It was either come here or go to a penal colony in Siberia."

"Seems like an easy choice. Why you, among all the deserters? Why did you get this opportunity?"

"I had a little fame, before the war, as an amateur sportsman. I did the luge—you know what that is?" He mimicked lying on his back, wiggling his body from side to side, and she nodded. She could imagine him hurtling along the ice, his big hands gripping the sled.

A slight smile lifted the right corner of his mouth. "Plus, I am handsome."

"That's what you think," she said, but she couldn't help it: she was smiling, too.

Slowly, Sergey took a seat at the little table where they had their meals. She lowered herself down into the opposite chair, legs shaking. "All right," she said, "I believe you. The camera—er, visio-telespeaker—is turned off. If this is a long con, it's a good one."

His face was serious. "Do you understand that they are paying us the same, Katherine? They do not place value on what I'm doing any higher than on you. In a sense, I am only here for the story, too."

She pulled her jaw back, surprised. Could it be true? "How do you know we're making the same salary?"

"Because I am making twelve thousand rubles per month, and so are you."

She was nearly speechless. "I am."

Another grin curved the side of his lips. She tried not to follow suit. "Does it make you feel any better, about the housework? The fact that we are on equal terms? It is the beauty of the Soviet Union, eh?" He gestured around with his long, muscular arms. "And up here, there is a nice view, yes?"

She brought her seat closer to his, gave him another small shove on the chest. "Convince me you're telling the truth about all of this." She pushed him a little farther. "How do I know I can trust you?"

He seemed nervous with her pushing him. "You can."

"I can trust you, a deserter? Why should I believe that?"

"Because I deserted for a good reason." He caught her palms in his hands. "I am not a killer."

"I know that," she replied, staring into his eyes. They studied each other for a moment. His eyes, hooded and serious, were like two matches struck aflame. "Neither am I," she added, her voice husky now with . . . She hesitated to think of it as desire, but it was something, something.

"I know that," said Sergey, his words coming out in nearly a whisper.

The table was small, and so he had only to reach those long arms around and scoop her into his lap, and now they were in the same chair. She had never been this close to him before, close enough to see the pores on his face, to watch his fiery brown eyes dart back and forth across hers. He smelled wonderful, of warm skin and sweet breath, like the dried cherries they'd just eaten, and his hair felt silky between her fingers. At first he flinched, reminding her how long it had been since either of them had touched someone, but then he exhaled slowly and let his warm hands travel the length of her back.

She realized how long she'd been staring at the blank, empty landscape, how it had made her feel dead and bleached inside. Perhaps she'd felt that way on Earth, too.

They began kissing, his soft lips moving against hers, his hands caressing her back. His fingers crept around to the front of her tunic, to unhook the three metallic buttons holding her bodice together: one, two, three. He bent down and kissed the skin between her breasts.

No one had ever mentioned prophylactics up here in their habitat, when they were showing her the hairbrushes and soap flakes and toothpaste, but she pushed that from her mind as a moan escaped her lips. She wrapped her arms around his warm neck.

She knew she shouldn't be doing this, but she had to, she had to, she had to.

13

I'd have been embarrassed to admit it to Glenys, but I went to see Eli Cohn the very next day. I'd called him as soon as I got back to my apartment after lunch, and he agreed to meet me at his office. He worked in the Hearst Building, at Fifty-seventh and Eighth, near Columbus Circle. All through the taxi ride through the park, past the Sheep Meadow and the Plaza, a route I typically enjoyed for people-watching, I gripped the seat. My knees bent at funny angles toward each other, and my heels tapped the floor of the cab.

The rumor, which I'd gotten out of Glenys with only a bit of prodding, was so sensational I couldn't believe she'd speak it aloud. She'd heard—from a friend of a friend of a friend, she was careful to tell me—that Joe was in bed with the Central Intelligence Agency.

Joe Martin, in cahoots with the CIA.

I didn't know much about the agency—no one did—other than that it was a new wing of government for a modern era, a network of spies in combat with the Russians using sneaky, back-door methods. The words "Central Intelligence" made me think of pith helmets, white men on camelback, the smoky private rooms of European restaurants; it made me think of men shaking hands in a jungle in South America. It gave me a shiver. The thought of Joe's being involved with them—sure, it made him a patsy, and a bona-fide square, but there was a certain glamour to it all.

And it made sense. Joe had been born in New Jersey, but his mother had emigrated from Sicily in her teens. He had a full-throated desire to be a true American, an American as valuable as the boys who won the world wars. I recognized this urge in him because I'd always felt it myself. It was part of what had made me fall in love with him.

By the time I boarded an elevator in the Hearst Building, my heart was thudding so strongly it made my ribs hurt. My haunted face stared back at me in the shiny brass doors of the elevator. If you didn't know me well, you'd have said I was my same old self. But I could see the darkness around my eyes. I could feel the tightness of my clothes, the ache in my chest.

"I'm here to see Mr. Cohn," I told the receptionist on the fourth floor. A plaque and directory behind her on the wall read WOMEN'S MONTHLIES.

She peered at me over her glasses. "Yes, he told me you'd be coming. Mr. Cohn is on the right, at the end of the hall." She pointed with her pen. "He's with *Good Housekeeping*."

Now I was curious. I took my time walking toward Eli's office, stopping to observe framed covers lining the walls and to nod at the secretaries at their desks outside the men's offices. All of the *Good Housekeeping* covers featured cherubic illustrations of children at play. I knew little of Eli, but from what I did know, it was hard to imagine him working for such a magazine. I'd spoken with him once, briefly, at a party, back when *Downtown* was gestating and he was still someone Joe and Harry seemed eager to cozy up to. At that point, Eli had been a junior editor at *Time*.

According to Glenys, Eli had worked under Whittaker Chambers at *Time*—*the* Whittaker Chambers, who'd accused Alger Hiss of being a Communist spy in front of the House, who essentially got Hiss convicted of perjury. The Un-American Activities Committee had called Eli in as a witness as well, and it was widely expected that he would verify Chambers's good character. But Eli had refused to confirm what Chambers said about Hiss, either pleading the Fifth or outright contradicting Chambers. He made things terribly inconvenient, as Glenys put it—everyone wanted Hiss to be the scapegoat, to believe Chambers's own days as a Soviet operative were over. But when Eli was asked to identify any Soviet spies in the room, past or present, he had said that the only one he knew of was Chambers himself.

That week, Eli had lost his job with *Time*.

Now here he was, working for *Good Housekeeping*. It was a wonder anyone would hire him. I found his office at the very end of the hall, beside a spectacular display of Stargazer lilies. He had no girl outside his office, which was only big enough for his desk, one uncomfortable-looking visitor's chair, and a low bookshelf. The place was a mess.

ELI COHN, the plaque beside his door read. BOOKS EDITOR.

"Miss Leithauser." Eli stood behind the desk, buttoning his jacket, and smiled at me. He extended a hand to welcome me in. "Please, come have a seat."

Maybe it was the pregnancy, but I felt myself flush. I'd forgotten what a toothsome fellow Eli Cohn was, with fuzzy black caterpillar eyebrows and high cheekbones. There was a passing resemblance to Joe, in fact, but Eli stood a bit taller.

"I won't take up too much of your time," I said as I sat gingerly on the hard wooden chair.

He sat back in his own chair and took off his glasses. "That's all right, I'm only pretending to work today."

We both laughed. I couldn't tell if he was kidding or not. He flashed me his white teeth, hands interlocked in front of him, waiting politely for me to speak. The wall behind him was all window, but he had the gauzy curtains pulled closed, so the room was awash with filtered noon light and floating dust and felt like at least a hundred degrees. The armpits of my cardigan were already damp. The side walls seemed to lean in toward me; a man of Eli's height must have constantly felt as if he'd bump his elbows. I wondered what he thought of this miserable little office, this new job. It all seemed a kind of punishment.

"What kind of books do you review, Mr. Cohn?" I asked him.

"Good ones, if I can help it." There was a warmth about him, an ease with which he smiled. I tried to picture him stonewalling the House Un-American Activities Committee, defying what they wanted him to do. "I don't only do women's novels. I review some quality fiction. Last month, I interviewed Salinger."

My left cheek twitched. "The women's novels, the quality fiction—these are discrete categories? Or do they ever overlap?"

His eyebrows went up, and he sat forward in his chair. I had his attention. "They overlap," he said, putting his glasses back on. Now his smile had gone from flirtatious to genuinely interested. "You caught me, Miss Leithauser. I shouldn't have put it that way."

"That's all right. Please, call me Louise."

"Louise. You can call me Eli. We have met before, haven't we? What is it that brings you to my office today?"

"I . . ." My mouth went dry. I scanned his desk for a lozenge. Nothing. Stalling, I let my gaze wander over the dusty bookshelf, the stuffy air, the cheap drop ceiling and old flat carpet. I thought of what Harry had said that night earlier in the summer—it felt so long ago—*they're listening, they have bugs everywhere* . . .

What were the chances they—whoever the hell "they" were—would be keeping tabs on someone like Eli Cohn?

"Would you, um . . ." I stood up so suddenly I made myself dizzy. My hand went to the edge of his desk to steady myself. "Would you like to take a walk?"

"You know, when you first came in," Eli said as we strolled, fifteen minutes later, "I thought you were going to ask me for a job."

I smiled, a tight-lipped smile. "I wish it were something like that."

We were walking the path beside the Sheep Meadow. People on their lunch breaks dotted the lawn on picnic blankets, eating sandwiches their sweethearts or wives had brought from home. When we reached one of the more tree-shaded paths, Eli stopped and leaned against the fence. A slight roguishness crept back into his smile. "Is this private enough for you?"

"Yes." I took a deep breath. "Glenys Billings suggested I contact you. She mentioned rumors about Joe. It seemed to me she was trying to talk me out of marrying him."

"Interesting, coming from Harry's wife. Are you and Joe engaged to be married?"

"Not yet," I said. "But I'm going to have a baby in the spring." Honesty seemed the only way forward here. If I expected him to tell me sensitive information, I'd have to give the same in return. "I still need to tell Joe about it."

Eli's eyebrows went all the way up, then all the way down. "Oh, I see," he said quietly. "I'll be discreet, Miss Leithauser." Gone was any trace of playfulness in his voice, in his face. His hand went to my forearm, resting gently on the wrist. A group of cyclists blew past us, and he shielded me, perhaps subconsciously. "Can we find you a bench?"

"No, thank you. I'm fine." My hands in their gloves were balled into nervous fists, clenched against my hips. "Please, just tell me whatever it is Glenys wants me to know."

Eli sighed, looking away from me toward the ground. "I'm not sure I have the information you're looking for."

"Just tell me what you know."

"Okay." He rubbed his palms on the thighs of his slacks. "I didn't go to Harvard with Joe; I was a few years ahead, at Columbia. A little older than the 'oldest man at the Game,' you might say," he added with a wry grin. I rolled my eyes. "But Joe and I ran in the same circles after he came to the city, and for a little while, before he got the capital to found his own magazine, we worked together."

"At *The New Yorker*?"

"Yes. This was when Joe was the low man, doing ad sales, and I was an assistant editor. I was a low man, too, I'm not claiming anything else, but, because I was in editorial and Joe in ads, I always thought he had a bit of an inferiority complex around me." He gave me kind of a sheepish look, the sun speckling his face through the branches of a pear tree above. "Sorry."

"It's fine. So—what did he do? Put a tack on your chair?"

Eli let out a sharp laugh. "No. I don't know how to put this, but . . ." He scrunched up his mouth, then started again. "I was the low man, right? *The New Yorker* never gave me a byline. But you'd be surprised how many articles I actually wrote for them." A gleam came into his eye, and he gave me a slight nod. "Actually, maybe *you* wouldn't be surprised, Louise."

Despite everything, I felt a rush of pleasure at having been recognized for what I'd written, even under a pen name. "No, I'm not surprised."

"Joe and I became friends in those early days; he'd ask me to go for drinks or watch a ball game. And he'd ask me what I was writing. Once, I showed him something I was working on about China. Even I knew it was pretty risky stuff, and could come across as sympathetic to Mao, or critical of Truman. I was trying to get it just right before I showed the bosses. So I asked Joe what he thought, and he gushed over it." Eli rolled his eyes. "That was a Friday. On Monday morning, they called me into the publisher's office, and they killed the story."

"So—what?—you think he tattled on you?"

Eli laughed. "Good word for it—'tattled.' Yes, that's what it felt like at the time. Like he'd told someone who had some connection to the powers that be, and they'd done what they had to do to keep me from saying something they didn't like about China."

"Someone who had a connection to the powers that be." I

felt as if I'd swallowed a bag of marbles. "Eli, there's a rumor about Joe."

"Oh?" said Eli.

For some reason, I felt silly saying it, watching his face for signs of skepticism. "Glenys has heard Joe might be involved with the CIA."

Eli didn't answer right away. Wind ruffled all the leaves above us at once, creating a curtain of sound.

At last, he laughed. "That seems a bit far-fetched to me. I assumed he'd told one of the bigwigs at Condé Nast about my article, and they decided they were too conservative for that sort of thing. But I've heard of crazier things than magazine-editor spies." He crossed his arms over his chest. "Does he act like a spy? Have interesting gadgets?" He was smiling, having fun with the idea now, making me feel sort of silly. "Is he ever a bit too fixated on people?"

"James Baldwin," I said quickly, thinking of Joe giving him the third degree in Rome.

Eli looked incredulous. "You met Baldwin?"

I told him about Rome, about our uncomfortable supper near the Colosseum, though I left out the part about Joe grabbing my wrists in an alley afterward. As I relayed the story—Joe's awkward questions, Baldwin's challenging responses—I felt a queasiness grow inside my stomach. What if Joe had been on a mission, led by our government, to silence Baldwin?

As I spoke, Eli nodded thoughtfully. He didn't say anything for a while.

"This stays between us, all right?" I said when I was done relaying the Rome story. "Please don't write a tell-all."

Eli shook his head. "Oh, I absolutely won't, Louise. I'd suggest you keep it to yourself, too, for your safety." He looked over his shoulder, as if to prove a point. "But I'm glad you told me. Makes a fellow feel a little less crazy." He shrugged.

"What happened after they killed your China story?"

"I kept my head down. Wrote what I thought they wanted. Next time an editorial job opened up, it went to Joe. The ad boy. I heard he was making more than I was off the bat. And then he and Harry left to start *Downtown*. Doors just seemed to open for Joe. And you see what's happened to me." Eli laughed. "Now I'm the one who sounds jealous. I suppose I am." He glanced up at me, a sad smirk at the corner of his mouth.

"Egads," I muttered. The glamour I'd initially perceived, when Glenys had first mentioned the CIA, had completely faded. Now Joe just seemed to me like some sort of snitch for the government. "When we were in Rome, he was meeting with some fund-raisers. They had a strange name. Could they have been a cover for the CIA?"

"Oh, yeah?" Eli asked casually, or, rather, trying to sound casual. "What was it, do you remember?"

We stared at each other for a while. I opened my mouth. *The Congress for Cultural Freedom*, I was about to say, but I stopped myself. A cool breeze rushed through the trees above us, sprinkling goose bumps across my bare arms. Behind Eli's dark silhouette, in the Sheep Meadow, the picnickers were packing up their blankets and baskets. I saw a girl about my age, slim in trousers and a gingham shirt tied at her waist, staring straight at me. She visored her hand above her eyes, which were locked in a hard gaze with mine, as her companion folded their quilt into a neat triangle. He stood and turned his head over his shoulder to look at me as well.

Perhaps I was only being paranoid, but those two gave me the willies. I looked back at Eli, whom I'd barely known half an hour before, whose hand I had been ready to take in sympathy as he bemoaned the disappointments of his career. What did I know about this man? How could I trust him? How could I trust anyone?

"It's just a rumor, though, right?" I said, shoving my fingers farther into my gloves. "Unlikely. As you said. Hearsay."

Eli regarded me coolly, his hands in his pockets. "Sure. It may behoove your sanity, and mine, to see it that way."

I stuck out my hand for him to shake. "Thank you so much for the information. And now I really must be going. I can't keep you from your work."

His face went blank. He stuffed his hands back into his trouser pockets. "Sure. Gotta get back to my work. So long, Louise."

"So long, and thanks!"

As I turned to rush toward the beckoning taxis on Fifty-ninth Street, I thought I heard him say, "Good luck."

I had the taxi driver drop me off a block from my apartment so that I could walk. Maybe I needed a chance to clear my head.

No, if I was being honest with myself, I didn't want him to know where I lived. A completely random stranger, this taxi driver who looked like a grandfather from Queens, and my paranoia had reached such levels that I didn't want him to know my address.

A warm, fine rain had begun falling. I wrapped a navy scarf around my hair as I walked, head down. In a few days, everyone I knew would be reading my interview with Hemingway. My brush with greatness, my own clever questions and observations wrapped around this celebrated man's words. My dream assignment. I'd gotten it because of Joe and his connections. His fund-raising. If Glenys's claim about Joe was true, it implicated me as well. But did it make us villains? I wasn't sure.

And I wanted, so badly, to trust Joe's instincts. Despite any misgivings, I had to admit I had it bad for the guy. I dreamed of him at night, got flutters in my stomach whenever we said hello. Not to mention I had a new person growing in my belly, and *Joe had put it there*. When I allowed myself to feel my rawest emotions, this gave me an unabashed, primal thrill.

"Oof!" Right in front of my building, I ran smack into the shoulder of a very tall man. "Sorry," I said reflexively. He turned to face me, his lip curled under a red mustache. He'd just been standing there, staring out at the street.

"Pardon," he muttered, and then he turned back to where a passing cab was approaching the corner and whistled for it so shrilly that I realized I'd been brewing another headache. I stuffed my fingers into my ears—at the moment, I didn't care if it was rude—and shoved my key into the door to my tiny lobby. The door felt heavy as I swung it open with effort, holding it with my hip.

"Doors *just seemed to open*," Eli had said. Doors for Joe.

Doors for me. What if I did nothing, said nothing? What if I let the doors continue to open?

My head pounded as I climbed the two flights of stairs. All I wanted was to toe off my shoes, peel down my damp, restricting stockings, and take a shower. A little reefer wouldn't have been bad, either, but I hadn't had any in ages. And, besides, would that be bad for the baby?

When I got to my apartment door, I saw someone had taped a hastily scrawled note, just above the knob, written on pink paper: "Call your mother. She's been trying to reach you on the party line." I crumpled the memo in my palm. Lena upstairs, I figured. The sound of our party line ringing for me sent her into hysterics, especially when I wasn't there to answer.

I swung the door open, into my dark apartment, still thinking about the baby. The baby, the baby. What in God's name was I going to do about the baby? I had to tell—

"Joe." My handbag dropped at my feet.

He was standing in my living room, holding my telephone to his ear. He looked almost guilty, his eyes big, his shoulders hitched up to his ears, as if I'd caught him trespassing. Which, technically, I had. I'd never given Joe the key to my apartment. It was even a joke between us—I could get into his whenever I wanted, but here he'd have to ring the buzzer like any old suitor.

"Joe," I said again. "What are you doing here? How did you get—"

He held up a finger, and took a gingerly step closer to me. Now I could see that he was crying, silently. Two wet tracks lined his cheeks. I could hear a voice going a mile a minute on the other end, a female voice, I thought, shrill and insistent. Joe took another step closer, reaching tentatively to me as if he were approaching an uncaged tiger.

"Yes," he murmured, into the phone. "She's here now. I'll give you to her."

Fear coursed through my body. "Joe, what's the meaning of this? What on Earth—"

He handed me the receiver. "It's your mother. Louise, it's your mother, it's—"

I lifted the handset as though pulling it through water. Six inches from my ear, I could already hear her sobs.

"It's your brother," Joe whispered. "I'm sorry, I'm so sorry."

I collapsed to the floor, onto my knees, and Joe knelt with me.

PART II

WINTER

1954

✧ ✧ ✧
✧ ✧
✧
✧

14

January 10, 1954

Dear Miss Leithauser,

*Hell of a hatchet job they did on the interview. You did
fine on the observation bits, but they chopped what I said to
pieces. Had a sense this was coming all along. Those boys are
deep into it with the censor lot. At least Clifton, that lousy
publisher of mine, lets me say what I will as long as the
writing's good. If it's not good, he sends it back with womanish
notes scrawled all over. Might as well use pink pen.*

*Am back in the country for a while. Came through New
York for a few days but didn't want to see anyone. Just a new
thing or two at the Met, time for friends, no journalists. Not
even you, even though you have the hat Mary gave me last
Christmas. Will notify you when we are back at home so that
you can return hat.*

*Now am in the West. Staying with an old friend with a cattle
ranch near Casper. I write for an hour and a half each morning,
and then, for the rest of the day, we hunt. Landed a bear last
Thursday, a great big male with gray in his muzzle. The
meat had the texture of wet yarn. But, daughter, thrill of the
hunt makes for mighty good sauce. There's that killer instinct.*

In any case, Mary and I have a sense we're all alone here. None of the busybodies on the coasts. Drinking has been fine, sunsets early and bright, and the guerrilla novel, which has turned out to be a marvelous long story, is flowing as quick as water.

Daughter, you've crossed my mind more than once since that day at the zoo and the Garden. Hope whatever trouble you had found yourself in has been resolved in a satisfactory manner, or that you're embracing trouble with clear eyes.

Tell them where they can put the interview assignments from now on. Keep up with your own writing. Remember not to get behind in the count.

Yrs,
E. Hemingway

P.S. The best of my novels is not <u>The Sun Also Rises</u>, as you said. It is <u>A Farewell to Arms</u>. There's the one I've got to outdo before my time is up.

I heard the bathtub begin to drain, and I jumped. Quickly, I stuffed Hemingway's typewritten letter—only the post-script had been scrawled in pencil—back into my purse. I'd had it in my possession for a week and had read and reread it a hundred times. The thrill of receiving word from him, even if it was just his way of getting his darn hat back, made my toes curl.

When Joe emerged from his bathroom in a towel, comb-ing his wet hair, he found me curling my eyelashes. I gave him a little smile. I sat at the vanity he'd set up for me in his apartment, wearing my new Chantilly lace nightgown with matching peignoir. The nightie was bell-shaped, ending just below my panties.

Besides the vanity, Joe had bought me an entire maternity wardrobe, assembled by the salesgirls at Barney's. The only caveat was that I had to keep these new things at his apartment. The maternity wear I'd purchased for myself looked far more pedestrian.

He came up behind me, put his hands on my shoulders, and kissed me on the cheek.

"Why won't you let me marry you today?" he whispered against my temple. "Head to City Hall, make it official. . . ."

My smile faded. I licked my lips and gazed out the window. Joe's apartment, at the corner of Forty-second and Tenth, faced north and west, with a view of the Hudson River and the low roofs of Hell's Kitchen. This morning, a light flurry of snow had just petered out, and the city looked like an elaborate cake, dusted with powdered sugar.

"Oh, silly," I said, pushing him away gently. "You know how I feel about City Hall weddings. Let's wait till I have my figure back, and I can wear a real gown."

He frowned and turned away, and I watched him in the mirror as I curled my round brush under the ends of my hair. I didn't give a damn about a real gown, and part of me feared Joe knew I was simply buying time.

"I'm also not in the most celebratory mood yet," I said quietly, toward my compact. "You understand."

Joe took a deep breath and nodded. "I do."

After my brother died, it had become immediately clear to me that I wanted to keep this baby—my flesh and blood, and Paul's, too. Joe had been there to support me, honoring my wishes, though he hadn't quite understood why I didn't want him at Paul's memorial service in Ossining. Whenever that subject came up, or if he started asking questions about my parents, I put him off with talk about the baby. To my surprise, he'd been supportive of the pregnancy in general, even eager; he'd gotten my engagement ring within weeks, and I'd accepted it. It was a bright half-carat diamond in a palladium band, the new "it" metal, which Joe had found at a jeweler's on Wall Street.

But when he pressed me to marry quickly, I'd demurred, even in the fog of my grief. I'd had the willpower to hold on to my own apartment and my job. For now, at least.

"And—what?—our child will be the ring bearer?" Joe asked from his dresser, rooting through his socks. "My mother won't exactly be pleased."

"Your mother doesn't sound as if she's pleased anyway, dear." I swung around to face him. "And since when do you care what your parents think? You run a magazine that prints photos of nude girls, for crying out loud."

He shrugged and smiled a wistful smile. He had undergone somewhat of a metamorphosis as a result of my pregnancy. He hadn't gotten chubby, exactly, but had filled out a bit more in the face, his cheeks fuller and manlier, more fatherly. Even his beard, shorn down now but visible underneath the skin, seemed to have thickened. It was almost as if something pheromonal was going on, my pregnancy and its aura taking him from juvenile to silverback in a matter of months. I had to say, he'd become even more delicious.

"If you can get a break at Mr. Franklin's today," he said, "maybe think of a few more questions for Malamud, would you? It'd be good to have a list for us to go over with Harry, when we get a minute this weekend."

I put some lotion in my hands and began smoothing it up and down my bare legs, aware of Joe watching. "I've got a few questions worked out."

The Hemingway article, butchered as it was, had been a great success for the magazine. The issue had come out right around the same time as Paul's funeral, so I hadn't been at peak form to argue with Joe and Harry, but they had indeed done a hatchet job on my work: gone was everything about Cuba, about the FBI, about Hemingway's reasons for living outside the States. I thought the whole thing came across as sophomoric drivel when you took all that out: a schoolgirl acting skittish about boxing and bullfighting (gone were my points about Korea) and babbling about word counts in fiction. But, apparently, readers had enjoyed it, as had the critics: *Downtown* No. 3, the issue in which my article had appeared, had earned Joe and Harry a Magazine Editors' Guild award nomination for best new monthly. We all were ecstatic, even I myself. After that, Joe and Harry had declared I was worthy of at least a bimonthly feature: Louise Leithauser, girl journalist, interviewing the great men of letters. Next up would be Bernard Malamud. I planned to ask him which seat in Yankee Stadium he thought King Arthur might choose.

"Did you get any writing done yesterday?" asked Joe, tugging a shoe tree out of his loafer.

"Sure, I did," I said without looking at him. I'd written, all right, but I hadn't been working on my questions for Malamud. I was still knee-deep in my story about Katherine and Sergey on the moon, despite what I knew Joe would think of it. It had taken on a life of its own; sometimes I couldn't type fast enough, and when I got to the end of a page I'd find I was out of breath, heart pounding. The two had become lovers, which had been my plan all along, but I was no longer sure Katherine would get the better of Sergey, bend him to her will, make an American of him. I was no longer at all sure where the story was headed.

I blew Joe a kiss as he made for the bedroom door, headed for the *Downtown* office. A second later, he was back.

"It's snowing pretty hard out there again. Let me get you a car to the office."

"I'll manage on my own. I have my snow boots here."

Joe frowned. "I'm only trying to keep you and the baby safe."

I shook my head. "We're getting along just fine. Oh!" I cried, catching him. He turned around. "Do you have a copy of *A Farewell to Arms*?"

"Probably. If I do, you know where to find it. Why?"

Subconsciously, I let my fingers flit to the leather handle of my purse, where I'd been keeping the letter from Papa. "Oh," I replied, reaching inside my robe to scratch the taut skin on my warm, round belly, "just something I've been meaning to read for a while."

Joe let out a nervous laugh. "Maybe you should wait until after you've had the baby."

"Why?"

"At the end . . . Well, I don't want to spoil it for you, honey, but it's not the best fit for the expectant mother."

"Let me guess. Disastrous childbirth?"

"You could say that."

I shrugged. "I'm not worried. I'm sure Hemingway's girl didn't have twilight sleep." Labor and delivery were the furthest things from my mind. It was a modern era, I would have anesthesia, people did it all the time. It wasn't in my plans to remember a thing. I'd go in with my hair done and makeup on, and I'd wake up a few hours later without even having broken a sweat.

Joe smiled. He came over to give me one last lingering kiss, on the lips this time, putting his cool hand under my nightie. "See you tomorrow at the awards dinner."

I waited until he'd left, listened for him to lock the door. Then I ran to the spare bedroom.

Joe's apartment was a two-bed—or a one-plus-den, to be more accurate. In the little den he kept his bookshelves and an old writing desk he'd bought at a thrift store in the Village when he first moved to the city. The desk came with a pedigree—it might have once belonged to Henry Jarvis Raymond, the antiques dealer claimed—but to me it just looked like a beat-up table, soft wood with an artificial orangey stain, dented and scratched in deep black grooves. Joe claimed that when he sat there he could feel the energy and drive Raymond must have felt when he was cofounding *The New York Times*.

I opened the drawers one by one, as I'd done on several previous occasions. Nothing new. The drawers were messy, full of Joe's memoranda and torn-off notes to himself, articles ripped from competing magazines, and aspirin, Alka Seltzer, and miniature bottles of liquor. I'd already combed through it all. In another drawer, a few boxes of Eaton's Corrasable Bond paper and some fresh gummy-pink erasers. And candy, always candy. I crunched some nonpareil chocolates as I rummaged.

I'd been doing this since the day I found out about my brother—that is, the day I'd spoken with Eli—fishing around in Joe's desk and bookshelves for anything to corroborate what Eli and Glenys suggested about him. Anything that would give me some insight into who, or what, might be pulling Joe's strings. Plain as day, Joe and Harry had edited my words and Hemingway's with a political bent, aimed at making Hemingway seem friendlier to the United States than he'd actually been. But why? It was easier for me to believe that Joe, with his naked ambition, was involved in a conspiracy than to conclude that his co-conspirators were members of our own government. We were on the side of freedom, after all. Freedom of speech, freedom of the press. That was what I'd always believed, and until I found some evidence that the CIA, or FBI, or any other government body was working to control artists' words, I wasn't quite ready to accept that.

So far, all I had found, surprisingly, was a lot of booze. Never had I thought of Joe as a lush—that was more Harry's role. Beyond the stocked liquor cabinet, which I'd been familiar with, I found bottles of bourbon, schnapps, even a half-empty jug of tequila stashed in the apartment. This morning, as I combed his shelves for *A Farewell to Arms*—it would be my cover, if he surprised me by coming back to the apartment—my fingers touched not one but two bottles of Scotch with sticky labels, a squat cinnamon schnapps used as a bookend, and a mini–vodka bottle flung on a high shelf, empty. For a while, I just stared at the bottle, puzzling it out.

Why would someone throw an empty bottle up into his bookshelf? It sounded like something that might happen at a party, but I knew there'd never been a party here—the place was just too damn small. And if there had been, I'd have been invited.

If he was drinking alone, I wondered what motivated this. Stress? Guilt?

Pushing the chair toward the bookshelf, I stood on the seat (unsteadily, my weight creaking the spindly legs) and pulled down an old hatbox where Joe kept his tax returns. Nothing seemed to have changed there, either. I was losing hope of ever finding anything. This didn't produce the relief I would have hoped, or the closure I needed to marry Joe. Instead, I felt even more unsettled.

I was just about to dismount the chair when I noticed a group of books shelved sideways.

"There you are," I said, reaching for *A Farewell to Arms*. For Pete's sake, when had I started talking to myself? Maybe I was starting to lose it.

As I pulled the book from the middle of the stack of paperbacks, the pile shifted, and a single sheet of paper emerged from the bottom. I picked it up to read.

The handwriting was large, cockily drawn in thick black ink. Right away, my eyes picked out my own name. I gripped the letter in shaking hands. My head went fuzzy, and when I held on to the bookshelf the whole thing wobbled. I managed to catch my breath and lower myself, one bare foot at a time, to the cold floor.

It was a memo from Harry, written on his personal stationery, dated right after my meeting with Hemingway.

Joe,

Here it is with the fixes. I'll leave it up to you to decide how much you want to put back in, if you think you'll be in the doghouse with Louise if we change too much. I don't think she's as bad a writer as you say, but it damn sure would've been best if she let him talk and didn't yammer on herself so much. At least she took good notes.

Well, he must've thought she was pretty or we wouldn't have gotten anything, and there's a little meat left here. It won't be a bad piece, but can we lead with it? I'm thinking maybe a last-page question-and-answer will be the better format. Ultimately, it will be up to you-know-who

The letter cut off there; the rest of it had been torn away. I smacked the paper. My cheeks were flaming hot. "I don't think she's as bad a writer as you say." My fists clenched, wrinkling the paper. I focused on the last part: "It will be up to you-know-who."

The boys had been scared to death of a mystery man lurking at their release party. Who the hell was it, and whom did he work for? This little torn slip of paper, which I stuffed into my handbag before dressing quickly for work—I was going to be late—might just have been the best proof I'd found that he existed at all.

With a splitting headache, I arrived at work a half-hour late. A bad move, since I'd decided I finally had to tell Mr. Franklin I was expecting. I knew he and Mrs. Whitacre had to have noticed, especially now that I looked as if I'd swallowed a small melon. I rapped lightly on his door when I heard him get off the phone with a client. Inside, I was still fuming, flustered, over having found the note from Harry. My news came out in an ungainly rush just after I'd closed the door to his office, shutting out Mrs. Whitacre and her pricked ears.

Kind as he was, Mr. Franklin pretended he'd had no idea.

"This is wonderful news, Miss Leithauser, just wonderful," he said. He went over to his decanter to pour himself a drink, gesturing to me with an empty lowball glass. I declined. "Especially after what happened to your brother."

I couldn't help it; tears sprang to my eyes. My ribs pushed against my womb as I took a long, deep breath. He reached over to hand me a tissue from his brass-plated tissue box. "Thank you, sir."

"Some of the happiest marriages I've seen have begun as . . ." He cleared his throat and adjusted his thick-framed glasses. The ice inside his glass clinked. "What I mean to say is, I'm sure you and Mr. Martin will have a very happy union. You know I've seen a lot in my day."

"A lot of unhappy ones, I'm sure," I replied, and we both uttered short-lived laughs. He took his seat behind his desk, across from me, and a silence fell over us. Behind him, the snow had stopped pelting the window. In its stead, a sad gray sky peeked through the brown blinds.

I let my eyes fall to the desk's surface. Neat, as always, but cluttered with memorabilia from his family: a sepia photograph of his wife in a 1920s bias-cut wedding gown and embroidered veil; a monogrammed gilt desk set, a gift from his children for his fiftieth birthday; a glass paperweight with two miniature blue baby shoes suspended inside. I wondered how a man's family remained so happy, at least from my perspective, when his entire career was predicated upon a reminder of so many other people's suffering.

I nearly asked him to share the secret to a happy marriage, but I could predict what he'd say: honesty, trust, communication.

Harry's words had been playing Ping-Pong inside my skull all morning: "I don't think she's as bad a writer as you say. . . . It will be up to you-know-who . . . ." There was no question: I'd have to confront Joe with the letter. I knew my voice would shake when I did it. I knew I might break into angry tears. But it had to be done.

I forced myself back to the present. "I'll get back to my work, then, sir."

Mr. Franklin had been mid-sip; the ice cubes fell against his teeth, and he spat one back into his glass, wincing. "In your condition, are you quite sure, Miss Leithauser? You're feeling up to the task?"

"Oh, yes," I said, and, to demonstrate, I stood and did a little tap dance I'd learned from watching Shirley Temple as a child—"Shuffle Off to Buffalo." Mr. Franklin didn't laugh.

"Well, all right," he said, looking very unsure. He pressed the buzzer on his desk. "Mrs. Whitacre, would you ask them to bring my car around? I have to be in court by ten-thirty."

I thought that was the end of it, until he caught me at the door.

"Miss Leithauser, when you get a chance, bring me the file marked 'Résumés,' from the Office Miscellany cabinet. We saved some of the other girls' contact information, you see, when we hired you. I'd like to start calling them so we can be sure to have your replacement lined up."

I felt queasy. "My replacement?"

"Of course! You don't intend to keep working for long, do you? After all, you and Joe plan to . . ." He gestured toward my engagement ring.

My lungs couldn't get enough air. I supposed I knew I'd have to stop working after the baby was born, but until then

I'd thought I could continue as I was. Without my job, I'd never be able to keep my apartment. Without my apartment, I'd have to marry Joe right away. And I'd just found that stinking letter.

"The baby isn't due until April, Mr. Franklin. Can I at least stay on until then?"

Now he looked squeamish. He adjusted his glasses. "You've seemed on edge to me lately, Miss Leithauser. Are you certain some well-deserved rest time isn't what you need?"

"Not at all, sir." I swallowed, thinking of the rent that would soon be due. "I planned on working right up until the baby's arrival."

He winced, no doubt imagining my water breaking on his Persian rug. "I think you'd better bring me those résumés, Miss Leithauser, just in case. These babies have a way of deciding when they'll come on their own."

"I'll get right on that."

As I gripped the doorknob with a sweaty palm, I heard him chuckle.

"And here I just thought you'd helped yourself to too many of those Hostess cakes you girls keep in the break room."

I bit my lip to keep from saying anything I'd regret.

When I came out of his office, I noticed Mrs. Whitacre adjusting herself in her seat, wiggling her behind as if she'd just sat down. No doubt she'd been eavesdropping. We gave each other tight smiles, without a word; as I'd begun to show, her demeanor toward me had cooled. I hoped she hadn't heard Mr. Franklin tell me to fetch the file. I wondered how long I could pretend I didn't know where to find it.

15

THE LUNAR HOUSEWIFE

The First Woman

Katherine lay across Sergey's warm, naked chest, gazing out the huge domed window at the Earth. From up here, it looked small and unremarkable, a featureless crescent. It was hard to believe that everything that had ever happened to her before this had occurred down there, on that bit of blue and white. All her grief, all her disappointments and humiliations. She could see none of it from up here, no signs of humanity whatsoever. The longer she spent in this quiet, lonely bubble, the smaller her home planet seemed, and the larger Sergey loomed in her consciousness.

She rolled over to face him. He was still asleep, or pretending to be; his chest rose and fell with each deep breath, but he was no longer snoring. She ran the back of her finger along his smooth cheek. The man still woke every day and bathed himself, shaved his whiskers, neatly combed his hair. At first she had thought it was vanity, all for the audience, but now she knew it was for her. It had been all along.

His hand caught hers. "A few more minutes, Katya," he whispered, his voice hoarse from sleep, his eyes still shut. His use of the pet name felt like the final step in her transformation from an American to something else. Not quite a Russian, but not an American anymore.

"You can't go home again," she murmured. She'd heard that somewhere. Sergey stirred.

She rolled onto her back, her naked breasts bared to the infinite universe above. When in human history had anyone been granted a view of the stars like this? She'd begun naming constellations she found on her own. She pointed them out to herself, her waking companions: the Cobra, the Butterfly, the Woman with the Child.

"Darling, what if . . ." She ducked under his arm, the soft hair of his armpit brushing her shoulder. He felt so warm, while she was suddenly chilled. "What if you faint at the sight of it—of the baby coming out? I'll be all alone. And what will I do then?"

Her hand went to her stomach. Her skin felt as firm as a medicine ball under her palm. She'd begun to feel the little creature stir.

Sergey laughed, a low, rumbling vibration under his ribs. "I told you, I was a soldier. I do not faint at the sight of blood."

She recoiled at the word "blood." He was a soldier, yes, but a deserting soldier. She wouldn't have said it aloud to him, but that's what he was, after all—a pacifist. A fine quality in a lover, not necessarily so in an obstetrician.

By her calculations, looking back through her journal, she was four months gone. She and Sergey were contracted to stay a year on the moon. The Soviets had enough oxygen and water to keep them there that long, and even the news of her pregnancy hadn't persuaded them to shorten the mission. Captain Kuznetsov had basic medical training, they'd informed her; he had been enlisted to oversee any medical emergencies that might occur in the lunar habitat, and this policy had not changed.

Katherine yanked the covers over their heads. They'd had to stop turning off the camera—the Earthlings, as they'd begun to call them, had complained—and so they found privacy this way: they'd duck under a blanket and whisper. It made her feel like a child, hiding from her parents.

"You can rely on me, Katya," Sergey said in the warm cocoon of the quilt. His eyes, finally opened, were dark and sleepy, squinty with affection. "I have tended to soldiers' wounds. I have endured hardship. I will not flinch when you need me most."

"I have endured hardship, too," she replied.

"What is it that happened?" he asked in a soft voice. "With you and the—the headmaster of your school?"

"The principal," she corrected him. She tucked her hands between her cheek and the pillow. Just speaking the word made her nerves jump uncomfortably. After several months of "tutoring sessions" at the motel in town, he'd asked her to run away with him. Meet at the dock, he'd said, the one where the kids fished for bluegill and smallmouth, and let's meet at night, when no one will notice we're gone until we're well on our way to Chicago. She'd been young, sixteen, and hadn't thought it strange that he wanted to meet her on the dock of the lake until he tried to throw her over.

"He interfered with me," she told Sergey. "Then he tried to kill me."

"How did you escape?"

"I threw him into the lake."

Sergey began laughing. It felt good to join him. She laughed and laughed, until tears ran down her cheeks. They dried quickly in the warm, close air under the blanket.

"Did he drown?" Sergey asked at last.

"No. He must have returned to his family sopping wet, though, and good and angry. He told everyone I'd invited him down to the water and pushed him in because I couldn't have him to myself. My parents were mortified. Nothing was the same after that."

"And now here you are," said Sergey.

"And now here I am."

"An outcast, with another outcast. Here we are."

"But we aren't outcasts anymore," she whispered. "We're valuable now. Everyone on Earth adores us. They want to see this baby born healthy."

It was true: their baby was the talk of every newspaper in Russia, and a recurring headline in most of the seedier American tabloids. The child had become a sort of royalty, to her and Sergey's excitement, the first human child to be conceived outside Earth.

She continued, excited: "I've thought it through.

We can demand a transport back to Earth, so that I can have the baby there. We offer a press conference as soon as it's born. Once it's old enough, we'll come back."

Sergey shook his head sadly. "And how old are you thinking is old enough?"

"I don't know. One? Two?"

"That's too long." He whispered so softly she could barely hear. "They would not send us back up here. They have thousands of volunteers. Our popularity is our curse. Central Command would choose another pair." His fingers caught a small snag in her hair, which he gently teased out. "We'd have to stay on Earth. And what is there on Earth for us now, my love?"

At the beginning of this mission, she'd never have dreamed she'd want to live on the moon forever. The longer she'd stayed, the more contained, confined she felt, the more she paradoxically dreaded their eventual return. What *was* there on Earth for her? A life in exile, in Russia? Would that be so terrible? They'd return a pair of heroes.

"I'd be fine on Earth as long as I could stay with you," she declared, but even as she said it, the confidence drained from her voice. On Earth, they would be at the mercy of other people. People like the Soviet officials, who could deport her at any moment if she stopped doing their bidding. Up here, they were safe. They could be the first man and the first woman.

"Of course you could stay with me," Sergey said quickly. He took her wrists in his hands and kissed the delicate skin above her crisscrossed veins. "But let us not cross that bridge. I can do it, Katya. I can deliver this baby."

His mouth crushed hers in a kiss so fierce she could no longer argue; she could no longer think.

· 16 ·

Onstage, a young woman in a gold lamé two-piece dress, a sliver of midriff showing above the skirt, bounced and flitted to the music of the orchestra. She stood behind her *Glasspiel*, which looked like a metal suitcase holding dozens of water goblets, each full of imperceptibly differing quantities of water. With wet fingers she caressed each one, producing a marimba tune that danced lightly over the orchestra's melody. The music carried nicely through the grand ballroom of the Hotel Edison, the site of the twelfth annual Magazine Editors' Guild awards. The guild had spared no expense: Miss Gloria Parker was the blond bandleader's name, a *Glasspiel* virtuoso. I'd seen her in some Soundies during the war.

"How do you think she tells them apart?" Joe whispered in my ear. "The water glasses, I mean. They all look alike."

We were sitting at a table for eight, toward the front of the ballroom, where we could feel the orchestra's vibrations in the soles of our feet. Plates of duck à l'orange and green beans almondine lay before us, alongside individual chalices of shrimp cocktail. The Louise of six months prior, the one who hadn't yet tasted an apple from the Tree of Knowledge, would have thought it was a gas when her taxi pulled up in front of the hotel's row of shiny doors and the white-gloved attendant helped her onto the curb. But today's Louise felt weighted down in complications.

For starters, getting dressed had been a doozy. A month ago, when I'd bought my gown for the occasion, black velvet with a wide shiny belt at the cinched waist, I'd only gone up one size, out of foolish optimism. Now the darn thing barely fit, even with my Charis maternity girdle. I'd had to settle for pulling the tiny waist all the way up to my ribs, letting the belt touch the undersides of my breasts. I'd decked my ears, wrists, and neck in big jewelry, hoping to draw the eye upward. Below the clavicle, I felt like a lampshade.

Besides that, the man at my left elbow was Mort Clifton, joined by his stunning silver-haired wife. Joe hadn't done me the courtesy of warning me ahead of time that he'd be coming, and now I was a nervous wreck. Sweat dripped down the back of my neck, sticking the chain of my necklace's clasp to my damp skin. All evening I'd been trying to think of the right way to remind him he'd told me to send my novel, but so far all I'd been able to do was ask him to pass the rolls and laugh pathetically at his jokes with a dry, nervous throat.

And, finally, there was my jet-bead handbag. The note I'd found from Harry was tucked into the inside pocket. Later tonight, when we were alone, I planned to put it in front of Joe and demand answers.

"Wonderful, just wonderful!" Clifton proclaimed when one song ended, jabbing me with his elbow as he began to clap heartily. I smiled and clapped along with him.

On the other side of the Cliftons were a bald, middle-aged man and his wife. The man was from *Newsweek*, which was nominated for the Best American Magazine Award. Harry and Glenys sat on Joe's right, each of them tapping their fingernails against the tabletop to the marimba music. Harry was signaling the waiter for another cocktail. He leaned to whisper something in Glenys's ear. She wore an ivory faille jacket; the color was high in her cheeks. For once, she and her husband seemed to be having fun together. He'd actually been speaking to her more than he had to Joe.

"How are your nerves, my boy?" Clifton said, leaning over me to speak to Joe. "What's your temperature on *Playboy*—is Mr. Hefner going to sweep it out from under you, or do you boys have this one in the bag?"

A blast of hot air came my way as Joe laughed deferentially toward the older man. "I've never thought I had anything in the bag, sir."

"It's the secret to his success," I said mechanically, filling my role as the dutiful fiancée. Joe put his hand on my knee.

When Clifton turned back toward his wife, Joe spoke into my neck again, raising the little hairs that had escaped my chignon. "I mean, did you ever think you'd be attending a party like this?"

I shrugged and shifted in my chair. The top of my girdle dug uncomfortably against my bottom ribs, and I felt slightly dizzy from the squeeze of the thing. I took a tiny bite of duck and dabbed the grease off my lips with my napkin. "I suppose you expect me to thank you," I whispered. "Unless you think it's my Hemingway piece that got us here."

Joe recoiled. He'd been grinning madly, his freshly shaved neck splotched in happy pink. Now he looked hurt. His eyes, merrily red from alcohol, almost looked as if they could cry. "What's gotten into you?" he said, just as the band's song ended. The "you" landed hard. "Of all the places to pick a fight."

Everyone around us applauded politely, with some whistles from the back. Gloria Parker moved on to the wooden xylophone, her padded mallets landing with a bounce. Her smile never changed.

I was watching Joe cut his food with the tines of his fork, his jaw clenched. He put his fork down and turned toward me, and I had the sense he was about to suggest we step outside for a moment when Mort Clifton saved us.

"Miss Leithauser, I seem to remember you write, is that correct?"

I turned on a thousand-watt smile, beaming my attention toward Clifton and his wife. "Why, yes, I do. How kind of you to mention it. I'm a contributing writer to *Downtown*, as a matter of fact." I had no official title, but I figured this would do. "I wrote the interview with Hemingway."

"Ah." Clifton gestured toward me with his fork, squinting one eye. "That's right, I knew it was a dame who'd written—"

"Well, that was a fine piece!" the man from *Newsweek* shouted across the table, and, despite the compliment, I felt like slapping him for interrupting. "This one's a keeper!" he yelled to Joe, sticking out his thumb in my direction.

I didn't look at Joe, but out of the corner of my eye I saw him smile stiffly. "She'd better be, I don't have much choice in the matter now!" He patted my stomach.

All three of the men laughed. I ground my molars. Clifton turned back to his wife, his attention on me and my writing having waned.

The awards began soon after. Two gentlemen from the

guild said a bit about each magazine as they called the editors to the stage to accept their trophies, book-shaped crystal paperweights about the size of a *Reader's Digest*. Every time one of the men they called up onstage took a little too long in tooting his own horn, I felt like booing. What lay before me this evening, once I finally got Joe alone, would be a confrontation, and as the ceremony dragged I dreaded it more and more. What if I was too tired to get my points across? What if all I got from Joe were more lies?

At last, we were down to the final three awards, for the best magazines of the year. They began with the best weekly. *Downtown*'s category would be next. "This is it, old chum," Harry said, reaching across Glenys to pound Joe's shoulder.

"Pardon, Miss Leithauser," Mort Clifton said as the presenters took the stage. "But have you heard from our mutual friend lately?"

For a moment, I was dumbfounded. He'd chosen an odd moment to ask me this. Our mutual friend—wasn't that Joe? I could sense Joe himself listening, as he took a careful sip of champagne. "I'm not quite sure who you mean, Mr. Clifton."

"Well, Mr. Hemingway, of course. He's at work on a very secret, infuriatingly well-guarded novel, and I haven't been able to get hold of him. Do you know where he's staying these days?"

"Actually, I do." I flushed as Clifton turned his chair toward me and Joe breathed down my neck. I hadn't told him about Hemingway's letter, wanting to keep it to myself until I was sure how I'd address what he and Harry had done to my article and why. But the allure of being the girl in the know, the one with the information these more powerful men wanted about Ernest Hemingway, was too much for me to resist. Against my better judgment, my tongue loosened by champagne, I replied proudly, "He's in Wyoming, staying with a friend."

"Do you still have Hemingway's hat?" Harry yelled at me from across the table, smiling blithely.

We all applauded politely as the "Best Weekly" editors returned to their seats, but I noticed Glenys had stiffened, her teeth exposed in a grimace. Joe turned to Harry as the noise subsided, a muscle flexing in his jaw. "Hemingway's hat?" he repeated.

"Sure, Louise's got it," Harry said easily, oblivious to the discomfort of the people surrounding him. "He left it at her place. She showed it to me one night."

"Just when he came over to pick up my article," I said loudly. "*Nothing happened.*"

I clapped my hand over my mouth. The room had gone very quiet. Glenys was squinting hard at me, playing with the little wooden sword that had speared her olives. A man onstage was ripping open an envelope.

"For Best New Magazine, *Downtown!*" the man at the podium said, gesturing to Harry and Joe to come up onstage. I tried to offer Joe a kiss on the cheek, but he just gave me a look as he stood, dropping his napkin on the table. He and Harry trotted up there in their tuxedos, a bounce in Harry's step; Joe climbed the stairs more slowly, head down, contemplative. A girl in a sparkling dress handed each of them a crystal paperweight.

"In Wyoming, you say?" Mort whispered in my left ear. "Did he mention where? Cody, or Casper?"

"Casper," I murmured back. My heart was beating hard as I realized I should've kept my damned mouth shut about Hemingway's whereabouts.

"Ah, Casper." Clifton resettled himself in his chair and began to cut a cream puff in half with his butter knife. "He'll be on Bill Jorgensen's cattle ranch." He chuckled to himself. "The old rascal."

My heart thundered against my cramped rib cage. Papa had trusted me, writing me that letter, letting me know where he'd gone. And where he'd gone was somewhere far away from, as he put it, the busybodies on the coasts. I had become one of those busybodies. I turned my attention back to the stage, wincing against the bright lights of the ceremony.

"These two young upstarts!" the man at the podium was saying. "I don't know where they get the chutzpah, but they've managed to produce a superb new magazine for the next generation. These fellas have taken it upon themselves to risk it all for this exciting new print venture, and, boy oh boy, did their risk pay off."

I clapped along with everyone else, my white-gloved hands not making a sound.

"From men's grooming tips," the emcee continued, "to interviews with the likes of Nelson Rockefeller and Ernest Hemingway . . ."

A sprinkle of applause, then the tinkling of silverware against glasses: the guests were demanding an acceptance speech, and the emcee looked ready to cede the microphone to Joe and Harry. There seemed to be a bit of silent disagreement for a split second, Joe and Harry looking at each other, unable to decide who would take the mike. I stared as Joe jutted out his right elbow, ready to push Harry aside.

Then, through the din, a voice broke out. It took me a second to realize that the man from *Newsweek*, the one sitting with us, had stood.

"You've got the writer right here!" he cried. "Here's the gal who interviewed Hemingway—why don't you bring her up onstage?"

"The gal who interviewed Mr. Hemingway!" said the man at the podium, leaning back toward the microphone. He squinted at our table. "You there, gorgeous, come on up and join the fellas!"

I found myself rising, my napkin slipping to the floor, as the crowd applauded, probably cursing the *Newsweek* man for letting the evening drag on even longer than it already had. Clifton raised his glass at me with a distracted grin. Carefully, I climbed the steps to the stage. My torso felt as if it would burst my zipper as I minced my way to the podium.

Under the bright lights, I could see almost no one in the darkened ballroom, save for Glenys, turned around in her seat, scowling.

"Sure is nice to have you up here, after one long gravy train of fellas," said the emcee, his hand on my shoulder. I stood in front of Joe and Harry, eclipsing them. I wondered if they really were seething at the moment, or if it was only my imagination. "Tell us, what was it like writing for these guys?"

"To be frank, sir . . ." I said into the microphone, my voice producing a bit of feedback. I took a deep breath and stepped back. "Writing for your own fella is a bit like wearing a girdle. Lots of restraints."

I'd nailed it; the audience, whose attention had been waning further and further, roared with laughter. The emcee wiped the corners of his eyes. He seemed to be enjoying this switch in roles, this transformation to television host. I couldn't see the looks on Joe's and Harry's faces behind me, but I could guess.

"Oh, is that so?" asked the man, making a "Can you believe it?" face toward the audience. "Could you tell us if you've got anything good coming up?"

Joe's hand went to my shoulder. I knew better than to mention Malamud before we had it in the bag.

"We may have another big celebrity interview coming soon," I said. "But who knows—these boys'll probably censor that one, too."

The mood in the audience shifted. I got a couple of laughs, but mostly silence. I could make out the dark silhouettes of people lifting their drinks to their mouths, the burst of lighters against cigarettes. The man had been leaning toward me, microphone eagerly placed right in front of my lips, but now he pulled back, stood tall again. Immediately I realized my mistake: I'd said "censor" instead of "edit."

"Well, you three are lovely young people, and I wish you the best with the next issues of the magazine." He turned back to the audience, but not without flicking a wrist toward one of the girls who'd been handing out trophies. With a swanlike gesture, she indicated where we could exit the stage. "Now, on to the big guns!" the man said to the audience, and I turned to follow Joe and Harry. Their backs were facing me. Neither of them had gotten to say a word.

Harry and Glenys followed us outside when it was time to go. It had rained while we were in the hotel, and the lights of

Times Square were magnified in shining puddles on the dark street. Joe's award felt heavy in my purse. Glenys held Harry's in both palms, her lip quavering. Our miserable mood had spread, it seemed, only to her; Harry seemed unaware of how ragged the rest of us were feeling. He used his lips to pull a cigarette from a soft pack he kept in his pocket, then gestured to Joe to stand between him and the wind so that he could manage a light. Joe's body seemed to be made of granite. He kept his gaze distant from all of us.

"What a night, my good man," Harry said, walking backward toward the avenue. Silently, we followed him. Glenys kept herself as far away from me as she could and would not look in my direction. I knew I'd only made it worse when I'd shouted, "*Nothing happened*," and I feared that anything I had to add would only make her more suspicious.

"No need for the festivities to end now, am I right?" Harry continued. "We could have a drink at the Yale Club, or P. J. Clarke's won't be closed until—" His voice cut out as he stumbled against a garbage can, laughing and cursing. His polished dress shoes splashed messily into a brown puddle.

Joe reached out, ostensibly to steady his friend, but I could see the vise grip with which he squeezed Harry's biceps. Harry winced.

"I think you've had enough to drink tonight," Joe said in a low growl. "Louise and I are going home." He held on for a moment longer than he needed to, then pushed Harry aside and continued on down the sidewalk.

"What the hell's eating you?" Harry called after us. Joe ignored him. The first cab that passed us he signaled to stop, without waiting to see if our friends could get a taxi, too. When I turned around, as I was getting into the back seat, I saw the two of them standing where we'd left them, by the trash can, Harry swaying on his feet as Glenys spoke to him, crying.

Our taxi smelled, unfortunately, of salami. Joe sat slumped against his door, not looking at me. I kept my hands wrapped around my pocketbook, perched primly on my stiff knees. "I feel as if I've entered the principal's office," I said at last, to break the silence.

"What's done is done," Joe muttered to the window. "I'm not going to shout at you."

"I didn't sleep with Harry," I replied.

His lips tensed. "I'm not talking about that. I meant your little performance onstage."

"My little performance?" I said, turning toward him. I tried lifting the knee closer to him onto the seat, so that I could face him better, but that hurt my belly. "Hell," I muttered, reaching under my dress to undo the zipper on my waist cincher. I breathed a sigh of relief.

Joe glanced at me and rolled his eyes. "Well, that's one 'restraint' of yours I'm glad to see falling away."

"Look at me," I said, and he did, begrudgingly. "We've never spoken about it, but we must. You did censor my interview with Hemingway. Don't laugh, it's true. Anything controversial you took out, without even consulting me. Don't you think that was unfair to me, to him? Don't you think you left out the truth?"

"What Hemingway thinks is true is not *true*," Joe said, chopping the air in front of him with one hand. "Castro and Cuba are a game to him. If we'd left that in, it'd be dangerous."

"Who told you to take it out?"

"What do you mean, who told us? Harry and I took it out."

The Times Square traffic was petering out, and we were getting close to Joe's apartment. I was running out of time. Without a word, I unzipped my purse. I pulled out the fragment of that letter and handed it to him. He blinked as he read it, his brow furrowed.

"Where did you get this?" he asked, looking at the letter, not me.

"It was in your bookshelf, right under *A Farewell to Arms*." I could see him cursing himself for forgetting it there.

"Louise . . ." he began. He turned his brown eyes toward me, suddenly contrite. "Harry wrote this, not me, you have to understand. I'd never have said you were a bad writer."

"Never mind," I said, even though that part still stung. "What's this at the end, about you-know-who? Who do you have to answer to? It's time you told me."

"As if I'm the only one with secrets, Louise. You're corresponding with 'Papa,' as you call him, right under my nose? What, you two are sending each other love letters now?"

"Love letters! You're being ridiculous."

"Where is he?" Joe demanded. "Where did you tell Clifton he's gone?"

"I . . ." That sense of dread came flooding back, soaking my conscience in acid. I'd told Clifton where Hemingway was, but Joe had been onstage. Maybe Clifton wouldn't do anything with the information. Would Joe? "I can't tell you."

Joe's face looked purplish with rage. "You can't tell me? *Me?*"

The taxi driver cleared his throat. We were parked right outside Joe's apartment. It had begun to rain again, and the windshield wipers made squeaking sounds as they dragged across the glass.

"Let's talk inside," Joe said quietly as he leafed through his wallet for the bills. He handed some money to the driver, then came around to let me out of the car. We stood underneath the awning, out of the rain.

"No, let's talk here. I can't tell you because I don't know what you're into, Joe. I don't know if you're in with the government, or something else. Someone's asking you to spy on writers, is that right? Someone's asked you to make sure they don't say anything that makes Uncle Sam look bad. They give you money, you print all the propaganda they want. It all makes sense."

"Ha!" Joe let out such a big laugh that he doubled over, then stood straight. His hands were in his pockets. "It all makes sense? That's the most nonsensical thing I've ever heard."

I crossed my arms. "Not really. It adds up: Two young men with little experience start a new magazine, and within a year it wins a major award. Fund-raisers line up to help them. Girl reporter discovers heavy instances of censorship inside the magazine's editorial process. I'd say it makes a lot of sense."

"Are you downplaying the work we've put into *Downtown*?"

"No, I know you've worked hard—"

"Are you really that ungrateful for the opportunities we've given you? You aren't as smart as I thought you were, Louise. You aren't that different from the other girls, after all."

His voice was growing louder. He seemed less concerned

than he had a moment ago about anyone's overhearing us; now his anger had taken over. I wondered how much he'd had to drink. There was no one else around, but I noticed that the taxi we'd taken hadn't budged from the curb.

"You're trying to make me feel crazy, and small," I said, my voice shaking. "But I didn't plant that letter."

"Forget the letter! It's how men talk when they think no girls are around. Think about all you have to lose. And stop. Saying. Stupid. Things. *Especially* into a microphone. You could've gotten us into a lot of trouble."

The taxi was still there. I came closer to Joe and plucked the letter out of his hand. "With. *Whom?*"

Before he could say anything, I turned and walked quickly toward the taxi. Out in the rain, the door handle was beaded with water, slippery in my hand. I let myself in and slid across the vinyl seat. "I'm going uptown," I told the driver.

I watched his eyes crinkle in the rearview mirror. "I had a feeling, miss."

Joe came to knock on my window, shivering in the cold rain, and I rolled it down an inch. "Come on, stop this foolishness and come inside."

"I don't want to see you for a while," I said. The reality, the consequences, of cutting Joe from my life felt like a monkey on my back. I'd have to address that tomorrow. For now, I simply could not go upstairs with someone bent on making me feel as if everything I'd uncovered existed only in my head. To go upstairs I'd have to be complicit. I'd have to pull the wool over my own eyes.

Joe looked stricken, and for a moment, something broke inside my own heart. This was the man I'd be giving a child. If only things could be simple.

"Louise, be reasonable," he pleaded.

"I am," I responded, and the cab pulled away so quickly I worried we'd run over his toes. I turned around to see him standing there in the rain, his arms wrapped around himself. I sat back against the seat and pinched the skin between my eyebrows. This was supposed to have been a celebratory evening, the best of his life.

"You made the right choice, miss," said the cabdriver a few minutes later, as he turned north on Eighth Avenue. "Guys like him'll do anything to cover up their indiscretions."

"Yeah," I said, watching a hobo ride his bicycle through the rain, his basket loaded with junk. "Something like that."

17

THE LUNAR HOUSEWIFE

Oxygen

One morning—or afternoon; they'd begun sleeping whenever they felt tired—Katherine woke to find herself alone. She sat up and stretched, looking around, expecting to see him just out of reach, that teasing smile on his face. But Sergey's bed, pushed up against hers, was empty, his pillow cold to the touch.

Of course, he'd be in what they laughingly called the canteen, the table and chairs beside the tiny cookstove. But no. The seating modules were empty.

She got out of bed, stumbling in her sleepy stupor. She pulled her dressing gown, the one drab gray garment they'd given her to provide some privacy, around her bulging stomach. She strode past the locked closet, past the camera, its impassive green light blinking.

Peeking through the circular window of the hatch, she breathed a little sigh of relief. One of Sergey's lunar-exploration suits was gone. He must have headed out to collect samples. When she went to the wide wall of windows, however, she couldn't see him. It was odd that he'd go out without her. They had a routine; she helped fasten the clips that kept his oxygen line secure over his shoulder, so that he wouldn't trip on it or lose the nozzle, and then, when he returned, she got him out of the suit and cleaned it for him. Maybe it did have something to do with the fact that they paid her just as much as they did Sergey, or maybe the love she felt for him made everything easier, but she'd never been so happy to do the same thing day in and day out in her entire life.

She scanned the pocked gray surface, squinting. He'd traveled almost to the horizon before, almost out of her range of vision, but she'd never completely lost sight of him. She mixed a little instant coffee and sat on the window ledge, waiting.

A voice inside her head spoke: *Maybe he's gone. Maybe he knew of a way to call for a shuttle home. This is what men do. When you're at your most vulnerable, and you are, Katherine, it's a repellent to them. They go.* The voice sounded remarkably like her mother's.

But it was what men did, wasn't it? They went. Or worse.

She shook her head. It was ludicrous to think he could have, or would have, gone anywhere. "Rubbish," she murmured to herself. "No way they'd be able to come and get him without waking me." She stirred the lumps in her passable coffee. "And now I know just how much I'd be talking to myself if you weren't here. Hurry home, my love."

Laughing a little, she glanced back at the vestibule, the hatch. Now she noticed what she'd failed to before:

both of the oxygen hoses, the hoses that kept Sergey tethered to the habitat and breathing, remained coiled to the wall.

A ripple of fear shot through her. She put her coffee cup down. Slowly, she stood, letting the dressing gown slip from her shoulders and pool at her feet. He couldn't have gotten far without oxygen, could he? Yet he wasn't visible, was he?

"Well," she said, her voice shaking, "ain't that something?"

There was only one thing to do. As she entered the key code to unlock the hatch, slid up the heavy bolt, and pulled open the handle with a light hiss, she realized just how badly she'd been aching to do this all along. It wasn't fear coursing through her veins, not even concern for Sergey, not exactly, but excitement. Her fingers trembled as she took the spare Exo-Shell uniform down from its broad-shouldered hanger. No question about its cleanliness—she'd sanitized it herself. Shaking, she eased her bare feet into the attached rubbery boots, then pulled the hard-cased trousers up over her legs. At its joints, the suit was made of flexible material—an impermeable fabric, she presumed—but the rest felt like coconut shells. Since it was sized for a man, she could get her belly inside, but barely. She had to suck in her stomach a bit, and as she did, she imagined the baby putting its hands against the walls to brace itself.

"Sorry, little prince," she whispered. "Or princess. We have to find your father."

The helmet was on, locked into the collar. She attached one of the oxygen hoses to the nozzle on the back of her helmet and locked it, then flipped the red switch on the wall. Oxygen flowed. For months she'd been doing this, day in and day out, and now she wondered if perhaps the Soviet command had in fact been training her to be the extra, in case of an emergency like this. Perhaps, in their own sly way, they'd been keeping her in the wings.

She made sure the hatch to the habitat was closed, and finally set forth to open the door to the vestibule. Before her, through another portal window, she could see the bright white land of that final frontier, beckoning her. When had she last flown, really flown? When had she last felt herself overcome gravity by her own power? That would be the first thing she'd do—take a huge leap. The biggest she could. She had been feeling so heavy, so weighed down by this new low center of gravity just below her navel. Now she would step outside, and fly.

After that, she would find out what had happened to Sergey.

There would be no *whoosh* of air when she clicked open the second door; she knew that. The feeling of airlessness was another factor she'd been curious about. With a deep breath—the boost of oxygen inside her helmet was making her dizzy—she slid the three latches open, then pushed down on the handle.

She hadn't been prepared for how bright it would seem out here—the habitat must have had light-filtering glass—and was that a *whoosh* she'd felt? One booted foot reached unsteadily out to land in the soft dust. Under her sole it felt like cake flour. She took another deep breath, then reached out with the other foot. It gave a light bounce—

Something clamped down hard on her right shoulder. A gloved hand. It whirled her around, twirling her in the air, and when she turned there was Sergey, in his suit. She could just make out her face reflected in the glass of his helmet, her eyes surprised and fearful, and behind that, there were his eyes, the brows furrowed in what looked like anger. He yanked her back inside the vestibule and pushed the door shut behind them.

He had his helmet off in a flash, and now he was pounding on hers, knock-knock-knocking like the police at the door of an outlaw's house. "Take it off!" he shouted, his voice muffled. Without waiting for her to move, he went around behind her and unplugged the oxygen hose. Then he twisted the helmet out of its groove and tugged it off her head.

"Katya! What in the name of hell did you think you were doing?"

"You were gone!" she cried, pushing him a little. "I woke up and you were gone! Where the hell did you go? And how did you do it without oxygen?"

He blinked a few times, as though he were trying to make sense of what she had said. "Without oxygen, what are you talking about? Look! I was connected. I was right there, right beside the habitat. I was collecting the dust in the shadow of our home. Don't you believe me?"

Did she? It didn't make sense. She'd seen the two

hoses coiled next to each other. She remembered wondering which one she should take, the one on the left or the one on the right. But Sergey was grinning at her, laughing a little now, and everything felt all right. Her belly was beginning to ache. She decided to laugh as well. "You were right there?"

"I was right there! If this was Earth, I'd have been your dutiful *cynpyz*, planting your tulip bulbs in our front garden bed." He reached for her. "Here, let me help you take that off."

She let him slip the heavy garment off her shoulders, past her belly—*ahh*—and down over her legs. She held his shoulders as she stepped out of the boots, thinking that now she would have to clean and sanitize two suits instead of one.

"Don't do that to me again," she said, pointing her finger at his face. He pretended to bite it. "Wake me before you leave. You know I like to see you off."

"Yes, dear," he said, and he turned so that she could help him undress. Now they stood in the small vestibule, stomach to stomach, both in their underwear, her round smooth belly grazing the trail of soft dark hairs that disappeared into his shorts.

"What does *cynpyz* mean?" she murmured, reaching up around his neck.

"Husband." He reached behind him and took both of her hands, brought them around to his warm mouth, and kissed them. "Don't you do that to *me* again, yes? *You* are not supposed to be out there."

Their eyes met above their interlocked hands. They stood still for a moment, staring at each other, taking deep breaths. She could see pale flecks in the irises of his dark-brown eyes.

Then Sergey broke her gaze and continued, kissing her fingers: "All could have been lost, Katya. All," he repeated, as he bent to crush her mouth with his, "could have been lost."

18

Dear Mr. Hemingway,

I loathe to write this, as I can feel you cringe at my words on the other side of this letter, but I must tell you that I've made a terrible mistake. At a dinner with Mort Clifton and the Downtown *boys, I let it slip you were in Wyoming. Mr. Clifton seemed keen to find you, particularly to dig around about your novel-in-progress. Though I was able to keep mum regarding the novel itself, I'd had a bit of drink and mentioned I'd heard from you and that you were in Casper.*

You may already know this; the man may already be calling you to nag about your writing, or to urge you to come back to New York for some god-awful meeting. Please, sir, I hope you will accept my deepest apologies for poking this great gaping hole in your privacy.

If you'll indulge me, I wonder if I might ask a bit more about that very thing—your concerns about privacy—even though our formal interview has ended. I most regret that the boys didn't let me keep the bits you told me about "the dullest men alive" listening to you and about your reasons for moving to Cuba. If it hadn't been for that Mr. England at the Garden, asking you all his silly questions, I might've pressed you further on that point, sir.

*Do you sincerely believe anyone is watching you? Do you
believe there are ill-actors right here in publishing, perhaps
in our own government, who would like to shut down our
opinions, who would like us reading—writing—from a script?
I'm not sure what to think anymore, and I'd be glad to hear
your thoughts on the matter. That is, if you feel comfortable
putting such thoughts down.*

*And, that is, if you forgive me for giving away your
location.*

*With deepest regret,
Louise Leithauser*

*P.S. To answer your queries, yes, I am embracing trouble, I
believe with clear eyes. At the moment I'm making a go of it
alone, though I haven't the faintest idea how I will survive
with a child or where I will have to go. It may be—heaven
help me—that eventually I return to my mother's house. She
has been asking for my company, as my brother was in fact
killed in action at Pork Chop Hill.*

*P.P.S. At the very least, my manuscript is coming along.
Through all of this, I haven't gotten behind in the count.*

For almost four weeks, I avoided all contact with Joe. I went
to and from my job in the wet snow, keeping myself small
and my voice quiet while in the office. Mr. Franklin limited
himself to overly polite, minimal interactions. It was beginning to become difficult for me to kneel on the floor beside
the filing cabinets, my back aching. I tried my best to work

even harder than before, so that no one could complain about the job I was doing. Mercifully—or so I thought—Mr. Franklin hadn't asked me to find the folder of résumés again, but one gray, slushy day in late February I realized that the file was no longer in its place in the Office Miscellany cabinet.

I came home from work that day feeling dejected, and more alone than I'd ever thought possible with another human taking up space inside my body. I couldn't call my mother to ask for help—all she wanted to know was when my wedding would be, and when she'd finally get to meet Joe. I couldn't tell her that he and I were on the outs. I was afraid the shame of my unwed state, coupled with her very raw grief over Paul, would crush her.

That left almost no one for me to lean on. Reaching out to Glenys felt risky, somehow. Her foremost loyalty would lie with Harry.

Besides all of that, I was convinced I'd squandered the best connection I'd ever made in my life. I'd been a waitress, and then I had become a girl who received letters from Ernest Hemingway. Then I'd blown it, in an effort to get into Mort Clifton's good graces. Mort Clifton, who didn't give a damn about me or my novel, who only wanted to know where he could track down his most important writer. I had no faith that I'd ever receive correspondence from Papa again.

I trudged up the stairs to my apartment, the smell of garlic as strong as ever in the hallway, planning to take off my shoes and reheat a bit of beef roast and carrots on my hot plate, when I noticed there was something pinned to my door, a pink slip of paper.

CITY OF NEW YORK
EVICTION NOTICE
FOURTEEN-DAY NOTICE TO VACATE PREMISES

My knees went warm and tingly, and for a second, I thought they'd give out. The baby responded with a hard kick against my right side. I put my fingers to the little foot, quieting it, as I read the rest. The reason the notice gave for my eviction was indecent behavior.

I yanked the paper off its thumbtack and marched upstairs, to Lena's apartment, and pounded on her door. Dogs barked and yelped inside. I could hear her banging pots around in her kitchen. I'd never even met my landlord. They had me drop off each month's rent in cash in a deli on the West Side, where a little box marked "Rent" sat beside the soda fountain with its forty-two flavors. I had no idea who owned the building, probably a slumlord. In any case, he'd never recognize me if he passed me on the street, nor I him. There was only one way he'd know if I was involved in anything indecent.

At last Lena came to the door, in her bathrobe, holding some kind of white terrier. The fur around its mouth looked wet, stringy, and brown. Her hair was up in a shower cap. "Oh, it's you," she said. "What do you want?"

I held up the pink piece of paper. "Mrs. Bunche, I'm being evicted."

She shrugged. "So?"

"So . . . it says I'm to leave because of indecent behavior. How, might I ask, would they know that?"

"For starters, you come and go at odd hours." She wrinkled her nose as if she had an itch. She wouldn't look me in the eye. "You've got this fella, that fella, here late at night." Her lip curled. Perhaps she wasn't as hard of hearing as I'd thought.

"I only have the one fella," I said through my teeth. Right now, I didn't even have him.

"Oh, yeah? What about the blond one?"

I closed my eyes. "Harry? He's only a friend." Damn him for having come at night.

"Huh. And now look at you, bacon in the drawer. How can you even know whose it is, eh?"

I took a step toward her, and she held up the dog to shield herself. Another one yapped at her feet. She'd been keeping it back with her foot, but now she let it tumble into the hallway, where it yipped warning barks at the hem of my coat.

I held up the pink sheet of paper in front of her face, and tore it to shreds right there on her doormat. Then I turned on my heel to go back downstairs.

"What's it matter, anyway?" she called after me. "With that fancy ring on your finger, I thought you were going to marry your fella!"

As I shoved my key into the lock, I could hear my telephone ringing, using my code for the party line. Another eviction notice, I figured. I came in and slid off my shoes, then let it ring out while I went into the kitchen and poured myself a glass of water. I stood in front of the counter for a minute, my hands flat in front of me, my head down. There was a jar of peanut butter inside the cupboard. I fished it out and found a spoon.

Life on Earth had grown more difficult for me by the day. No wonder I'd found myself writing about a girl with nowhere to go but the moon. What would I do if I lost my apartment, my job? I could move somewhere no one knew me, pretend to be a widow, I supposed.

Mouth full of peanut butter, I shook my head sadly. Then what would I do: Wait tables again? Bus empty cocktail glasses?

I put the sad little jar of peanut butter back into the cabinet, the spoon in the shallow sink. I missed Joe. Life with him had been simple, cozy, everything provided for. What had I been thinking, cutting him off like that? I could be interviewing Bernard Malamud right now, using all the baseball trivia I'd stuffed into my head in preparation, instead of plugging away at the surefire failure that was *The Lunar Housewife*. I wondered if they'd found another girl to meet with Malamud, if she was perhaps a girlfriend of Harry's.

The telephone began ringing again. Two short rings, one long one. My code. Lena pounded on the floor with what sounded like an umbrella. "Answer it, will you?" she called.

The last thing I wanted was to satisfy her, but I went to the phone, taking off my coat and draping it over the sofa before I picked up the handset. "Hello?"

"Louise. Thank God you came to the phone. Oh, Louise, I have to tell you something."

"Joe," I said breathlessly. I hadn't spoken to him since that night after the awards ceremony. It would have been good to hear his voice, except that he sounded frantic, as if he'd been crying. It reminded me of the day I'd come home to find him here with news about Paul. I sat down.

"What's the matter?" I said in a low voice, and then, before he could answer, I remembered Lena upstairs. "Be careful. Someone could be listening in." I tried to make out any breathing on the line.

"It's Harry," he said, his voice hoarse, and before he could go on, I knew. "He's dead."

My teeth began to chatter. I gathered my cold feet up onto the couch. Harry—dead? It was impossible. I thought of him at the dinner ceremony, full of life. Holding Glenys's hand. It couldn't be. "What happened?"

"I don't know, I . . ." Joe stopped to get himself together. "He used some dope, some bad dope."

"That can kill you?" I tried to remember exactly what Harry had looked like. Unfathomable, that I'd seen him in his tuxedo just weeks ago, and now he was gone.

"I guess. I guess so. If you're a goddamn knucklehead like Harry." Joe let out a small sob. I heard him blow his nose. "At least he didn't have to die alone."

"Let me guess." My throat was beginning to hurt from the news. "Beverly was with him."

"Yes," Joe said. "It's a funny thing—she's been quite a help to Glenys in the last couple of days. She's been helping plan the funeral."

I swallowed, imagining Glenys and Beverly spending all that time together. Talking to each other. I felt as if I were swallowing glass. I forced myself to focus. "Joe," I said, "he's been dead a couple of days, and you're just telling me now?"

"I wasn't sure you'd want to speak to me, after the way we left things."

"Of course I'd want to speak with you at a time like this."

"Lou . . ." Joe began, his voice sounding young, wistful. "Would you mind if I came over? Or would you like to come here?"

I thought of the eviction notice, of Lena pounding on the ceiling upstairs. Of my cold radiators, which would rattle for hours after I finally let them have some steam. "I'll come to you," I said quickly, and in no time at all, I was back in my coat.

Henry Crawford "Harry" Billings's funeral service took place at Madison Avenue Presbyterian, with a private burial to follow on Martha's Vineyard a few days later. The reception after the service felt every bit like one of his parties, only better, because all the glitter he'd collected over the years had assembled itself into a final shimmering farewell. Truman Capote took up a prime spot on the sofa, chain-smoking Pall Malls with Peggy Guggenheim, he in a velvet bow tie, she in furs. From my vantage point beside a potted fern, I spotted Norman Mailer, one of the younger Rothschilds, and William Holden betting on a game of blackjack. A celebrated war photographer held forth by the bar cart, flanked by his chilly German wife.

The noise level felt no different from any other party, and the mood tended more toward festive than somber; nobody mentioned the cause of Harry's death, but the consensus seemed to be he'd gone out on a happy, if irresponsible, note, so why not keep the party going.

At one point, Capote gave an impromptu speech in that pinched voice of his: "If ever a man could make terrible scarves look good—and he did have *terrible* taste in scarves— it was Harry Billings. . . ."

The only solemn presence at the party took the form of Harry and Glenys's children, who, despite being in their own home, seemed out of place as they stared, stunned, at the party guests when they were prompted to come forward and say goodbye. Then they were herded to their rooms by an aunt. The poor kids, I thought, looking at their tired freckled faces, their sagging bobby socks, the shadows that should not have been under their eyes. Maybe I shouldn't have thought ill of the dead, but I wondered how well they'd even known their father.

Glenys, for her part, appeared dazed, probably drugged, almost grateful to be the center of attention for once; it was as if she knew that, for this one day, she'd be allowed to serve as a surrogate for her husband and collect all the admiration he'd cultivated without her. She sat on the davenport opposite Capote, between her mother and Gloria Grahame, who'd collected her Best Actress in a Supporting Role trophy last March and was already, rumor had it, a has-been. In her Broadway days, I'd heard, she had a thing with Harry.

As for everyone else, proving how well they'd known Harry personally had become a kind of sport. The rooms thundered with a sea of competing stories, the voices growing louder and more frantic as the afternoon wore on. Snippets leapt above the surface, like flying fish enjoying brief moments in the sun:

". . . when he brought that girl Sheila from the Anchor back to Durfee!"

". . . told him a thousand times it wouldn't float, but, listen, we were half in the bag . . ."

". . . asked me to marry him right then and there. Sorry, Glenys, it was all a joke. . . ."

It was all making me sick. Besides, no one had offered me a chair, despite my aching belly. I kept pushing the baby's feet away from the right side of my rib cage, which only made its bottom push back at me on the left. Still, I didn't want to fight for a seat. Then I'd have to interact with people, and I wasn't much in the mood to speak to anyone. Instead, I clung gratefully to the conveniently placed plant and watched Joe through the fern's fronds.

Even he seemed more at ease now, after he'd spent most of the service gripping my hand, his face white as death. He'd found a circle of men with gray hair and mustaches, round bellies and tailored suits, and even though I wasn't certain who they were, I had a feeling they were big wheels in publishing. They were talking animatedly in their tight group, gray and black petals on a closed-up flower. After a minute, Joe looked over his shoulder to find me. Our eyes locked, and he offered a little wave.

I'd spent two nights in a row at his apartment, then last night at my own place, so I'd be able to get ready. I knew he felt grateful, and relieved, to have me back by his side, and in general I felt relieved as well. But something about seeing him among all these men brought back an unsettled feeling in my stomach. In a minute I'd have to find a bathroom, just to get away from all this. I was about to make a break for it when one of the men broke from Joe's pack, with a face that looked as serious as I felt.

He caught my eyes, and his thick, dark eyebrows went up. It was Eli.

My first instinct was to turn away. He'd spilled some very sensitive information to me, and what had I made of it? Still, when I glanced back in his direction, he was smiling. I smiled back, then subconsciously reached down to smooth my black pencil skirt. I'd paired it with a black Peter Pan–collar jacket with pearl buttons, and had a single pearl in each ear. Leaving the house, I'd felt pretty, but now, among the likes of Gloria Grahame, I felt like a tent you'd take camping.

Eli blinked a few times, then, with the slightest gesture, inclined his head twice toward the balcony. I looked to Joe, who was deep in conversation, then back to Eli.

A hand squeezed my elbow. "Louise."

I jumped to see that it was Beverly. "What is it?" I hissed, recoiling.

"I need to speak with you."

Beverly looked even worse than Glenys, gray-pale, in a subdued navy turtleneck sweater and long skirt. I'd seen her at the edges of the reception, whispering with the waitstaff and quietly collecting used napkins from beside the coffee service. It seemed Joe had been right, about Glenys and Beverly planning the funeral together, which would have struck me as oddly beautiful, even sort of European, if it all hadn't also made me want to scream into a pillow.

I glanced back at Eli, who'd rejoined the conversation around Joe. "Whatever you have to say, you can say to me now," I whispered to Beverly.

She shook her head. "What I have to tell you is best told in private. Would you come out onto the balcony with me for a moment? It's cold, but you can have a seat."

She took me outside and got me situated in a cushioned chair under the awning, gently fluffing the pillow behind me. I liked her more than I wanted to. She stood in front of me with her arms crossed against the chill, gazing out over the foggy city. Behind her, a cluster of pots held a depressing collection of dead plants. One wizened vine lay encrusted over the thick stone railing. Beverly nudged one of the nearer pots with the toe of her flat.

"Have you told Joe the truth yet? Does he know you and I worked together?" She glanced up at me with a patient face.

Now I could admit it: I could see what Harry had seen in her. She was not only lovely in form, she was also intelligent, even refined. She'd helped Glenys and had kept my secret. For someone who'd seduced Harry, a married man, she somehow felt like the one with the moral authority here, rather than me.

"No," I said.

"Why not?"

"I don't know," I admitted, tears springing to my eyes. "If I admit I was at that party working, a waitress, I'll have to tell him about everything. About who my parents are . . . who I am . . ."

Beverly tilted her head to the side. Her eyes were stunning, light blue-gray, now shot through with red. "Who are you?"

I sniffed, looking back at my hands. "I'm the daughter of a housemaid. And a drunk."

She snorted. "Aren't we all."

For a moment, we both watched traffic shear through puddles on the avenue, far below us. I gathered myself together. "What was it you wanted to tell me?"

Beverly took a deep breath, her rib cage rising and falling. "There's no way to sugarcoat this, Louise. Harry was getting ready to throw you under."

A cool blast of wind, shot through with mist, hit me in the face. "Me? What are you talking about? How could he throw me under?"

"You *and* Joe. Do you remember the Hemingway interview you did?"

"Of course I do."

"Harry did all the edits to that story. Joe let him do it because he said he was too close to you to alter your work."

Beverly looked through the French doors for a second. "I can't stay out here much longer. Harry had taken whatever it was he cut from your Hemingway piece and was going to publish it himself, as an exclusive. Just a week or two ago, he went and pitched the idea to *Harper's*, or *Harper's Bazaar*—I can't remember which."

A shiver passed through my body. "He was going to scoop me."

She nodded. "The crux of it was that Hemingway is working on a secret novel that'll be explosive, that he's hiding out in Cuba and I guess Wyoming now. Harry was hoping it would be a big story for him, that it would come out this summer. That was going to give him enough time to part ways with Joe first."

"Part ways with Joe?"

"Harry had been complaining a lot about *Downtown*. It isn't fun anymore, he said. It's turned into something else. 'As unexciting as any other branch of government,' he called it, whatever that means." She shrugged. "As for the article, now that he's dead, I don't know what they'll do. I'm handling some of his affairs, so I suppose I should dig up the name of the editor and find out."

"Please do find out," I said. "And get me a copy of that article, if you can."

"All right." Beverly shuffled her feet nervously, looking in through the glass doors again. "You can come get it at my apartment. He kept a file there of projects he was working on, things he didn't want other people to see."

"The goddamn crook," I said aloud, then looked back at her. "Sorry."

"He is dead, Louise," she said simply. I couldn't read the

expression on her face. "Remember that." She stalked over the wet paving stones toward the French doors.

"You don't think . . ." I said, stopping her just as she reached for the handle. She didn't look at me, and I guessed there were tears in her eyes. "You don't think this had something to do with his death, do you?"

Beverly let out a sharp laugh, and when she finally did look over her shoulder, her cheeks were wet. "He had some bad dope. That's all. I don't see how it could be related." She slipped back into the party.

I stayed out on the balcony, processing what she'd told me. What if Harry's death hadn't been an accident? What if someone in power had decided he'd been trying to say too much? I wished I could place a call to the afterlife and ask Harry what had happened. And then—wring his neck.

A click behind me, and the rise of voices and laughter. I turned, expecting to see Joe, but it was Eli who had come out to join me. My heartbeat quickened. "Eli," I said, trying to stand up, but he stopped me with a finger over his lips, then pulled another chair close. It made a screeching nose, metal legs on slate.

"Forgive me, Harry," he whispered, taking a sip of his martini.

"Screw him," I said forcefully, and Eli's brown eyes shot up in surprise. "Listen. Harry's mistress just told me something interesting. I think you should know."

He leaned toward me. "Go on."

"Apparently, Harry was trying to run with a stolen story—stolen from me, by the way—about Hemingway writing a secret novel, something sympathetic to the Commies." As I explained what Hemingway had told me about his new novel, what he'd said about Castro and Korea and all that had been cut from my interview, Eli listened thoughtfully, his gaze trained at my knee. "Beverly said he took it to either *Harper's* or *Harper's Bazaar;* she couldn't remember which one. *Bazaar* is Hearst, isn't it? Have you heard any rumblings about this?"

"I haven't, but nobody tells me much of anything," Eli sighed. "I can put an ear to the ground if you want, though."

"Please do." My heartbeat had gotten a little closer to normal. He reached for an afghan on one of the chaises and handed it to me. The expression on his face was tender, leading me to wonder if the guy wasn't a bit sweet on me.

"How are you, Louise?" Eli asked, sitting with his hands interlaced between his legs and leaning his face, open as a book, toward me. With his chin he gestured back toward the funeral gathering. "This has to be pretty upsetting for you. And Joe."

"Yes. Joe seems quite broken up. Almost—"

The doors swung open, both at once, and there was Joe, his cheeks aflame. He looked from me to Eli and back again. "Louise? Everything all right?"

Eli stood coolly, putting his hands in his pockets, as I scrambled to find the pocketbook I'd dropped on the slate. "Actually," I replied, "I was just getting a headache. I think you should find me a taxi."

"Good idea," Joe said, and with a curt nod at Eli, he took me by the hand and led me back into the apartment.

The headache was a ruse, but I'd had enough of this damned party—I'd just learned that the deceased had been willing to cheat me, and still I felt I had more right to mourn him than half these hangers-on. I wanted to go home, put on some Pond's, and go to bed. No one had moved since I'd been outside; in fact, the festivities seemed to have escalated. Capote was now lying across Peggy Guggenheim's lap, blowing smoke rings onto her chin, while everyone laughed.

Under the din, Joe murmured, "I wasn't aware you knew Eli Cohn."

"I met him right here, as a matter of fact."

We'd reached the little foyer. Joe turned me toward him, took both of my upper arms in his hands, and loosened his grip. "I'd like you to come home with me, Louise, all right? Please."

"Joe . . ."

"Please, Lou. It's been so good to spend this time with you, despite the circumstances. Don't leave me alone tonight." His eyes welled with tears. He looked exhausted. "Let's all stay together."

As he spoke the last sentence, he put his hands on the top of my belly. I closed my eyes. "I'll have to go home again, to fetch some of my things."

"Fetch your things. Fetch everything."

"Joe, I . . ." I couldn't help reaching out to cup his cheek. He leaned his face into my hand and kissed the side of my thumb. "All right, I'll pack a bag and come over."

"I'll come with you," he said in a hurry, then left to say his goodbyes.

I put on my coat, my mind swimming with what Beverly had just told me. Harry's treachery and his sudden death had occurred uncomfortably close to each other. I reminded myself to look for the simplest explanation, which would be that Harry had simply bought some bad drugs. I was tapping my toes nervously beside the door when Glenys found me, her mascara running down her cheeks.

"I knew it," she hissed, stabbing her finger back in the direction of the living room, toward Beverly. "You've been going behind my back all this time, Louise. Not with Harry, but with her! You're friends with her! Oh, I can just imagine it, the two of you laughing at me, the silly wife."

"I'd never laugh at you. I only went to dinner with the guys and her once, and I didn't realize—"

"You went to *dinner* with her?"

"Glenys, please." I put my hands on her shoulders, but she shrugged me off. "It's not what you think, and, besides, I thought the two of you were . . ." I searched for the right words. "I thought you and she had . . ." My words fell feebly on my own ears. That Glenys and Beverly had maintained some sort of peace surrounding Harry's funeral didn't mean Glenys would want to imagine Beverly at dinner with Joe and me.

Beverly chose the absolutely wrong moment to stride up to us right then, acknowledging Glenys with a comment about when the caterers had to leave. Glenys's eyes were green fire. Beverly leaned in close to me and whispered in my ear, "Come by my apartment next Wednesday around lunchtime to pick up the article." She pressed something into my hand, a hot, damp triangle of notebook paper, then swept back into the party to continue her bizarre role as co-hostess. Glenys and I both watched her go, a stunning figure even in drab mourning clothes.

I stuffed the paper into my pocket, knowing without looking that it contained her address. The last thing I saw as Joe led me out the door was Glenys's blotchy face, all the hatred, grief, and frustration she must have been feeling since Harry's death pouring, like lava from the top of a volcano, toward me.

19

Beverly's Greenwich Village apartment was indeed not far from Minetta Tavern, or from the black-and-white checker-board exterior of the White Horse. Just looking at the place gave me a residual hangover. I'd been there with the guys a few times, in what now felt like my past life, for a late-night cocktail and to gawk at Dylan Thomas.

The driver let me out at the corner of Bleecker and West Eleventh. I'd taken a taxi straight down the West Side, claiming a doctor's appointment so that Mr. Franklin would allow me a long lunch. In the time since Beverly had passed me her address, Joe had convinced me to move into his apartment. I'd left the second eviction notice on my kitchen table, and he'd read it the day of Harry's funeral, then insisted the baby and I move in with him. Admittedly, it hadn't taken that much to get me to capitulate; I was weary of the feeling that time was ticking against me. If I'd tried to fight the eviction and lost, I'd have been kicked out of my apartment today.

But the sense of the walls closing in hadn't dissipated with my move to Forty-second Street. Rather, it had increased. Most of my pieces of furniture, which had been castoffs before I'd acquired them, had ended up on the curb. Now that I owned nearly nothing, I felt like a kept woman. All that I'd moved to Joe's were my clothes, some kitchen items, and the filing box in which I kept my manuscript. I'd had to hide that on a high shelf in his office.

On the corner near Beverly's place, a tiny grocery advertised fancy fruits and five-cent Coca-Cola. I headed west on Eleventh, toward the river, which I felt I'd never truly smelled until now. Dead fish, garbage, marine-engine oil. My purse tucked under my arm, I made my way past row after row of neat brick buildings. The rain, followed by unseasonable warmth and sunshine for the first week of March, had brought the first periwinkle blooms peeking through the wrought-iron rails.

"Oh, for Pete's sake," I muttered to myself, when I realized I had at least half a block to go. "Should've had him drop me off farther down." A group of teenagers snickered at me over their cigarettes as they smoked on a stoop, but I didn't care. My belly felt as tight as a basketball, and just as heavy. The space between my legs throbbed.

At last I reached her building, 333 West Eleventh, a handsome four-story with a shiny green door. I stared up at it, wondering how she could afford a place like this. Perhaps her relationship with Harry had progressed to the point where he'd set her up in a pad.

As I approached the steps, I realized she was waiting outside, smoking. Her hair was tied up in a scarf, and she wore some kind of coverall contraption, a gray one-piece, like a glamorous housepainter. Her face was bare except for bright-red lipstick, which left a stain on her cigarette. She took a few quick, nervy drags to finish, then gestured me inside.

"Come on," she said by way of hello, "I'll get you a drink."

Inside, her slim gray bottom disappeared up the dark staircase like Alice's rabbit, leaving me to trudge after her. I figured she had to be on the second floor, but, no, she led me up, up, all the way up to the fourth floor, and by the time I arrived I had sweat pouring down my brow. "Oh, sorry," she said, waiting at her door when I finally arrived. "No elevator. Your doctor probably told you not to do that."

"You could've had the article," I said, between breaths, "waiting for me downstairs."

"Oh," she said, her face falling a bit, and I wondered if she was lonely. "Yes, I suppose I could have."

She led me inside. The apartment was a studio with a Murphy bed in the far corner, a postage-stamp-sized kitchen with a coffeemaker and toaster oven, and a love seat and little TV with rabbit ears askew. The two tall windows were decked in spider plants, their offspring strewn over the radiator and onto the floor, and a soft-looking gray cat sat with its tail twitching on one of the sills. The whole place stank of stale coffee. I noticed a red typewriter on a TV tray, fresh paper on the platen. As I got closer, I caught a glimpse of a few words she'd typed.

"You're a writer, too?" I asked, aghast.

She made a move to get between the typewriter and me. "Of course I am," she said in a hurry. "Why else would I have been with Harry? Why else would either of us have requested to work those parties?"

"Good point," I said. It made sense now, the way she'd challenged Harry to get Hughes or Baldwin to write his Harlem piece. I should have known.

"Please, sit down." There was only one place to sit, so I took up the middle of the love seat. Despite myself, I let out a long sigh.

I pointed at the typewriter. "Did you really think he'd help you?"

Her thumbnail found its way between her lips. "I don't know. I guess I thought, just being around him, just being with an exciting man like that . . . something would rub off."

"You sound like Glenys," I replied, and Beverly pulled a face. She brushed something I couldn't see off her thigh, then cleared her throat.

Her question caught me off guard. "Did you really think Joe would help you?"

"I . . ." For so long, I'd convinced myself that what existed between Joe and me was different, that we'd fallen in love by coincidence, even though he was a powerful magazine editor and I had been a struggling writer-cum-waitress. I hadn't wanted to believe that the allure of his connections had had anything to do with my attraction to him. But the two were intertwined, weren't they, as difficult to pull apart as braided strands of taffy. Were girls ever free simply to fall in love, without considerations of power, connection, access? I wasn't sure.

"Yes," I confessed, collapsing a bit in fatigue. "Yes, I suppose I did. He has."

Beverly handed me an ice water in an etched green glass, which I gulped greedily. She pulled a stool from the kitchen, then perched on it with one knee bouncing, thumbnail in her mouth.

"What happened?" I asked softly. "The night . . . the night of?"

She took a few breaths in through her nose, shredding the nail with her teeth. Her eyes were unfocused, staring at a dusty corner of the baseboards. "I've been thinking about it a lot," she said, and I got the sense this was the real reason she wanted me here. She had no one else to talk to. "It was so strange. Sometimes Harry and I will go get some dope. We usually go down to see the Italians in Sheridan Square. You know, Mafia kids."

"You go with him?" I said, and she answered with a smug look, a what-kind-of-writer-are-you kind of look.

"Yes, I go with him. Well, this time, the guys met him here, right outside my place, which made me sort of nervous that my landlord might see. I said, 'Come on, Harry, let's meet them around back of the bar,' but Harry told me it'd be quick. These two guys, older guys, about my father's age, showed up and gave Harry a bag, and that was it. He must have paid them ahead of time. I'd never seen anything like it."

"Dope," I said. She already thought I was a square, so I figured I'd ask the question. "Dope, like mary jane?"

She shook her head. "Most of the time, yes. I thought that's what he was getting, but he told me when we came inside it was H. Heroin. Harry thought it would take him to a higher level intellectually—that's what he called it, a higher level. But he told me I didn't have to try it." A huge sob racked her body, and she squeezed her eyes tight. "And I didn't. I didn't want to try it. I almost did, just to keep him company, but I didn't want to try it." Her eyes were wide, scared, as if she'd just stepped into the path of an oncoming bus and someone had yanked her back at the last second. "So . . . I let him smoke it alone. He got really affectionate, really laughy, and then sleepy. We put on—we put on *I Love Lucy*—he said I could pick. I fell asleep next to him, and when I woke up, he was cold and—and he'd gotten sick all over my shoulder." Her face constricted in tears.

I felt dizzy. My swollen hands throbbed. I couldn't imagine waking up like that, Harry's heavy, cold body lying against my shoulder. Surely Glenys resented Beverly for having been with her husband in his last moments, but I could see that this had been no privilege.

The cat leapt down and rubbed its body against one of the legs of Beverly's stool as she wept. It fled when I got up to hand her a tissue.

"Thanks," she said, and blew her nose.

Someone down on the street was yelling, his voice shrill, about where to put the cooler of fish. When I went to close the window, I looked down, meeting the eyes of a man in a dirty white apron and hat. He squinted up at me, and the hairs on the back of my neck lifted. I crept slowly away from the window.

"What did the men look like?" I asked her.

"I don't know, one was . . . small, dark-complected, Italian or Puerto Rican. The other was big—as tall as Harry, I'd say. But older, at least fifty. He had a mustache."

"A red mustache?" My mouth felt as if I'd been chewing cotton. I'd seen a man with a red mustache, and recently. I just couldn't pinpoint where it had been.

Beverly frowned, wiping her nose with the back of her hand. "I don't know. It was dark. But . . . maybe." She began to nod. "Why?"

Our faces had grown close as we leaned into each other over the ash-strewn coffee table, as if we were old friends or co-conspirators planning a coup. I sat up. The stench of coffee was overpowering. I had to get out of here. I felt a roaring begin behind my ears, a rushing of blood.

My thighs edged forward on her scratchy sofa, the weight of the baby pressing me down, and I reached for her hand to get myself up. "Listen," I said, collecting my purse with shaking fingers. "Don't tell anyone I came here. And be careful, Beverly. Watch yourself when you come and go."

She crossed her arms. "Now you sound like him. He was so paranoid." Her voice belied her nervousness. "Always watching his back." She reached down for the cat and squeezed it against her chest, clutching its tail.

"I sound like him. He sounded like Hemingway. I've heard too much lately about people being watched, people being followed, to believe it's all a coincidence. I think there could be a . . . a plot under way." I was talking quickly now—babbling, perhaps—and she watched me as if I had two heads. "I'm just not sure— *Ouch*."

My hand shot to her arm, to catch myself, and I squeezed my eyes shut as a rolling pain passed through me, a hot wave like a curling iron being dragged across my stomach and down through my legs.

When I opened my eyes, Beverly's were wide as a guppy's, her mouth hanging open.

"Don't worry, it was only a Braxton Hicks. I'm not going to have a baby here on your rug. It's due to come April Fools' Day. I have nearly a month."

She led me to the door. "The joke's on— Oh, wait!" She ran and grabbed a manila folder from her coffee table. "I almost forgot, the entire reason you came here. This is the thing Harry was working on when he died. I'm not sure who else has it, but here you go."

It said something about my state of mind that I'd almost left without the pages. " 'Castro's Favorite Yanqui,' " I read. "Not a bad title."

Beverly sniffed. "He couldn't really write," she admitted, her shoulders falling a little in relief. It was her bitterness talking, I thought as I shoved Harry's work into my handbag. Everyone knew the man was brilliant. With a tight smile, Beverly closed the door, and I heard two locks slide into place.

I made for the stairs immediately, taking them two at a time in places, my hand sliding along the old, worn banister. Tiny splinters pierced my glove. My thoughts raced from one scenario to the next, like a little game piece hopping around the Monopoly board. Could Harry's death have been no accident? Was it possible he'd been killed just for writing the wrong kind of article, for picking the wrong celebrated writer to expose as a pinko, or was that crazy talk? Or could Harry have been involved in deeper schemes than any of us realized?

And what did Joe know about it all?

On the second-to-last flight of stairs, my right shoe slid out from under me.

I cried out, landing hard on my left hip and wrist. My purse skidded against the far wall. Harry's article lay fanned around its paper clip on the dusty floor. Breathing heavily, with rivulets of sweat pouring down from my hairline and into my big maternity brassiere, I sat there waiting, listening, praying no one would come out of their apartment to check on me.

All was quiet. I could hear a radio droning inside the nearest apartment, 2B. Beverly's door remained closed upstairs.

My stomach contracted. Another hot red wave crested, as though someone had flipped up a switch and sent one long bolt of electricity through me. I shut my eyes, bore down with my chin toward my chest. In a moment, it stopped.

Out on the street, I found a pay phone to place a call to Mr. Franklin. I had to call collect—strike number one—and tell him I wasn't feeling well and couldn't return to the office today—strike number two against me. Already I was skating on thin ice, I knew it, but never in my life had I wanted more to shut myself in, bolt the door, and pull a blanket up over my head. My entire body was shaking, and I hoped to God the fall hadn't damaged the baby.

The problem was, I didn't have a home to return to. I had someone else's home. And even though it was not yet three in the afternoon when I got to Joe's apartment, I could hear him inside as I turned the key in the door.

"Joe?" I called tentatively, hanging my jacket on one of the hooks on the entry wall. I tried to keep my voice steady. "What are you doing home from work so early?"

He didn't answer. I could hear pages turning in the little study. I turned the corner and there he was, my "Lunar Housewife" manuscript strewn over his lap and the desk, his face flushed.

So he'd gone snooping, as well. I put a fist to my hip. "What is this?"

"I should be asking you that!" he sputtered. "Is this how you've been spending your time? Writing this, this nonsense—"

To hear him speak this way of my pet project, to see him

tossing pages aside as though they were so much junk, cut something loose in me. I'd planned to broach the subject of Harry's betrayal tactfully, shrewdly, to extract as much information from Joe as I could, but now I slapped Harry's article on the desk in front of him. "Maybe *you* can tell *me* what the hell this is."

His lip curled as he looked down at the papers. "Never seen this before, and I'm in no mood to play guessing games."

I poked my gloved finger into his lap. "It's Harry stealing my work, that's what it is. It's an article he was working on about Hemingway. It's terrible, I might add." During the ride downtown, I'd read it, and I'd been flabbergasted to find Beverly hadn't been kidding. The thing was a piece of crap, disorganized, childish in tone. At one point Harry had even used the wrong form of "your"—"Hemingway is not you're typical literary icon."

Knowing I'd done such better work with the same material filled me with even more rage.

"He stole the stuff you two cut from my interview," I shouted, spittle flying from between my teeth, "everything Hemingway said about surveillance, and the FBI, and the Castro brothers. Did you know Harry was sneaking behind your back?"

Joe's hands came down, slowly, and he gathered the pages into a stack. Ducking his head, he tried to hand them back to me. "I don't even want to see it."

"Joe," I said quietly, the pads of my fingers pressed into the desk. He didn't look up. "Someone must have found out about this. Someone had him killed."

Joe ran his hands through his hair. "Do you hear yourself? You sound crazy."

"He bought heroin from two men who Beverly thought didn't look like drug pushers."

"Beverly? What are you doing talking to Beverly?"

"You cannot tell me who I'm allowed to speak to, Joe Martin. You cannot call me crazy and expect that to shut me up." I winced. A bruise on my hip, from the fall, had really begun to smart. "Who are you involved with? Why did you need to cut that stuff from my work in the first place?"

He glowered at me. "Your piece went too long. Any writer worth his salt knows how to take some cuts."

"No, no, I won't accept that as an explanation. Not this time, especially not now that Harry's dead. Are you working for the CIA?"

"Oh, Christ. The who?"

"The CIA." I took a second to catch my breath, to make sure what I had to say came out right. My blood was beating madly in my temples. "I've been thinking about Harry's Harvard-Yale essay. If you consider it in a certain way . . . I'm trying to remember the quote. . . ." I closed my eyes. "'What the new radicals don't understand is that things like boycotts only result in fewer people getting to enjoy a bus ride.' He's encouraging young people to accept the status quo. And his language about that damned football game—like he was describing a holy experience. Do you know what it reminded me of?" I was really on a roll now.

"What did it remind you of," Joe said, his mouth pinched.

"Goebbels."

Joe's eyes popped. His lower teeth came forward. "Goebbels. Propaganda, you mean. You sound like a crazy little girl." He grabbed a handful of papers, my novel and Harry's article all mixed together, and shuffled them onto the desk in a heap. "Goebbels! For God's sake. This is all a nice attempt to distract me from how silly you've been. Good try."

"Excuse me?"

"Writing this Russian fantasy nonsense, which I've already told you is a bad idea. No one will want to publish this, Lou. Can't you see that? Meanwhile, you've got your own fellow eating out of the palm of your hand."

Eating out of the palm of my hand? Then why was I the one who'd been feeling controlled, manipulated, managed lately? "How so?"

"I pay you more per word than I pay any other writer, male or female, to write the kind of features everybody's dying to write."

He'd effectively pushed me into the living room. With each step he took forward, I took one back, until I was pinned to the sofa. The room was dark. The sky outside, stretching vast over the Hudson and Hell's Kitchen, had thickened with rain clouds.

Joe had his finger in my face. "I do everything in my power to get you what you say you want, real work as a writer, and you fritter your time away writing girly nonsense and cooking up crackpot theories. Harry wasn't killed; he was a reckless blockhead who finally got what was coming to him."

In all our time together, I couldn't remember that Joe and I had ever fought like this. We were both breathing heavily, his face still the color of a ripe beet, tears in his eyes.

"You can't mean that," I said, my voice catching in my throat. Another Braxton-Hicks contraction gripped my belly. I let it roll past me, ignoring its white heat. "You can't think Harry had it coming." An awful realization came to me then—what if Joe, even some part of Joe he'd hidden from himself, had *wanted* Harry dead? I remembered how hard he'd gripped Harry's arm after the awards dinner, as if he'd meant to hurt him. "Do you hear yourself? You can't possibly think that."

"No," he said, his voice suddenly quite small. He put his face in his hands. "No, I didn't mean it."

"He's just another dead young man." I was crying hard now, in pain and exhaustion and grief. "Another American casualty. Just like Paul."

Joe peeked at me from between his fingers. "I'm sorry about Paul, Louise, but you're wrong."

"What did Paul's death accomplish?" I gasped between sobs. I was changing the subject, I knew it, but I'd been bottling up my heartache over Paul for so long, and it all came spilling out. "The borders didn't change. They're calling it a proxy war, did you know that? As if the infantry were toys. It's an outrage. And you wouldn't even let me write . . ." My voice went out. Another contraction came over me, this one even stronger than the last, doubling me over. The pain was intense, ripping me open from the inside out.

Joe's hands went to my shoulders. "Here," he said, his voice still stiff, but slightly melted, "let me help you to the couch." I waited, and he followed suit, as the pain crested and rolled away. When I went to stand up straight, I felt a *pop!* between my legs. Something warm began gushing down my stockings, pooling in the heels of my shoes.

He was still trying to lead me to sit. "Stop," I said, and pointed downward. I had my eyes closed. I could hear him gasp.

"We're taking you to the hospital," he said. "I'll call a car.

Don't move. Louise, you hear me? Don't you move. And don't look down."

But I did. He left me, suddenly shivering, standing in a puddle of fluid, and when I opened my eyes and couldn't resist glancing downward, I saw that the puddle was a deep red.

· 20 ·

The lights were bright in the emergency room. I wasn't supposed to be here. I wasn't supposed to be remembering this, but I would, I knew I would. I was stripped from the waist. The table felt wet. I looked at Joe through blurred eyes. Joe was supposed to be reading a newspaper with the other expectant fathers, tucked into a waiting room with a coffeemaker.

Joe was sawing at my hand with something, something metal.

Someone was moaning, "*Please*, please, please, make it stop"—that was me.

A nurse: "Oh, goodness, she's awake again."

"I can't—I can't get it off!" Joe wiped at his forehead with his sleeve. "For Christ's sake, don't you have anything sharper?"

The nurses flocked around me, so many nurses, all in white, all moving quickly, all scared, and there was a doctor somewhere: I could hear him calmly putting on his gloves.

"No, and you'd better hurry," one of the nurses snapped at Joe, "or she's gonna lose that finger."

"Please, God. Oh, for God's sake, make it stop. I'll do anything."

"Louise." Joe's tearful face was right above mine, his hand

pushing my hair back from my forehead. I didn't care about seeing him or whatever he was doing to my hand. I didn't care about the baby. All I wanted was for the pain to stop. He was saying something about my engagement ring, about blood transfusions. He pulled my face toward him.

"Louise, you're going to be all right, I promise."

"Just take the baby out, just get it out, just make it stop. Make it stop, I'll do anything."

"The baby's already here, Louise, she's here, she's beautiful. Louise? Louise!"

"Mister, her finger!"

I could hear Joe weeping, trying to catch his breath, then the sawing, sawing at my ring finger began again. At last I felt a pinch against that finger on my left hand, and then something gave way. Something broke. Someone stuck something into my upper arm, and I was gone.

I awoke in a sunny room. I'd expected a common ward after giving birth, rows of tired and happy new mothers convalescing together in our mutual sighs, but this was a tiny room of my own, white walls, green linoleum floor.

Joe was sitting in a chair, staring out the window, his face swollen and eyes red. I summoned some strength and cleared my throat, letting out a dry cough.

He sprang to life. At once he was by my side, holding my left hand. "Oh, Louise," he said, brushing my hair from my forehead. My hair, I realized, was balled up in a disgusting, sweaty mass. "Jesus, you gave me a scare."

Tears were forming in my eyes. I had flashes of memory from the night before, or two nights before—time had become slippery, I knew both too much and too little. Perhaps I didn't want to ask what had happened. My right hand went to my stomach. It felt like a partially collapsed balloon, a painful, swollen, raw balloon. "The baby—is the baby all right?"

"She is. She's got black hair, Louise, all standing straight up. She's in the nursery. They said you can see her when you're awake, which you are—thank God, you're awake." He kissed me. "I'll have them get you a wheelchair."

"I need water, too," I croaked. "Joe . . ." I caught his sleeve, as he was getting up to reach for a pitcher beside the bed. "What happened?"

He took my hand. "The doctors aren't sure why, but something inside you—the placenta?" The word brought color to his cheeks. "It partially detached, it seems, before it should have. I thought I was going to lose you, Lou, and that scared me." He brushed my sticky hair back from my forehead.

I managed a tiny smile. "Did you save the ring?"

The corners of his mouth raised a bit. He patted his breast pocket. "It's just fine. Mangled, but the band can be repaired. You, on the other hand . . . There was a minute when I thought you couldn't be saved."

"Oh," I said quietly. We were both crying now. I dabbed the corner of my eye. "I'm all right."

He nodded, his hand resting at the back of my neck. He held my gaze with his brown eyes. "You scared me more than anything ever has."

Of all the memories that came flooding back to me those first few days in the hospital, I couldn't remember the baby coming out, although I was told later it happened right there in triage. They'd had to get her out as quickly as possible. And so, when I first saw her, in a nurse's arms with a pink ribbon in her hair, she was a stranger.

"Look at that," I said, pointing at a sign above the rows of wire bassinets. " 'Babies are displayed at this window between ten and noon, three and five.' They get a union break."

"Isn't she beautiful?" Joe asked, his breath fogging the window.

"I can't see her very well," I said from the wheelchair they'd put me in. It wasn't exactly true—I could see her just fine—but I couldn't tell her apart from any of the others. They all looked like wrinkly little newborn guinea pigs to me, all with the same downy spiked hair and red, uncomfortable faces, their pacifiers huge against their tiny mouths.

On the second day, my own mother spoke to me over the phone, in tears. She was relieved and even a bit tickled, it turned out, to have spoken to Joe. He'd called her after I was out of the woods. My mother promised to visit and help me once we were home with the baby, which I was doing my best to forestall.

During our stay in the hospital, I lay in bed, eating grayish hamburgers and black-bean salad to get my iron up. The nurses who'd tended to me, none of whom I recognized, fluttered around us. They didn't seem to know what to make of me, an unwed mother with a doting father at hand. Several mentioned that there was a chapel right there in the hospital, if we wanted to tie the knot. They seemed nonplussed when I demurred, but I knew they meant well. "You were knockin' at heaven's door!" one older Irish woman kept saying. Every time she repeated it, I felt like crying.

Joe went home every night, to sleep comfortably in his own bed, while the baby—still nameless—suckled Vitaflo bottles in the nursery and I shivered in my cotton gown, dreaming vividly from the morphine. Once in a while, they took me to the nursery to see her, and I peered at her through the glass as a sturdy nurse held her confidently, one hand behind her neck, one under her squirming, tiny legs. I couldn't for the life of me imagine leaving here with her, without any of these women to help. I felt we'd drown.

The night before I was scheduled to go home, I had a dream about Harry.

"Hiya, beautiful," he said, descending the steps of an airplane. We were both on the tarmac, our hair blowing in the wind from the propellers. I had the sense that the plane was headed somewhere special, a tropical island perhaps, and that I should get on, but my shoes seemed nailed to the ground.

"You shouldn't do that," I said. He was standing on one of the wings, arms outstretched. There was also something I should ask him, I knew, but in the dream I couldn't remember what it was. "It's not safe up there."

"I'm knocking on heaven's door," Harry replied, and I woke up in a sweat, panting.

I sat bolt upright, like a vampire, then gasped—there was someone sitting at the foot of the bed.

"Joe?" I said, my eyes adjusting. I could sense it was morning, but the sun hadn't come up yet. The light filtering through the slats in the blinds was pale blue. "What are you doing here so early?"

He turned toward me, his lower lip between his teeth,

which were drawing the blood out of the skin, blanching it white. "I have to talk to you."

"Okay." I sat up against the pillows.

Joe took a deep breath. His eyes looked hollow, shadowed, as if he hadn't slept all night. "You were right about some things. I . . . When I thought I might lose you, I knew I'd never forgive myself for keeping you in the dark."

My heart was beating wildly, pumping blood to my face and limbs. Other people's blood: I'd had two transfusions. I couldn't stop thinking about that.

He took a deep breath, keeping his eyes low, focused on the bed. All I could see were his dark eyelashes. "Listen. There are some men in the government, good men, who've taken it upon themselves to offer grants to worthy artists and publications. We happen to be one of them. The grants can't be made public; otherwise, it would look as if they were favoring one political ideology over another."

"When, in fact, they are," I said. "And they're censoring the ones they have in their pocket, aren't they? They're telling writers what they can and cannot say."

"No, that's ridiculous. To think the government would bother to"—he sputtered, looking at the ceiling—"send agents out to do copyedits, that's horse crap."

I clenched my jaw. This was supposed to be a coming-clean conversation, yet I still felt as if I were talking to a wall. "How can you claim that? I've seen it myself; my own work has been compromised to fit the agenda."

"Well, Lou, it's really my work. I gave you the Hemingway assignment. I'm giving you Malamud. You don't have to take them."

I crossed my arms over my chest. My breasts had been

bound to stop my milk; they felt like two small boulders, hard and itchy, under the gauze. "So *Downtown* is part of some psychological-warfare effort."

He ran a hand over his beard stubble. "How do you know that term—'psychological warfare'?"

"Must have learned it from *Popular Science*," I said sarcastically. "Answer the question."

"No, *Downtown* is not some propaganda machine." His voice dropped, and he shifted closer to me on the mattress, his weight against my hip. "It's a regular magazine, just like any other."

"The Congress for Cultural Freedom," I said. "The people you went to for funding, while we were in Italy. Are they CIA?"

"No, not at all," said Joe, but he looked worried. He seemed to be realizing I'd connected more dots than he'd hoped. He wiped sweat from his hands on his pants. "And that's it. That's all there is to tell."

I watched a silverfish slip down one of the walls. He was acting as if I hadn't read the letter from Harry myself, the one in which he'd written, "It will be up to you-know-who." Joe was referring to an oblique "they," as if he had no part in it. "And what about you? You had an awful lot of strange questions for James Baldwin. You've been rather harsh to me about my Russian novel. How do I know you're not CIA?"

"Keep your voice down. You know I'm not CIA because you know me. I am not a CIA agent." If it was a lie, it was a lie confidently delivered. He never broke my gaze, keeping his eyes steady and open wide. Maybe he had been well trained. Or maybe he was telling the truth, about this at least.

After a minute, his fingers traveled over the white bed-spread, toward my limp hand. His pointer finger tapped once, twice, on my middle knuckle.

"Your turn," he said.

I pulled my hand away. "My turn?"

He nodded. His eyes were wide, brown, and clear. "Your turn to tell me a truth." The tip of his tongue poked between his lips in an almost teasing smile. "I've always thought that was funny—you hear 'tell a lie' all the time, but not 'tell a truth.' It's only, 'tell *the* truth,' as if there's only one truth to tell. All I'm asking is for you to tell me *a* truth. Pick one."

"That's the most writerly quibble I've ever heard," I said, to buy time. Adrenaline coursed under my skin.

His gaze didn't budge. "Tell me a truth, Lou."

I breathed. "You spoke to my mother."

"Yes, your mother was very kind. And concerned about you."

I huffed, "Sure she was. Now that Paul's gone, she has a little bit of concern left over."

"She mentioned that she had to work yesterday. Seems she's a housekeeper?"

"Yes. There's my truth. I'm the daughter of a housekeeper."

"So what? I'm the son of a seamstress."

"Sure, but your father sold insurance. Mine hasn't worked since I was a little girl."

His hand wrapped around my wrist. "So—you're the daughter of a housekeeper and an unemployed man. I think you know that's not the truth I'm after."

An announcement crackled over the hospital's loudspeaker system, rousing the patients. Soon they'd be in to take my vital signs, to bring my breakfast. It had been nine days. In all likelihood, they would be discharging me that afternoon. I would have to go home, with Joe.

Slowly, I sat up in bed and stretched my elbows behind me for support. I pulled my neck tall, so I'd be eye to eye with him. "Seems you already know something. You're just asking for me to confirm it."

He dropped his eyes. The lids were shiny with perspiration, shadowed with exhaustion. "I know you were working, at the party where we met."

I tried to read his expression, but his face revealed nothing. "Who told you?"

"Oh, you don't give yourself enough credit, Louise. I noticed you right at the beginning of that party, with your bright red hair. When you took off the apron and stayed, after all the other staff had left, I thought it was some kind of game. I thought you'd laugh about it later. But you never mentioned it again. Next thing I knew, you were a law clerk. I wasn't sure what to make of it."

Something dawned on me then. Something incredible. "You thought I was a spy, didn't you?"

He began waving this suggestion away with his hands, brushing it off like dust. "No, no, I'd never have thought that. Who would you have been spying for? You have spies on the brain, Lou. It's making you crazy. No, instead I wondered, after all this time, why you never mentioned your past as a cocktail waitress. At times I thought you might be using me."

"Using you?"

"Yeah, giving me the runaround." His lower lip came out, just a tad. He looked pitiful. And handsome. Despite everything, I wanted to reach out and touch the smooth part of his cheek, run my thumb over that lip. "Getting close to me so that you could get closer to, say, Mort Clifton. Hemingway."

"I was not using you," I said gently. "I always loved you."

He gave a little start, as did I; I hadn't meant to say "loved," in the past tense. Somehow I couldn't make myself correct it, though. I couldn't force my lips to form the words "I love you." I still felt there was a wall between us, a scrim of some sort. I could see through it, I could see him, he was close enough for me to embrace, but something, some unspoken thing, kept us at arm's length from each other.

For a moment, we said nothing, both of us staring in the direction of the window. Thin gray light penetrated the curtains.

"I've thought of a name," Joe said finally.

"A name for what?" I said, lost in thought. I'd been biting my pinkie nail to shreds.

His eyes turned sharp, alarmed. "For the baby, of course."

"Oh." The baby had been the furthest thing from my mind.

"I was thinking 'Aurora.' It means 'rebirth,' as well as 'dawn.' And with what just happened to you, with us . . . I thought we could use a fresh start."

We certainly could, I thought. "It's nice," I conceded. "How about if I choose the middle name?"

"Of course," he said. His face had relaxed now. He looked relieved. I decided to give him the opportunity to tell the truth one last time.

"Joe. Was Harry's death an accident?"

He let out a long sigh, rolling his eyes to the ceiling. "*Yes*. He was reckless, you know that. He bought some bad dope, and that's the end of it."

A nurse knocked on my door. She entered without waiting for a response, as they tended to do. I looked up, expecting a breakfast tray, but instead she was holding the baby. I pushed myself farther back against the pillows, ready to make an excuse for why Joe and I had to be left alone so that we could continue our conversation, but before I knew it, the woman had put the little bundle in my arms.

"Oh" was all I could say, looking down at her. The baby was asleep, black eyelashes fanned over her downy cheeks. She had a wide button nose covered in what looked like tiny white pimples. Her lips were delicately formed, the soft peach of a spring flower.

I leaned down and kissed her. She had a buttery-sweet scent, and when my mouth touched hers she wrinkled her face up and yawned, a little kitten yowl escaping her lips.

"Her name is Aurora Francine," I said, "after my grandmother."

"Aurora Francine," said Joe. His hair brushed my forehead, and I realized how close he'd come. He was practically lying beside me.

"I'd like to be alone with her for a minute, if you don't mind," I said quietly.

Joe's arms snapped straight, pushing him up from the mattress. He looked almost as if he'd touched a light socket. He stared at me for a moment, resentment distorting his face. Then he excused himself to go sort out the hospital bills before we were discharged. I supposed our effort at a rebirth hadn't yet taken.

———

Aurora—or Francie, as I'd secretly begun thinking of her—cried all the way to the curb, her face bright red, approaching purple. Joe ran ahead to open the door of the long black automobile waiting for us, which surprised me: I'd been expecting a Yellow taxi.

As I approached, I noticed the big car had a surprisingly plush interior, leather club seats, a bottle of seltzer with rocks glasses. "Fancy," I muttered. "Did you call this boat?"

"Only the best for you, my dear," Joe replied, without warmth.

I slid inside and shouted over the baby's screams, "Get me the baby bottle, will you?"

Joe obeyed, then came around the car to sit beside me in the back. The silence between the two of us felt thick. The driver began pulling away from the curb as I tried stuffing the nipple into the baby's mouth. Her lips stayed dilated, her tonsils vibrating from the screams.

"Oh, for Pete's sake," I muttered. I let out a deep breath, watching midtown pass by us. People were still living their ordinary lives, meeting co-workers at the deli, working to fix a pothole. It was incredible, after all the death and birth I'd been involved in lately, to think these last few weeks could have been like any others for so many people.

"Here, let me try." Joe did his best, tapping the nipple against the baby's tongue. A few drops of formula dripped out, and she clamped down for a second. We both breathed a sigh of relief. Then she spit it out and began screaming again.

"For crying out loud," said Joe.

"When you get home," the driver butted in, "dip it in sugar water. That'll do it."

Who asked you? I thought, but I tried to remain polite. "Do you have children?" I replied, just a bit icily.

The driver laughed. "Yes, ma'am. I've got six." He adjusted the rearview mirror so that I could see his face. "All six of them rascals."

"Six!" Joe exclaimed, still wrestling with the crying baby and her bottle. His upper lip was beaded with sweat. "Never knew that about you, Bob."

As for me, I couldn't respond. It had taken everything I had not to gasp when I saw the driver's face in the mirror.

He was the man with the red mustache.

21

The man with the red mustache lingered for a while after he brought us home from the hospital. He lent a hand in carrying my suitcase and setting up the bassinet in our bedroom, and then he helped himself to some jam croissants and doughnuts Joe had bought at the bakery downstairs. All the while, I hovered around the corners of rooms, clutching the baby, who would finally take a bottle as long as I offered it while standing. I fed her and watched Joe and Bob eat casually, chatting about this and that.

I felt cold. I'd told myself Joe couldn't have been involved in Harry's death—he'd seemed so upset by it. His tears had been his alibi. Now I wondered if he'd been reacting out of guilt.

"Louise, come sit with us," Joe urged me from the little kitchen table, white confectioner's sugar dusting his chin. "I'll make you a cup of tea."

"No, thank you," I said, making an attempt to laugh it off. "Baby dictates that I stand, and baby gets what baby wants."

"That's a dangerous habit to get into," said the man with the red mustache. Bob. He and Joe were on a first-name basis. The guy had a jovial air about him, as though there were nothing strange about his being here at all. As though I had never seen him before.

"She's less than two weeks old," I replied as politely as I could. "I'd hardly call anything a habit yet." Her tiny face lay drooling on my shoulder as I moved my body in awkward, jerky motions to keep her still. My brain sizzled, trying to remember everything I could about Bob and the first time I'd seen him. I had been coming home from somewhere, hadn't I, when I bumped into him. He'd been standing directly in front of my apartment, I remembered that for sure—it had been my apartment, not Joe's. Then he'd whistled, ear-splittingly, for a cab.

Joe held up an éclair, licking his thumb on the other hand. "Come on, Lou, honey, have a doughnut. You're looking pale."

"Just give me a second." That day Bob had whistled in front of my apartment—was it the same day I'd come home to find that Joe had let himself in? Could Bob have been warning him I was coming? Joe and I had never discussed how he'd gotten inside. That was the day we found out Paul had died, and any thoughts about forced entry or snooping had been crushed by my grief.

But my suspicions came through clearly now.

Joe's telephone rang right next to my ear, and I startled so profoundly that Francie began crying. Joe got up from the table, wiping his mouth, to reach for the phone. Something led me to hand him the baby instead.

"I'll get it," I insisted, as Francie burrowed her milk-drool lips against his collar. He gave me a bit of an odd look—I never answered the phone at his apartment—as Bob reached for another cruller at the table.

"Joe Martin's place," I said when I answered.

The voice on the other line came through loudly. "Miss Leithauser, I presume?"

A quivery feeling came into my knees. It was Papa. "It is," I replied, my eyes fixed on Joe's. In the daylight angling through the kitchen window, swirls of dust motes floated between us.

"Ah, good! Was hoping I'd catch you and not Eager Eddie, or his mother. He seems the type of boy whose mother comes to dust the baseboards and take out the bathroom trash, am I right?"

Unexpected laughter burst out of me, not a graceful laugh but a nervous, relieved gurgle. Joe was still watching me, swaying the baby. Bob looked up from the table.

"Yes, I believe that is right," I replied. I almost added *Papa*, but stopped myself. Instinct, that quiet but clear voice, told me it would be better to keep the caller's identity to myself.

"I'm calling from our hotel. Mary and I are back in the city. We fly to Miami in a few days to spend time in the Keys. Then home to the farm in Havana. They miss us, the cats, the dogs. And the pigeons."

"Uh-huh." I wasn't sure where this was going. Part of me wanted to cut the guy off, but you couldn't just cut off Hemingway.

"Time in Wyoming cut short by surprise visitors. Unwelcome guests. You think you're covering all bases, keeping an eye on the man on first, then, out of nowhere, someone steals third."

I didn't follow. "Steals third?" I said aloud.

Joe's eyebrows shot up. *Who is it?* he mouthed. I held up a finger.

Hemingway went on, "They found me. First I get a call from that sissy Mort Clifton, at my old chum's ranch, even though my chum's got an unlisted number. So does your pal

Joe, did you know that? Only way I could track you down was to ask a few mutual friends. Your Joe's off the books."

"You don't say," I replied, glancing at Joe and Bob before turning my face toward the wall. Winter sunlight angled past me, bright polygons on the white paint.

"So—call comes from Mort. Then the finks arrive. Always give themselves away. They're the ones wearing penny loafers in the snow, pretending to hunt. When, really, it's all about checking on me, seeing what I'm up to."

They're the ones pretending to read a newspaper in Italian, I thought. *They're the ones taking you home from the hospital.* They were everywhere.

"Oh, I am sorry," I said with a sinking feeling. Papa hadn't gotten my letter before he'd fled. He didn't know I was the one who'd told Mort Clifton where he'd gone. Otherwise, he never would have called me. In a few days, though, his chum in Wyoming would receive it and forward it to him. It would be waiting when he arrived back in Cuba.

I didn't have much time left to be Ernest Hemingway's friend.

"Nothing new," he grunted. I could hear jazz playing faintly in the background, two women's voices chatting. "Nothing surprising. Well! I'm at the Plaza, daughter, not too far from you, could come by this afternoon to pick up my hat. Will have to be in a couple hours. We've just gotten room service—snails and an ice bucket, waiting on champagne."

I closed my eyes, my cheek against the wall. I felt as if all of my limbs were chained to the floor, each by a different fetter: the mewling baby, Joe, Bob, my still-healing, achy womb. Joe's apartment, though sunny and warm, might well have been a cold prison. After I hung up, I'd be interrogated.

I'd be handed back the baby. I felt like lingering on the line forever.

In my mind I pictured writing on the moon, in the dust: *Send help! S.O.S.!*

My spine straightened. I had an idea. I whirled around and swallowed the lump in my throat. "Oh, no," I said brightly. "I couldn't possibly, Mother."

"*Mother?*" Hemingway repeated.

"Mm-hmm," I said. Joe kept watching me, and I smiled at him with my lips shut. Bob had gone back to his doughnut, though he looked to have his ears perked.

There was a pause on the line. "Turn that down, will you?" Hemingway shouted to someone, and a second later, the music disappeared. "Listen, Leithauser, are you in trouble? Say yes if you are."

"Yes," I said.

"I knew it. I knew there was something off about that son of a bitch." Hemingway actually sounded excited. "We can come get you now, Mary and I can. Say yes if that's the game plan."

"Oh, no," I replied. "Thursday."

"Thursday. That works beautifully if you can wait until then, daughter. Tomorrow Mary is picking up a car. Wants to drive out to Montauk to see her sister. Thursday at ten sharp, that's ten in the morning, Mary and I will be there."

"Thursday, yes," I said as breezily as I could. "That'll be a great time for you to meet the baby."

"The baby? Oh, Louise eh-Light-hau-sah, trouble has found you."

I forced a casual laugh. "Yes, yes. And you remember Joe's address, right, Mother? Oh, silly, I'll tell you again."

I gave Papa Joe's street and building number before I hung up. I wiped my palms on my dress, then reached for Francie. Joe held on to her for a second. "Who was that?"

"Who do you think it was? My mother. She's coming at, um . . ." I calculated quickly. I hoped Joe would go to the office as usual on Thursday morning, so that I could jump into the Hemingways' car and have them take me somewhere, anywhere, without his knowing. "At three in the afternoon on Thursday, to meet Francie." I peeled her gently off his shoulder, at which she started to fuss.

"I thought we agreed on 'Aurora.'"

"We did. It's just a nickname." We stared at each other a moment, until I broke the silence with a loud kiss on Francie's forehead. "I'll just lie down with her in the other room. Will you hand me that bottle, and the burp cloth? Thank you."

I took Francie into the bedroom and shut the door behind me. My rib cage went up and down with each breath, and I forced myself to take a big inhale, all the way down into my aching gut. The men murmured to each other in the kitchen for a while as I fed Francie her bottle. Her tiny rosebud lips wrapped perfectly around the nipple; her translucent eyelids closed as she drank. She went right back to sleep, and I laid her on our pillows so that I could go to the vanity Joe had set up for me and brush my hair.

My eyes, in the mirror, looked hollow and dark. Freckles stood bold against my bluish-pale skin. I looked haunted. I heard one of the men go into the bathroom. Then the bedroom door creaked open. My eyes shot up, watching the door in the mirror. It was Bob.

"What on—" I whispered. He put his finger to his lips.

"Shh. You'll wake the baby." He came over to kneel beside where I sat at the vanity, a tender gesture, it would seem, until his face took on a twisted smile. "Who was that on the phone?" he said, almost inaudibly.

My stomach squeezed in fear. "My mother. I told you already."

Bob cocked his head to the side. "What was that about stealing third base?"

"Just something my father said in the background. Please, will you leave me be? I'm trying to have a moment to myself."

Bob licked his bottom lip, then the top one. His bristly mustache moved in and out of his mouth. I tried to imagine him selling bad dope to Harry and Beverly. I wanted to ask him if he'd done it. If he'd sold it, if he knew it was bad.

"Baseball season hasn't begun yet," he whispered. "It starts April 13." He smiled and pointed to himself. "Giants fan."

"What's going on here?" Joe shouted from the doorway, and immediately Francie began to cry.

Bob stood. "I was only talking to your wife," he said. Neither of us bothered to correct him. I went, trembling all over, to get Francie. Joe opened the door all the way, pointing toward the hallway.

"I think it's time for you to leave," he said, and Bob did, with a slight tip of the hat toward me as he went. I tried to catch Joe's eye, but he avoided me, frowning as he showed the man out.

At ten in the morning on Thursday, the front door to Joe's apartment burst open. I hadn't heard the buzzer, hadn't even realized I'd left the door unlocked, but here Papa loomed on the threshold, this time in a fishing cap and a big turtleneck sweater the color of mustard. His cheeks, above his beard, were sunburned, and he had a darkly scabbed cut below his lip.

I felt like crying in relief at the sight of him. I'd been standing in the middle of the living room before he arrived, wringing my gloves in my hands. Francie was taking her morning nap.

"My hat?" he demanded, skipping hello. "Very important hat, you see, Christmas gift from Mrs. Hemingway."

"Oh, yes, of course," I said, and went to fetch it from the back of the top shelf in the closet. He grunted his thanks.

"Where are your bags?" he asked.

"My suitcase is right there—behind the door." For the last couple of days, I'd been quietly piling our necessities in a corner of the office: Francie's glass bottles and nipples, cleaned and dried; her tiny baby outfits; two nightgowns for me, and enough clothes, if I kept them clean, to last me a few five-day cycles. After Joe left for the office that morning, I'd shoved them all into the suitcase.

Hemingway appraised me. "You're dressed for the part, Leithauser, which I appreciate. A bit like Bonnie Parker on the run from the authorities, but nice."

I felt myself blush. I had on a powder-blue dress with a wide sailor's collar and a red rose appliqué on the shoulder. Some part of me had known that if I stayed in a housedress I'd never find the strength to go. "Oh, Papa, thank you for coming for me. If you only knew—"

He held up a hand, shutting me up. "Listen, Mary's double-parked down there, and it's a rental with out-of-state plates, so we'd better move." He reached for my bag. "Where's the little one—is it a boy or a girl?"

"A girl." I could hear his wife in the car, down in the street, laying on the horn. *Blap blap blaaaaap*. "She's asleep, but I'll fetch her."

"Good. I'll take this suitcase; you grab the baby and meet us down there."

I went to the bassinet, where Francie was sleeping soundly, one tiny hand curled over the top of her pink blanket. I hated to wake her, but of course she did wake up as soon as I lifted her limp, tiny body into my hands. I bounce-stepped her into the kitchen to find Hemingway helping himself to a few taralli cookies.

"May I?" he asked, eyes twinkling, crumbs in his beard.

"Of course," I said. "Take heaps of them." Joe's mother, a stout, well-dressed woman, had come by earlier in the week, to meet Francie and to drop off loads of food: a tray of chicken francese, baked pasta shells, sweets by the bundle. She'd held Francie but hadn't been able to look me in the eye. "You're still going to be married, right?" she'd asked in a panic, confirming my suspicion that she both loathed me for having a baby with her son out of wedlock and also wanted me to marry him as quickly as possible. The paradox, I supposed, of propriety.

Francie was wailing by the time I *click-clack*ed down to the curb in my heels and ran toward the big maroon Packard. The skies over midtown looked low, pillowy, a gray duvet. Hemingway leaned with one hand on the rental car's frame, talking with his wife inside. I caught a glimpse of her gripping the wheel, a wiry blond woman with a sharp gray gaze. Her mink coat took up the entire front seat. She appraised the baby and me, then gave us a welcoming nod.

I couldn't believe we were doing this. Leaving Joe, getting into the car with Hemingway and his wife.

"All set?" Hemingway asked me. "You brought something for that one to suckle while we drive, I hope?"

"Yes." I felt dizzy. I had a bottle of formula in my pocket, sloshing around.

"Where are we taking you?"

"Ossining," I said breathlessly. There was nowhere else to go but my parents' home. I'd called my mother the day before, and she'd been surprisingly thrilled, if a bit overwhelmed, at the idea of having Francie and me come to stay.

"You hear that, Mary? Ossining."

You'd have thought the fourth Mrs. Hemingway would balk at the idea of driving me, a complete stranger and much younger woman, all the way to Ossining, but all Mary did was crack her knuckles in their leather driving gloves and comment, "Oh, Papa, the oysters. Remember that time, with the oysters?"

Hemingway nodded. "Penelope's is the restaurant. Last there in '47, with Jim Porter and wife."

"Papa, let's go have baked oysters for lunch, what do you say?"

Something about it soothed me, listening to them casually talk about oysters as though this were merely a tourist's outing, and I weren't running away from the father of my child. Mentally, I checked my packing list. I had the diapers and bottles. I had my engagement ring, still broken, zipped into the secret compartment in my purse. Mrs. Hemingway pulled the car away from the curb as soon as Papa had settled next to her in the front.

I sat up quickly. "Stop!"

Mrs. Hemingway braked hard. My hand shot out to stop Francie and myself from crashing into the back of her seat. "What is it?" She peered at me through the rearview mirror, as if to say, *This had better be good.*

"I don't have my manuscript," I explained.

Hemingway wheeled around. "You'd better go and get it!" He elbowed Mrs. Hemingway, then said in his pet accent, "Louise eh-Light-hau-sah want to be big-time writer. Working on manuscript, top secret. Go get that work of yours, daughter. Here, hand baby to Mary. Mary loves babies."

Mrs. Hemingway didn't look sure she loved babies as much as her husband claimed, but she took Francie into the furry driver's seat and allowed me to run back into the building. With a stitch in my side, breathing hard, I flew into the apartment and went straight to Joe's office. I dragged the desk chair over to the bookshelf and stood on it so that I could reach the filing box with my manuscript inside.

The box felt three times lighter than I'd been expecting, which almost caused me to lose my balance. I was shaking, my teeth chattering, when I knelt on the carpet and opened the lid. I had to take my manuscript with me, or I might never see it again.

Only I was too late.

My manuscript was gone.

I heard the sound of a key being entered into the front door of the apartment. "Lou?" Joe called.

I cleared my throat and stepped out into the living room. Joe had been leafing through the mail, but he stopped when he saw my outfit. "Where . . ." He let out a nervous, unbe- lieving chuckle. "Where are you going? Where's Francie?"

I tightened my lips. "I'm leaving."

"What?" Joe took a step closer to me. "Lou, you can't be serious. With the baby? Why on Earth would you leave? Where could you go?"

I couldn't look at him. I spoke to the window over the sofa. "I'm going to my mother's."

Again, that incredulous laugh. It was beginning to feel like ridicule—how could I possibly think I'd survive without him? "Your mystery mother. The one you're so embarrassed by, you won't let anyone meet her. And now you want to live with her?"

"I love my mother," I said, tears spilling down my cheeks. "And she wants what's best for me. That's more than I can say for you."

The horn started again. *Blap blap blaaaaap. Blap blaaaaaaap.*

At the sight of me crying, Joe seemed to realize this was really happening. I was actually planning to go. "Louise. Jesus Christ. You aren't serious. You can't leave."

"I no longer feel safe here, Joe."

"You no longer feel safe? Are you serious?"

"Harry is dead. He's *dead*. And you knew it was coming."

Joe blew a puff of air out of his lips and looked away. "That's not—"

"Don't lie to me. You lie, and you lie, and I won't stand for it anymore."

For a while, Joe considered this, his eyes trained on the fabric rose pinned to my shoulder. He looked at my gloves and the matching blue hat. I'd brought my purse in with me, and it was sitting beside my feet. It was full of diapers. Something about the bag of diapers hit him like a strong wave. His face collapsed.

"Louise, please. You are safe. You, Francie. Of course you're safe with me—I love you."

"I'm not so sure that I am. Safe, that is." I took a step toward my purse. "My physical person may not be in any peril, but there are other ways to do damage to someone's life. You've taken something very dear to me. Something I can never recover."

He cast his eyes to the side. There was my confirmation: he'd destroyed *The Lunar Housewife*. He'd taken it straight to an incinerator, or a paper shredder, and the worst of it was, he'd have told himself it was for my own good.

I took another step, bent down slowly, and grasped the handle of my pocketbook. I could still hear Mrs. Hemingway, or maybe it was Papa, laying on the horn. I was tempted to tell Joe whom I'd be leaving with, but I restrained myself. "Goodbye, darling," I said in a strangled voice, and then I walked out the door.

22

"It is a shame they were out of beluga, Papa," Mrs. Hemingway said a few hours later, when we were all sated and tired. She dabbed the corners of her mouth with a white napkin. "We'll have to see if we can order some back at the Plaza."

Hemingway sat back in his chair. Behind him, the early-spring sun was beginning to set upon the Hudson. I felt myself stifling a yawn. "Of course the Plaza will have it, the Plaza never runs out of caviar." He signaled the waiter. "Double bourbons all around."

My mother moved quickly to cover her glass. "Oh, no, not for me, thank you."

Hemingway winked at her. "Mrs. Leithauser, I like you. You know when to pull the pitcher."

My mother's face turned crimson, and she responded by burying her nose in Francie's neck.

In a very real sense, this scenario was both my mother's nightmare and my own. At the Hemingways' insistence, we were eating in a restaurant that was not half a mile from the house in which I'd grown up, but which we'd never been able to afford. Since I reached adulthood my mother had accused me of putting on airs and social climbing, and now I'd shown up at her house with a famous writer and his stylish wife. I could see the look on my mother's face when we burst through her storm door: irritation, confusion, a sense that I was rubbing something in her face. Like an uncontrollable tic, her hand had flown to cover the right side of her mouth, where she was missing one incisor. Her eyes had flitted nervously upstairs, where, without a doubt, my father was sleeping off a violent hangover.

But then her gaze had landed on Francie, and she softened. She'd agreed to come out with us, and she'd held the baby, mystifyingly placid in her arms, in the back of the car. Still in a stained housedress, she'd barely spoken a word or eaten a bite during the meal; Hemingway had had to order for her. But even though she still showed signs of shell shock, her expression glazed over with happiness every time she looked down at the baby.

"You all right, Miss Leithauser?" Mrs. Hemingway asked me just before our plates were to be cleared. "You keep looking over your shoulder."

"She's making sure we didn't pick up a tail," Hemingway answered for me.

I laughed nervously. I had been scrutinizing every customer who came into the restaurant, especially anyone who sat near us or lingered by our table for too long. The two young men sitting beside us were, I thought, suspiciously quiet and dressed unusually blandly; the woman who kept walking a young girl to the window to look at the water had made eye contact with me one too many times. "Just looking around for old classmates, I guess," I said, feeling daft. "I haven't been to Ossining in quite a while."

"Oh, shoot," Mrs. Hemingway proclaimed, rifling through her purse. "Papa, we were going to buy more aspirin. It was on the list. Regina, dear." She put her hand on my mother's arm, and my mother stiffened. "Did I see a drugstore a couple doors down from here?"

"Yes, that's right," my mother said in a small voice, mostly to Francie. Part of me wanted to shake her—these people didn't care about her housedress. They didn't care that she cleaned homes for a living.

Then I remembered—I cared about those things. I never would have introduced her to Hemingway if I'd had a choice. I still hadn't introduced her to Joe.

"Perfect." Mrs. Hemingway popped out of her chair, flipped her mink coat back onto both shoulders in a neat shrug. "Game" was the adjective that came to mind as I watched her fluff her blond hair, wink at her husband. She seemed game as hell. I supposed you had to be, to sign up as Ernest Hemingway's fourth wife. "Papa, what do you say, a candy bar for the road?"

"Baby Ruth," said Hemingway, with a kiss on her hand.

With Mary gone, some of the energy left the table, and we fell into a stunned silence. My mother responded by taking Francie, who'd just woken up and was making staccato motions with her little tongue, to the window to watch the sunset.

"At last," Hemingway said, leaning on the table with one firm elbow. With the meaty pointer finger of his other hand, he stabbed the air at me. "We'll speak quickly. Never enough time. You need a meeting at the mound, daughter."

"I know." With *my* index finger, I plucked at a tiny barnacle cleaved to one of my discarded oyster shells. "What will I do without Joe?" I wondered aloud.

"Joe! Good riddance!" Hemingway scoffed, which led to a small coughing fit. His big chest heaved. "Can't trust a man who thinks he should be operating the crane while the others are on the ground with hammer and nails. By God, that boy fancies himself a crane operator."

"But I'm all alone, with a baby. And you can see I have no family money."

"Don't need money. Just smarts. Listen to me, daughter, there's great freedom in being a girl."

Watching my mother, who was pointing out at the horizon and murmuring to Francie, I had been wondering what would become of us all. Having a pity party, really, thinking how rotten we'd all been treated by the men in our lives. "Freedom?" I repeated. "In being a girl?"

He huffed, "You all bellyache about being the 'second sex,' but listen. Great thing about being a girl is this: *no one pays attention*. Whatever's in this book of yours, whatever radical stuff, you'll get away with it. The censors won't give a damn."

The waiter had come back with our double bourbons. I took too big a sip, winced at the burn. Hemingway drank his with a napkin wrapped around the glass. Emboldened by the liquor, I leaned forward and put a hand on his forearm, warm and hairy. "What do you think the powers that be are after, Papa? What's their game?"

"Their game is just what you think it is. Control. They like to control all writers, no imagination allowed, only bald-eagle Harvard Yard bullshit."

"Do you believe they'd kill to maintain that control?"

He licked his bottom lip, squinting. "Any of us could kill, at any time."

Bells tinkled at the front of the restaurant. Mrs. Hemingway had come back in, and was now chatting loudly in Spanish with the maître d'. Francie was beginning to fuss. Hemingway replaced his glasses and jabbed the tabletop with his fist. "Louise Leithauser, you listen to me. You're outmatched. You can't swing at these fellas and all they've got backing them; they're punching above their weight. What you need to do is duck, under the arm. Get on the inside, and then you hit with everything you've got."

He didn't seem to care who overheard him, but I lowered my voice, hoping he'd follow suit. "What does that mean, Papa?"

"Forget the New York publishers. There's a Joe in every goddamn one of them. Instead, find the silliest publisher you can, the one with the bright-pink paperbacks, and bring your manuscript to them. It'll get printed, mark my words."

Mrs. Hemingway strode back to the table and put her hand on her husband's shoulder. "Getting dark, Papa. We'd better head back to town. Traffic's going to be murder."

"This lousy town and its traffic. You'd think they'd be clamoring to get *out*. Here, my dear, drink your bourbon."

While Mary drank, I watched my mother nervously. She was starting to get that panicked look from before, when our ragtag gang had arrived at her house, but I had a couple more things to say to Hemingway. I took another glug from my own glass.

"Papa," I said, my voice creaky from the bourbon, "what about your novel? The one about the guerrilla. You think they'll let you go through with it?"

Mary was giving me dagger eyes, I realized too late. "Huh!" Hemingway said. "Clifton already knew about it, probably thanks to your boys and the bits I told you in the interview. Already suggesting mon-u-men-tal changes to manuscript. I tell him maybe I find new publisher. And maybe not."

He shrugged. Mary was shaking her head, tsk-tsk-ing her tongue.

When I heard Clifton's name, my mouth went dry. "I have to tell you something, Papa. It was my fault they came looking for you in Wyoming. I mentioned it to Clifton."

The noises in the restaurant seemed to increase as I faced the silent Hemingways. Dishes clinked in the kitchen. The chef shouted in French at a waiter. Mary had gone from a bird on his shoulder to a snake, her eyes and nostrils narrowed. Hemingway considered me thoughtfully, his big chest going up and down with each breath, the ribs on his turtleneck sweater expanding and contracting, like the belly of a whale. Finally, he spoke.

"Loose lips sink ships, Leithauser."

"I know, I'm so sorry—"

"Tell you what. Can use those loose lips of yours to play a little game. Tell your Joe, tell Clifton, tell whomever you want, there's a secret Hemingway novel in the works. Could be guerrilla novel, could be something you make up. Tell 'em I buried it in Cuba, somewhere on the grounds of the Finca Vigia. Say it's under the livestock if you please, maybe under the corner where all the shit collects."

"Oh, that's good, Papa," Mrs. Hemingway said, descending into a fit of giggles. She was his little parakeet again. "That's a good one."

"They'll be looking for it," said Papa. "They'll be looking for it long after I'm dead."

The last sliver of red, shimmering sun dipped below the horizon. The light in the room went from bright red to muted mauve. Waiters came around, lighting candles. Mrs. Hemingway had a far-off look on her face.

"I will, Papa," I said.

"They'll be looking for it." He wasn't smiling. He lifted his glass to his lips and downed the rest of his double bourbon in a huge gulp, drenching his beard. "That's just the counterpunch to do them in."

· 23 ·

THE LUNAR HOUSEWIFE

Outcry

Katherine opened her eyes.

The blanket of tiny stars stared back at her, unchanged, above. Beside her, Sergey softly snored. How long had it been since they turned in for what they termed night? Her hair felt dry, her body still cool. They had probably been asleep for only an hour or so.

There it was again. She sat up, wincing. An invisible hand ran a searing-hot iron over her body from ribs to knees. It passed in a wave, cresting at such pain she nearly cried out, then subsiding, slowly, to nothing.

"Sergey." She brushed a lock of hair away from his ear. At this point, she felt nothing but excitement. They would be fine, two pioneers out on this lunar prairie. Joseph and Mary alone in the manger. Now they were two. Soon they would be three. "It's beginning."

Sergey's eyes, red from sleep, popped open. "Oh, darling, oh, oh, oh," he said, sitting up, fumbling with her hands, attempting to be more awake than his current capabilities allowed. He rubbed his eyes, then felt her belly.

"Yes, your womb feels tense. You must sleep, my pet," he said. "It says in the book."

They'd sent a book, an obstetrics manual, which Sergey had been perusing. Katherine hadn't seen it arrive; it had come one morning while she was still asleep, along with their tanks of oxygen, packaged dried food, and water. The book was in Russian, but Sergey refused to translate most of it for her. "Here is a quote," he'd said. "'The young mother must allow only the most harmonious images of birth to pass upon her impressionable mind.' Let me be the one to prepare."

She'd scoffed at this. "I am perfectly capable of reading the medical literature on this process I'm about to go through," she'd told him. But, in truth, she felt she didn't have to. Women had been giving birth for millennia. Animals lay behind trees and in caves and labored unassisted, and their calves and pups and hatchlings took their first steps within the hour. If her time on the moon had taught her anything, it was that people were capable of surviving with fewer luxuries than they had come to believe possible. With Sergey's love filling the limited space that had become her entire sphere, she did not feel she needed anything else.

Now he stroked her hair. "The book says the first time for a woman may take a while, and it is best to go into it with as much rest as possible." Shyly, he swallowed and looked down. "This is your first time, yes?"

"Yes," she said instantly, reminded of how little they

knew of each other, even after all this time. In the absence of other people, busybodies and tax collectors and work colleagues and intrusive aunts, there really was no reason to talk much about one's history. "It's yours, too?"

"Yes," he said. "There is only you, and you"—he pointed at her stomach—"for me."

Another wave hit her, stronger this time, so strong that she had to grab his shoulder and squeeze hard with her eyes closed. Sergey tried something—something he must have read about in the book—grabbing her hips and pushing them in toward each other. It felt wrong, and she tried to stop him, but she found she couldn't speak. A strange cry came from within her, a raw, primeval sound, the first of its kind ever uttered on this celestial body. She screamed herself hoarse until the wave finally subsided, and when it did, she realized that the bulky cotton knickers she wore beneath her tunic were wet.

Slowly, she opened her eyes. Her vision had changed. It was crackling at the edges, it was all static; a blurry Sergey was visible only in outline, in the center of the picture. She couldn't see his eyes. She felt as if she were looking into a television that needed to be tuned.

She was in between stations. She needed her antenna fixed.

"Katya. Katya!" His hands were back on her shoulders, and he was trying to get her to answer.

"That time . . ." She gasped. "That time it didn't go away. The pain—it still hurts. It was only the second—why does it still hurt?"

Sergey gasped, and she realized he was looking down between her legs. Her legs felt wet and sticky. "*Bozhe moy*," he muttered. "*Bozhe moy, bozhe moy!*"

"What does that mean?" At last, she looked down at her lap. She was sitting in a puddle of red.

Sergey lifted her into his arms and laid her on his bed. When he stood back up, his white sleeping shirt was stained. "Stay here," he said, his voice shaking.

"Sergey!" Her body thrummed with pain, a low, dull ache. She had a horrible inkling that he'd leave, he'd put on his suit and disappear, as he'd done before. "Please, come back!"

When she heard his voice she realized he hadn't gone far. He was shouting in Russian. "*Pomogi! Pozhal'sta pomogi!*" She squinted, then realized he was bent over the camera, crying into the lens. "*Eto srochno, pomogi!*"

Another contraction was beginning. She could feel it start to rise, a tingling in the toes, a tsunami still off-shore. Quickly, it built. "Sergey, please!" She reached for him with outstretched fingers. "Don't leave me—" The ability to speak disappeared. Her eyes rolled back, away from him, staring in pain at the forbidding white landscape and the black sea of sky beyond. There had never been a pain like this before.

Or perhaps there had. Perhaps it had been felt by a million women before her, and the animals, too, oh, those animals. . . .

Perhaps this was the secret no one spoke of, the secret of life's creation: that it was built on the anni-hilation of the female body.

Sergey was at her side. She could feel his warm

fingers wrapped around hers and combing through the now damp mass of her hair. "*Bohze moy,*" he said again as he felt her belly and between her legs.

She felt him take a deep breath, his chest expanding against her upper arm. He let out a small sob, and then he screamed, in English this time:

"HELP!"

The last thing she remembered before everything went black was the locked door bursting open, and the men, so many men, rushing inside.

· 24 ·

Soon after arriving at my childhood home, I realized that Joe's act of destroying my manuscript had been a blessing in disguise. Feverishly, after Papa's encouragement, I worked to re-create *The Lunar Housewife* at odd hours, while Francie napped on my mother's lap. As I did my best to write from memory, I discovered everything that had come before had a hidden meaning. The locked door had been there all along, but I'd never been sure what to do with it.

Now I saw it clearly. Katherine had never been on the moon.

My parents' house, a tiny, shabby A-frame on a street that sloped down toward the Hudson, might well have been on another planet from Manhattan. Twice, a raccoon scared me out of my wits as I took out the evening's trash, and then there was the animal form of my father, who was in his cups by two every afternoon. After that, we had to tiptoe around him as he snored on the saggy front porch. Francie slept better in the old wooden crib than I did in my narrow childhood bed, where I lay awake thinking about Joe. During the day, however, whenever my mother had time between cleaning houses, I managed to write and even to rest. Regina had stepped into her role as grandmother with shocking enthusiasm. She wouldn't take Francie for walks—too many prying neighbors, she said, who'd shun her if they found out I wasn't married. But she had managed to fashion a sling out of an old bedsheet and used it to tie the baby to her chest while she cooked or vacuumed her living room, something that frightened me until I saw how peaceful Francie's tiny face looked, smushed up against my mother's freckled chest.

One night, warm for April in Ossining, my mother and I managed a glass of wine on the porch after my father roused himself and trudged, grunting, up to his own bed. My mother had gotten Francie down for the night, or the next few hours at least, with a warm bottle of formula.

"Her teeth may be moving already," my mother said, swirling her wine. "Her cry sounded different today."

The cry sounded different today? Who was this model of maternal affection? I'd barely seen her between the hours of eight in the morning and five at night, my entire childhood. She had never been warm or attentive, not to me at least. Paul, sometimes, but not me. I'd always assumed it was because I was a girl. Fathers were meant to dote on daughters, like mothers to sons. My father had always been angry or asleep. Now my mother seemed completely smitten with my young daughter, and I couldn't understand it.

Perhaps a little part of me felt jealous.

"Motherhood looks good on you," I said.

My mother sighed. Around me, she didn't try to hide the gap in her smile. She looked older, but in a comforting way: softer, her cheeks covered in a fine down. "I have been enjoying Francie," she said, "in a way I was never able to enjoy you and Paul."

It was the first time Paul's name had passed between us since the memorial. I couldn't look at her. I stared out over the grass, at the neighbors' dark houses. "What do you mean, you couldn't enjoy us?"

"Oh, it was so hard. I had twins, I was only twenty-one when you were born. My own mother was dead, we lived far away from any other family. Your father was no help. People always say how sweet babies are, and I had the sweetest babies." She sniffed.

I put my finger to the corner of my eye.

"But I couldn't enjoy my time with you. Not while you were babies. So . . . now. Francie." She shrugged, having spent her quota of sentimentality. She took a sip of her wine. "Well?" she continued, after a pause. "Are you going to tell me what happened?"

"With what?" I said, picking at a thread on one of the chair cushions.

"With this Joe of yours. This fella who was soooo swell you couldn't risk having him meet us."

My eyes fell. I hadn't wanted to feel guilty, but, seeing her in this time with Francie, I couldn't help it. "You didn't miss much, Mother. He was . . . He tried to control me."

"I can tell. You look like you've been through a war yourself." She sniffed again. "That's what they do, you know, these rich guys. They find a girl who's beneath them and treat you like Eliza Doolittle."

I studied her. It sounded as if she was speaking from experience. I wondered what kind of life she had led before my father came along. "I didn't know you knew *Pygmalion*."

Standing, she rolled her eyes. "I'm not as uncouth as you think I am, dear. Can't I get you something to eat? There's leftover goulash in the refrigerator. You're so pale and thin these days; you've got to get some color back in your cheeks."

"No, thanks. Good night, Mother." I hesitated. "I love you."

"I love you, too."

After she left, I stared out at the damp lawn. I knew I should go to bed, get a few hours' sleep before Francie needed a bottle, but the porch was so quiet. I could bring my typewriter outside and bang out a few hundred more words. I was dying to take Katherine past the discovery that she'd never left Earth.

"Oh, Louise," my mother said, coming back onto the porch, interrupting my train of thought. "I was thinking tomorrow you could pick up some groceries for me? We need mustard."

"Fine, I'll go to Cantucci's."

"No, not Cantucci's. Lovett's, over on the avenue."

I dropped my chin, making a face. "The mustard at Lovett's is different from the mustard at Cantucci's? Spill it, Mother. Who are you trying to get me to run into?"

She pursed her lips. "Fine. Terry and Barb Morris's son is back from California, and he's taken over management at Lovett's. Still single, from what I gather."

"You mean Glen Morris?" I'd heard Glen had gone to culinary school, which suggested a certain refinement, but all I could imagine was his reign of terror as football captain at our high school, his alleged torture of freshmen. "No, thank you. I'd rather die a spinster."

My mother shook her head. Her curlers did not budge. "I'm just saying. One of these days, you're going to have to put on lipstick and catch another man. Otherwise, I don't know what you and Francie are going to do."

"You mean you don't know what you'll do," I growled.

"You're too embarrassed by us even to take Francie for a walk."

"I am protecting you, Louise. If people catch wind of this, you won't be able to show your face here again. Even worse—they'll be asking me if I plan to ship you off to one of those homes for unwed girls. They'll expect you to give Francie away."

"Okay," I muttered. I wanted her to stop talking. "Glen Morris. I'll think about it."

After she headed up to bed, I went to get my typewriter from the living room. I stopped at the door from the porch to the house, my hand frozen on the knob. Something my mother had said—putting on lipstick and going to see a man. Hemingway had scoffed that there was a Joe on every editorial board—but what if there was also an Eli?

I telephoned Eli first thing the next morning, to see if he'd be willing to meet me. As I spoke, my heart hammered against my rib cage, but he answered with an easy laugh.

"Well, sure," he replied. "I could see you tonight, if that's all right. But first, I believe congratulations are in order?"

"Yes, thank you. I've got a lovely little girl, Francie."

"Would it be easiest for me to meet you close to Joe's apartment?"

After I explained, simply, that I would be coming from Ossining, Eli paused. "Since you'll arrive at Grand Central"— I was relieved that he didn't ask for details, at least not yet—"how about meeting at the Palm steakhouse on Second Avenue, at six? It's on my way home. I live in Kips Bay."

I felt myself blush. "We don't have to go to the Palm;

that's too expensive." A steak dinner—did he think this was a date? I was aware of my mother, feeding Francie a bottle at the kitchen table and watching me.

"Nonsense." Eli's voice held a little smile. "I'll get Hearst to pick up the check. All I have to tell them is that I'm meeting with a writer. You did want to discuss your work, didn't you?"

"Well, yes," I replied. I felt as if an elephant had been lifted off my chest. I'd been wondering how I'd bring up my manuscript, which was almost complete. I'd rubber-banded the pages and put the whole thing carefully in a big leather bag.

"Stupendous, Louise. See you there at six."

That evening, I took a half-empty train into Manhattan. It hadn't been much more than a month since Francie was born, and I still felt like a rag doll stitched loosely together. My stomach jiggled under my girdle. My old shoes were now too tight, leaving me with blisters on both sides by the time I walked from Park to Second Avenue.

When I reached Second, I turned and stared uptown. A warm wind blew down the avenue, brushing my curled hair from my face and jostling my little hat. My old apartment was right up there, nearly fifty blocks straight up. I could almost imagine that the old Louise still lived there, carefree, vigorous, and ignorant, waxing her legs and clattering away at her typewriter as if writing were some kind of sport and not a matter of survival.

It made me mad enough to spit. Mad at all these men and their secrets and lies. They'd stolen my old life from me.

For a Wednesday, the Palm was hopping. The group in front of me at the door were four women, their mingled perfumes heavy in my nostrils. They seemed to be co-workers, the way they were casually gossiping, their makeup a little faded from having put it on early that morning, their lipstick fresh. Their gossip dissected a memo their boss had sent around regarding inappropriate office attire. Each of them had a different theory as to the intended recipient.

They laughed and laughed, not a care in the world. One of them kept peering over the heads of the people behind me, likely searching for a particular fellow.

My envy felt so thick it was as if I'd swallowed something hard. I began breathing very quickly. I ducked my head and turned around, pushing past a few couples in line behind me, and I found a bench close to the avenue where I could sit and catch my breath.

In slapstick films, someone handed you a paper bag to breathe into in moments like these. I wished I had a paper bag. I tried forcing myself to hold my breath for one . . . two . . . three. . . .

A hand landed gently on my upper back. "Louise?"

I squeezed my eyes shut. *Please, don't let Eli be early, too.*

I opened my eyes and tried to make my face bright, professional. "Oh, hello!" He was kneeling in front of me, his face looking concerned. I fumbled for my purse and made to stand up. "Just got a bit dizzy there."

"Here, let me help." His hands were strong and warm under my arms, and once I felt steady, he put a cautious hand to my waist as he guided me past the crowd waiting to get into the restaurant. "Let's stroll for a bit before we go in."

We began walking, side by side, Eli's hands in his pockets, me clutching my leather bag. He shuffled his feet as he walked, looking down at his toes, and as soon as we were able to turn right, he gestured toward East Forty-fourth. This street felt a bit quieter than the avenue, which was crowded with white delivery trucks and waiting taxis. The air felt pleasant, just a bit cool as evening approached, and there was pink sunlight still visible over the tops of the buildings to the west.

"Are you sure you're all right, Louise?"

"If you must know, I'm not." I took a deep breath. "I was feeling rather angry."

"Oh?" He guided me toward a bench under a streetlight. "Tell me about it."

We sat down, straight across from the swinging black doors of an Irish pub. One of the doors hung loosely on its hinges, and with every customer and waiter going in and out, warm blasts of beer and stewed beef blew into our faces.

"You were right about Joe," I told him. "I can't trust anything he says anymore."

"What was I right about, exactly?" Eli asked. He held his right elbow and knee at angles so that he could face me straight on. His eyes were sharp, attentive. "Do you mind me asking?"

"No, not at all." I told him what Joe had confided in the hospital, about the government funding his magazine. "He claims that's all it is, that they have no control over what he prints. I think that's a load of nonsense. And then there's this Bob character."

"Bob?"

Eli's eyebrows rose as I told him what Beverly had said about buying the drugs that killed Harry, about the fact that I'd seen the red-mustached man before, about his giving us a ride home from the hospital.

"Well," said Eli, "you've certainly been doing your detective work."

"It hasn't taken that much work, actually. It all just—spilled out in front of me."

"Sounds as if you've been having a difficult time." He smiled, and inched a bit closer to me. "I'm sorry things didn't work out with Joe."

"That's all right." The way he was smiling at me, I wondered how sorry he actually was. It felt nice to have a handsome man pay attention to me like this, but I also wondered how I could steer the conversation back to my writing.

I was surprised when Eli brought it up himself. "Especially now that you've become a mother. Incidentally, how has this affected your art? Are you finding time to get your fingers on the keys?" One of his arms came slowly to drape across the back of the bench, nearly but not quite reaching my shoulders.

For a while, with the hum of Second Avenue traffic beeping and whooshing behind us, we discussed our work habits. I told him about the typewriter I'd been lugging around my parents' house, dropping it into whichever room I found the quietest and then moving it once again, how I'd once tried to perch it on a slab of granite in the park near their house and ended up with a splat of bird waste on the page.

I'd never been able to discuss writing in this way with Joe, I realized; at heart, Joe was more an accountant than a writer. And he was always so serious, nervy, worried about something or other, convinced his magazine would fail. It was exhausting. By contrast, Eli seemed perfectly relaxed, at peace with the fact that he'd been relegated from a rising star at *Time* to the books editor at a ladies' monthly. He wrote short stories, he confessed, which he didn't expect would ever warrant a glossy page, but which helped him wring the creative juices from himself so that he could sleep at night.

"I'm sure your stories are better than you think," I said. The street was turning dark, but the lights were on, and the night had that pleasant springtime feel: enough warmth to sit outside, but with no bugs or pea-soup humidity. I found myself leaning toward him with my hands laced in my lap, my left shoulder now unmistakably in contact with the edge of his right thumb. "Have you tried to have them published?"

Eli pursed his lips. "I'm not sure I have a name people want to print."

"Oh," I said, remembering the Un-American Activities Committee and all that. I watched a kitchen boy come out of the pub and place a green trash can near the curb. "I'm sorry to have mentioned it."

"As for you, why don't you tell me more about the novel itself? You'll remember I have become somewhat of an expert in women's fiction."

A taxi behind us beeped, and I jumped a bit. This was what I'd come here for, after all—to ask him for help in getting my novel published. I hadn't wanted to lead with it, though, in case he'd think our friendly rapport wasn't genuine, or that I'd been using his flirtation to my advantage. I pulled out my novel in its rubber band and handed it to him without a word. I watched him read the title, and his thick eyebrows lifted. He licked his finger and turned a few pages.

"Is this about a girl and a Soviet spaceman?"

"It is. It's a romantic fantasy. But there's more to it than that." I fumbled my words, trying to make him understand too many things all at once. "There are hidden meanings, it turns out, and things—things I didn't even know I was writing about until I'd written them."

Eli whistled. "It sounds very inventive."

I exhaled in relief. "I'm excited about it. I think it's quite good." I watched as he flipped forward a few more pages, and decided, my stomach clenched with nerves, that if I didn't ask now, I never would. "You must interact with a whole heap of women's publishers in your line of work. Can you think of anyone who might be interested in this? Is there anyone to whom you could introduce me?"

Eli smiled and began shuffling the pages back together, then snapped the rubber band into place. "Sure, I think I could do that. I know someone at Heinemann, someone at Clifton Books . . ." He rattled off a few more, but I was awestruck at having heard him give the name on the spine of *The Black Moth*. I felt like standing on the bench and shouting in triumph. "I'll contact them in the morning to gauge their interest, in which case they may reach out to you to ask for the manuscript, when you're finished."

"Oh, thank you, Eli."

"You're very welcome." He smiled. "May I hold on to this?"

It took me a second to realize what he meant, that he still grasped the thick white block of my novel. "Well," I began. I swallowed. The first version had been destroyed, or at least stolen. There was no copy. I felt a physical reaction to the idea of trusting another man, even if it was Eli, with my hardwrought work. "Well," I said again, "shouldn't I finish first?"

"Of course," Eli replied easily, and he handed it back to me. Once I had a grip on the pages again, I could relax.

"Goodness," I said, checking my watch. "We've blown our dinner reservation. Please accept my apologies."

"Don't even mention it," Eli said, handing me my purse. His hands lingered on it for a moment, both of us holding it together. His dark eyes were intense, staring into mine, and, not for the first time, I felt myself flush. "This has been quite a stimulating conversation, better than any old dinner. I'll reach out to those editors I know tomorrow."

As I walked to the train, I felt near drunk with possibility. How fortunate, that I'd found an insider who'd help me get my book in the right hands, and how ironic, that I'd met him because of Joe and Harry.

On the train, I took a window seat, ready to lean my head against the glass. My stomach growled. I glanced down at the pile of newspapers the previous rider had left on the floor. On top was the newest issue of *Downtown*.

My hair stood on end. It was as if Joe and his mysterious bedfellows had planted the magazine there, to watch my reaction. To remind me they were always there, in the background. I looked around the train, at all the men in their hats minding their own business. Then I picked it up.

There was a caricature of Harry on the cover, with his side-parted blond hair, buggy eyes, and big, toothy grin. "Harry Billings, 1925–1954." It made me ill. Joe had printed this. Joe may have had a hand in his death.

Despite myself, I flipped to the center story, one written by Harry. His parting words, the magazine declared: an essay about his having ridden along with a lobster fisherman and his sons for three days in Maine. The story's title was "Notes from an Amateur Lobsterman."

I stared at the story for a minute, dumbstruck. When had he had time to write this piece about lobster fishing, while he was busy scooping me?

"Last August I had the pleasure of sliding on my old waders and joining the crew of the *Anna Fitzgerald*," the essay began. "Her captain is Carl Casey, veteran of the Great War and . . ."

I shut the cover, shaking my head. No, I wouldn't read it now. I wouldn't let Harry and Joe spoil my evening. I slid the magazine into my leather satchel, on top of my manuscript, and turned back to the window. And my mother thought I needed to kowtow to the manager at the local grocery store—ha! I spent the ride daydreaming about what I'd wear for my author photograph.

For the next few days, I floated as if on a cloud. I enjoyed Francie as I never had before; at five weeks, she was beginning to smile at me, an open-mouthed, dribbly smile. At the start of her life, she'd been thin for a baby, her legs as spindly as those of a little chicken, but the cans and cans of Gerber formula she'd been slurping had done their work. She now had dimples in her elbows, chubby rolled thighs, and cheeks that begged for kisses, which I happily gave.

In the afternoons, as she slept, I wrote, and read and reread the latest issue of *Downtown*, especially "Notes from an Amateur Lobsterman." In luminous prose, Harry rhapsodized about the early mornings, the meager earnings, the rugged beauty of the painted buoys labeling lobster traps in teal, yellow, navy blue. Harry poked fun at his silver-spoon upbringing, his soft hands, which he'd sliced with a bowie knife after he made an unsuccessful tack knot. Still, he'd managed a feat of derring-do when he had to leap into the frigid water and disentangle a line from the propeller.

The average reader might have thought "Amateur Lobsterman" simply a mawkish ode to an old-fashioned way of life. But now that I had been clued in to the secret of some of *Downtown*'s donors, I could see, like an X-ray technician, the hidden layers of propaganda in the article. All of the men Harry interviewed for the piece were veterans; all of the young lobstermen in the pictorials vigorous, handsome, blond. The best of the New England transcendentalists were quoted throughout: Thoreau on the two colors of water, Whitman on the way stars look from a boat. The story ended with Harry feasting on lobster thermidor and prime rib at none other than the Palm. He mused about how the lobsters caught by his humble Mainer friends ended up on fine china in Chicago, in New Jersey, how they rode in refrigerated trucks all the way to Las Vegas. The article painted a picture of a beautiful, thriving American ecosystem, all working in harmony to provide us a different piece of the Dream.

It haunted me, not only because these were Harry's last words in print, but also because I knew why they'd been written, what they were intended to do. They made America and its capitalist system seem so unblemished, so pure. It all felt phony to me now.

"You seem to have turned a corner," my mother said one morning, when Francie and I came downstairs after a surprisingly decent night's sleep. We'd found her drinking coffee on the porch, bare feet up on the faded floral ottoman.

"I suppose I have." I peered down at Francie to hide my grin. "Seems my little plan to support myself might pan out after all."

"I see." My mother took Francie from me, and I stepped down onto the lawn to stretch my legs. "There's more coffee on the stove. And Joe called."

"Ugh." Now I felt itchy all over. I imagined bugs creeping against my ankles in the grass. "What does he want?"

"I think simply to hear how his daughter's been." My mother tilted her head to the side. "I don't know, Louise, maybe you should call him. Maybe the two of you can patch things up."

"Fat chance," I said, attempting nonchalance, even as the thought of speaking to Joe on the phone made me tremble all over. I brought my mother a fresh bottle and a burp cloth, and then I went upstairs to call him back.

My mother's bedroom was shaded and cool, the ceiling fan still running slowly. I took several deep breaths as I sat on her nubby white coverlet. I watched the drapes rustle in the breeze from the fan, yellowed lace curtains that I hated. They made me want to be back in sleek Manhattan. I watched a shiny black bug caught between the curtain and the liner; then I finally lifted the brass handset from her phone.

"Number, please," said the operator.

I gave her Joe's apartment's number. It was a Saturday; I figured he'd be at home. He answered on the first ring.

"Hello?"

Despite everything, I felt a little chemical rush of love at the sound of his voice, a fizzing sensation in my knees. "Hi, Joe."

"Louise, what have you been doing? I've called and called."

So my mother must have been shielding me from his calls. I didn't know whether to be grateful or angry. "It's been a bit busy. I have the baby, remember."

"Yes." His voice sounded pained. "Of course I remember. I miss her terribly—oh, Louise, you don't know what you've done to me."

"What I've done to *you*?" I got up, holding the receiver and stepping over the cord, so that I could close the bedroom door. "What about what you did to Harry? You know the man who killed him, or had him killed. Am I to trust you with my safety, and with Francie's, after that?"

He huffed into the phone, so loud I had to pull the handset away from my ear to protect it from the static blast. "Oh, it's you who can't trust me? That's rich. You're the one who's friendly with him."

"Friendly with him?" Bob, with his odd smile, flashed into my mind, and I shuddered. "I wouldn't say that. I'm polite to him because you are. But not anymore."

Joe huffed again. "That's not what I hear. What have you been telling him? Wait, don't say it over the phone."

"Telling him? I've barely spoken to the guy!" Downstairs, I could hear the screen door swing open. My mother's voice floated up the stairs as she sang softly to Francie. Hands shaking, I stood to examine some of the costume jewelry atop my mother's dresser, necklaces and bracelets piled on a dish with a crystal finger in the middle, stacked with rings.

"Oh, really?" said Joe. "Well, whatever you did tell him got Bob fired."

I fell silent. A stack of magazines collected dust in a basket beside my mother's dressing table. *McCall's, Good Housekeeping*.

"Wait," I said. The floor of my stomach felt as if it had dropped, an elevator with its cable cut. Slowly, I sat down on the hardwood floor, taking the handset and receiver with me. "Hold on a minute. I thought we were talking *about* Bob. When you said 'you're the one who's friendly with him,' you meant Bob, right? Right?"

"I did not mean Bob," said Joe.

The bug was still struggling, trapped in the curtain, fluttering its wings.

I covered my mouth with my hand, to keep from screaming.

Not Eli. Eli wasn't on their side. Eli had lost his job at *Time*, he'd had his China story blown up, he'd refused to testify. "Did you mean . . ."

"Shush. Don't say anything over the phone. I'm coming." I heard something like the jangle of keys in the background. I heard Joe putting on his shoes. "Don't say anything to anybody. I'm coming to Ossining."

With that he hung up, leaving me sitting on my mother's bedroom floor, clutching the telephone.

I met Joe at the station two hours later. I watched him get off the train and glance around eagerly in his white oxford shirt, sleeves rolled up, and tan trousers. He scanned the crowd, eyes passing over me once before he spotted me. I'd wrapped my hair in a dotted scarf and put on a big pair of my mother's cat's-eye sunglasses to cover my eyes, which were swollen from angry tears. I was also smoking a cigarette. It wasn't the first.

Part of me felt like a spy; the rest of me felt silly for even thinking it. He approached me quickly, his mouth open and ready to talk. But I'd been brooding these past hours, going over and over exactly what I wanted to say, what I needed to ask, and I wasn't about to let him take the lead.

I held up my hand: *Stop!* "Walk with me," I said.

I led him down through the riverside park, around a gazebo, and out onto the pier. The early-afternoon sun was beginning to slant over the water, turning the surface orange, highlighting the crests of the little waves in the river. Tulips were beginning to bloom in red and yellow in planters at the end of the pier. When I got to the end, I leaned against the railing and crossed my legs in their peg trousers at the knee. Joe made to lean beside me, but I wouldn't let him get any closer.

"You stay where you are," I said. I wanted him standing alone in the middle of the pier, as if this were an interview, he in the hot seat. I didn't remove my sunglasses.

He scratched his forearm, squinting. I noticed he had no satchel or anything else with him. He must have thrown his wallet into his pants pocket and run out the door.

"Eli Cohn is a CIA agent," I said. It was a question, but I didn't phrase it that way.

Joe took a long breath. He looked back up the pier. Besides a couple of children playing by the shore as their mother watched with the baby, we were alone.

"I can't confirm that, Lou," Joe replied. But when he saw the look on my face, he cleared his throat and whispered, "He is."

I pressed the heels of my hands to my eyebrows, then took one last, long drag from the cigarette and tossed it into the water. I'd told Eli everything. I'd almost let him keep my manuscript. My body vibrated with anger. Toward Eli, mostly, but he was not here. Joe would have to bear the brunt of it.

"So Hearst employs spies now. Are they aware that's what he does?"

Hesitantly, Joe nodded.

"Is that why they gave him the worst office on the floor? To try to hide him?"

"You've been to his office, then." Joe snickered. "Got to know the fella pretty well, did you? He made you into one of his assets and everything."

I felt like throwing up. Here I thought I'd been using Eli to my advantage. I was a damned fool after all. "All of you," I muttered. "All of you. Goddamn the lot of you." Was there anyone left to trust?

"Essentially," Joe continued, "you handed him a field report when you told him what I told you. I could be in a lot of trouble."

"He told me *you* reported *him* for a story he wanted to write about China."

Joe's left hand went back to scratching his right forearm. He gazed out at the water as he spoke. "It's cute that he told you that. It was a ruse, Louise. They were testing me. Eli himself was probably the one who came up with it. After I went to the editors about his China piece, he welcomed me into the fold. He's the one who recruited me. When we were at *The New Yorker*."

Joe almost sounded proud. And he would have been; he'd begun his life the son of poor Italian immigrants, neither of whom had gone to school past the third grade. He'd found himself at Harvard, then being recruited by the CIA. No wonder the guy wouldn't admit there was anything untoward about what he was doing.

"But Eli lost his job at *Time*," I said. I felt embarrassed, almost, at not having been able to put the pieces of the puzzle together myself. "He wouldn't corroborate what Whittaker Chambers said about Alger Hiss. He accused Chambers of still being a Soviet spy. . . . Is that true?"

Joe shrugged. "I don't know any more than you do. It's possible Chambers still was a Soviet spy, and that, even though the FBI made a deal with him to bring down Hiss, the CIA wasn't happy about it. My general impression is that sometimes the right hand doesn't know what the left is doing. Or it could be that, by publicly shaming Eli, getting him fired from *Time* and planted at Hearst, they were offering him even deeper cover and influence. Who knows?" He glanced back up the pier. "God, I can't believe we're discussing this."

"Worried they'll have you killed?"

"No," Joe said firmly. "They don't do that. It would never come to that. But they could send me to jail."

We stared at each other a moment. I was glad I could see his eyes and he couldn't see mine. His looked weary.

"They'd send you to jail? For talking? For printing the wrong words?"

"Possibly. Pipe down." Joe came a step closer. "What they're doing isn't wrong, Louise. It's a small part in the war against Communism. You know it's not wrong. Your brother died for this. If we can change a few minds, if we can keep young people on our side, through art . . . isn't that better than fighting another war?"

"I don't know." I didn't, anymore. The more I thought about it, the more it seemed to me that Paul had died entirely in vain, which was heartbreaking. "If we're talking about 'Un-American Activities' . . . is this not it? Censoring, controlling artists. Using them. Do you know who else does that?"

"Of course I do. That's why we have to beat them at their own game."

"What are we even fighting for if we're giving up our freedom of speech—isn't that the very first amendment? Who have we become?"

Joe smiled a little. He had a quick reply. "We're promoting art that's pro–freedom of speech. That's all."

"Listen to you, talking in circles. Maybe I just don't

understand how an essay about baiting lobster traps will really do anything for world peace." Part of me was trying to be insulting, to dismiss his magazine's work. But as I said it, as I smelled the fishy aroma coming off the river, the hot wood scent of the dock, something clicked inside my mind. Harry's essay had ended with a reference to eating lobster at the Palm, the restaurant where I'd met Eli. I'd just thought it was a coincidence.

"Oh my God," I said.

"What?" Joe took another step.

I took off my sunglasses. I had to get a better look at his face as I said this, to gauge his reaction. "Eli wrote that story. The one about the lobster, Harry's last work. Eli wrote it."

"Pssht," said Joe, tossing his head, but he didn't deny it. I watched his cheeks turn pink.

"He did, didn't he?" I said, coming toward him. "And he wrote the big one, too, the one about the Game. Eli's a writer, but he told me his work isn't published anywhere. He was lying. It *is* published—only not under his name."

I'd come very close to Joe, my finger pointed at his chest. I could see a tiny bit of toothpaste in the corner of his mouth. He started to say something, then stopped. Slowly, almost imperceptibly, he nodded.

"Aha!" I shouted, punching my fist in the air. I'd figured it out. The thrill of discovery faded quickly, however. I lowered my fist, then my shoulders. "I told him about my novel." *Loose lips sink ships.* My face landed in my open palm. How could I have been so stupid?

Joe shook his head, looking out over the river. "I'd give up any hope of the book being published, in that case. As I've been telling you all along."

I turned away from him and put the sunglasses back on. "At least he didn't shred it."

"No," Joe said. "He'll have done you one worse than that."

I went to the railing and stared out at the river's brown water. Joe came up beside me and crossed his arms over the edge. He rested his chin on his forearms, his body bent forward. We stared out at the water, side by side. I felt as if we were a pair of salt and pepper shakers that had been separated. We were, after all, someone's mother and father, and he was the only person who knew just what I'd gone through in bringing that little girl into the world.

"I'm sorry," he said quietly.

I didn't say anything in reply. We stood there awhile, watching white sailboats pass by, as the cruise boat to Bear Mountain cut through the waves.

"Louise. Louise, look at me." I did, reluctantly. His eyes were rimmed with red. "After all we've been through, you've got to promise me this. You won't get any notion in your head of spreading this around. In fact, you've got to promise not to say anything to anybody. I'll go to prison."

I pretended to mull his words, though he had to have known I wouldn't do anything to risk his being sent to prison. He was Francie's father, and always would be. And, despite myself, there was still a strong instinct urging me to give him a hug.

"What happened to Harry?" I asked, after a while.

Joe stood upright and sniffed, wiping his nose. "I told you," he said. "It must have been an accident."

For the first time, I wondered if Joe wasn't lying—if they'd kept him in the dark, or if the plan all along hadn't been to kill Harry, but to embarrass him, or scare him, or coerce him to confess to something, and all had gone horribly wrong. I wondered, too, if Joe didn't want to learn the truth. If it would be too much for him, would challenge his pure notions of patriotism.

Still, I began walking backward, away from him, toward land and my mother's house. Toward Francie. "At least there's one thing," I said.

"What's that?"

"Eli, Clifton—they'll never get the better of Hemingway. He's got his latest novel buried, somewhere on the grounds of the Finca Vigia. Really explosive stuff, apparently. All about Cuba, and Moncada, all with a guerrilla's-eye view. Don't know what he plans to do with it. Maybe he'll have Mary publish it after he's gone."

Joe raised one eyebrow, slowly. He had the look of a man who wanted to know more but didn't want to let on. "How do you know this?"

"He told me," I replied, "over oysters. Said something about burying it under the . . . the cows? Somewhere near the livestock."

Joe's features jumped, eyebrows raised and lips parted in such boyish curiosity that I felt bad for a moment. For just a moment. "Goodbye," I said, my voice catching. With a little salute, I turned away from him. My gait felt strange with him watching me, as if I were performing an imitation of a real person's walk. But I didn't turn around. I kept on going.

The first thing I did when I got home to find my mother and Francie asleep in a chair on the porch was walk back up to her bedroom and free the insect stuck inside the curtain. I don't know why I did it, but I had to do something, and, sure enough, after I tiptoed upstairs and past my father snoring in his own room, I found that it was still there. It had stopped fluttering, but it was alive. I carried it out onto the little widow's walk inside my cupped hands, but when I opened them, it wouldn't fly off right away. It had been captive for so long, it seemed, it didn't know how to free itself. Finally, I nudged it onto the railing, and it took to the sky. I watched it disappear into the trees.

What would Francie and I do now? What would become of us? Would I have to marry the grocer? I had Joe's ring, still hidden in the lining of my pocketbook, but how much money could I net from a small diamond? How long would it last me?

I stayed out there for a long time as the sky turned purple. When, at last, I ducked through my mother's window, back into the bedroom, I felt light-headed, but a little bit better. Then I noticed the bedposts.

My mother's old-fashioned bed had four knobby maple posts, the tops of which came unscrewed in the event that one wanted to add a canopy. Paul and I used to unscrew them when we were playing house as kids, put them in a basket, and call them bread rolls. I noticed now that one of them sat a bit crooked on the post, as if it had been recently unscrewed.

Silently, stealthily, I went over to check the bedpost. I unscrewed the top.

Nothing inside. Only a thick metal screw. Feeling ridiculous, I checked the other three. Then I went into my childhood bedroom and peered into the corners. I unplugged the hallway telephone, looking for extra wires.

Ultimately, I decided what I needed was a stiff drink.

As I walked down the hall, past my mother's bedroom, I noticed something tucked between her mattress and box spring. I knelt down and pulled it out.

It was a book, a pocket-sized paperback with gaudy gold lettering. The cover felt flimsy and cheap, the pages—and there were many—already yellowed. The title, *The Flight of the Fair*, appeared over the figures of what looked like a Revolutionary War soldier holding hands with a woman in a ruffled cap and a low-cut ball gown.

I stifled a laugh—my first of the day—imagining my mother reading this alone at night, then hiding it from my father under the mattress. I turned the book over to read the description on the back. About what I'd expected: chaste Virginia, orphaned by the war, finds comfort and safety in the arms of Samuel, a Son of Liberty. I scrolled down to the name of the publisher, which was one I'd never heard of: W. P. Fullerton Books, based in Paramus, New Jersey.

Find the silliest publisher you can, the one with the bright-pink paperbacks.

I hugged Virginia and Samuel to my chest. It felt too much to hope, but maybe. Maybe Eli's reach didn't extend all the way to little W. P. Fullerton Books in Paramus.

· 26 ·

THE LUNAR HOUSEWIFE

Rest and Revelation

Katherine awoke in a hospital bed. She could tell by the flimsy mattress, the thin blanket. Behind her head, something beeped faintly and steadily.

The first thing she did was sit up and gasp. "The baby—where's the baby?"

Someone was sitting in a chair at the foot of the bed. A few different someones were here with her. They'd drawn the blinds, leaving the room dark, lit only by a single long fluorescent bulb over the sink. She rubbed her eyes. Three men, the same Russian men who'd hired her in the first place, had been watching her sleep. Two leaned against the greenish wall, their arms crossed. They wore dark suits. The one sitting close to her, the bald one with glasses, had on a white lab coat.

"The baby is fine," said the bald one.

She put her hands over her face and wept. Shadowy memories came back to her. They'd put her in a big car or truck of some sort, where she'd lain across the back seats, screaming. The pain had been like nothing she'd ever felt before; it had been so engrossing and hypnotic in its power that she'd been unable to worry about the child until now. She'd been unable to grieve over what they'd done to her, what Sergey had done to her, unable to berate herself for not having figured it all out sooner. She had been unable to do anything but scream for the doctors, when, finally, they brought her here, to put an end to the pain. She'd gladly have had them put an end to *her* if that would have made it stop.

She'd been close to death. She could sense it now. The membrane between life and death felt thin, a gossamer curtain, and still close; she could reach out and touch it if she wanted. She could still step over that cliff, if she wasn't careful.

She wiped her eyes and inhaled. It seemed impossible for the baby to have survived. "The baby's fine?"

"Yes, it thrives, in fact. The nurses have been taking extra good care of him."

"Him!" It had been a boy, all along. A boy tucked under her rib cage as she'd slept on the moon. As she'd slept on what she'd *thought* was the moon. How could she trust anything they told her from now on? "Bring him to me," she insisted, trying to sit up further. Tubes and wires connected her to the bed. "Prove he's alive. My baby."

At once one of the men who'd been standing was at her side, pressing her down by the shoulder against the pillows. "No, no," he said, an infantilizing grin on his face as he ticktocked his finger back and forth at her.

"We have some particulars to discuss first, Miss Livingston," said the bald man.

"I'll say you do." She lay back, looking at the drab ceiling. She'd heard the hospitals in Russia were poorly run, dirty, crowded, and it seemed the rumors were true. Water stains marked the ceiling in a kind of map. She thought of the craters on the lunar surface, the ones Sergey had supposedly been measuring.

Sergey. He'd dissuaded her from asking for a star chart. He'd pretended he didn't know what lay behind the locked door. What else had he pretended?

"Captain Kuznetsov," she muttered. She clenched the threadbare blanket in her fists. "He knew all along. He was part of this."

The bald man cleared his throat. "Yes, he was aware of the true nature of the study."

"The study?" Her bosom ached. Her body felt as if it had been blown up, like a balloon, and deflated; now she ached with the force of the stretch. She wanted the baby.

She realized, as her eyes adjusted to the room, that she desperately longed to be back in her lunar habitat as well. It had been home to her for more than a year. And now even this dark chamber provided far too much stimulation, with its beeps and lights and people. The ceiling felt too low and crowded, the blanket was not her hibernation sack, the pillow was not her pillow. There was no Sergey beside her, no baby in her womb. Her breathing came fast and hard. "It was a study?"

"Yes, an isolation study. You and Captain Kuznetsov thrived in isolation far better than anyone expected." He didn't laugh, nor did the other two men, but she could hear the humor in their voices. They'd watched everything that had occurred between her and Sergey. It had all taken place in a lab.

"Why in hell wouldn't you simply have told me that? Why couldn't I willingly participate in a study?"

"We had to see how you would behave if you believed without question that you truly were separated from all humankind but one. Call it an . . . Adam-and-Eve re-creation."

The other men snorted.

"If you'd known we were watching, you might not have behaved with such a . . . lack of inhibition?"

She turned her face to the wall. She felt as if she might be sick.

"If you'd known there were doctors and nurses on just the other side of the wall, you'd have called them in much sooner, yes?"

"Sergey knew. Sergey didn't call them in. You put your faith in him, but not me."

"Ah, but Sergey did call us, did he not? The man lost his nerve." He mumbled something in Russian to his comrades, who chuckled under their breath. "What he wanted from us was obstetric training. He demanded we let him out of the soundstage for a few hours once."

So that was where he'd gone, the morning she couldn't find him. "The visio-telespeaker." She cleared her throat. "The camera. Could you see us when it was turned off? Could you hear us?"

She watched the man's face. A twitch of irritation appeared under one eye. "At those times, no. Captain Kuznetsov was given specific orders not to turn off the visio-telespeaker, only to pretend to do so. At times he obeyed us. But at times he did not." His yellow teeth showed, a simpering, pitying smile. For her. "It appears he is either a very good actor, or he did care for you a bit, *Katya*."

"Don't you dare call me that." She clutched her hospital gown closed. The idea of them watching her made her want to change her skin. "So . . . the newspapers, the public's reaction—all of that was a lie?"

The man's smile disappeared, and the two men behind him shifted. They seemed to grow a little bit taller. "This is the other particular we would like to speak about. In the eyes of the public, the pilot lunar program was a reality."

Katherine crossed her arms. "I can't imagine what's stopping me from disabusing the public of that notion." But even as she said it, as she watched the men looming over her, she knew that they could do anything they wanted to maintain her silence. They'd arrange to have her killed, here and now. She'd be no more than a smudge on a Soviet sidewalk. They could tell the world she'd passed away in childbirth. It happened often enough. It could have happened to her.

None of the men said anything. They waited in

silence, allowing the reality to settle, like a cloud, above their heads: she had no power here.

"My dear," said the bald man, "you cannot say anything, because no one would believe you."

"Not in the USSR, perhaps, but in my country, people would believe me. I'd tell them I was tricked by the Soviets. The U.S. would just love to break the story that the Soviet lunar landing had been faked."

Again, that simpering smile. Again, the men were silent, allowing something to settle over her, but what?

"You aren't going to let me leave, are you?" she asked. "You're going to ship me to Siberia."

Still no response. The men waited.

She was beginning to grow restless. Her lungs worked overtime. "You'll let me take the baby with me, won't you? Oh, please, will you let me take the baby to Si—"

Her hands had been grasping the rails at either side of the bed. Her thumb had brushed a little sticker on the rail, the manufacturer's sticker.

NILSSON'S HOSPITAL EQUIPMENT, the sticker read. LINCOLN, NEBRASKA.

The men continued in their silence as her eyes darted around the room. A clock ticked quietly on the wall, made by the Boston Watch Company. There was a tray beside her bed, holding a thermometer and a bowl of green Jell-O. She reached for the thermometer with a shaking hand. It measured degrees in Fahrenheit. On the wall, a map of the hospital, clearly marked exits—in English. How had she not seen it before? How had she missed all the signs, again?

"I'm in the United States," she whispered.

"Bingo!" the bald man burst out, clapping his hands together. "That is what Americans say, yes? Bingo?"

"I'm home." Her voice was barely audible. She didn't know whether to laugh or cry at this news.

"Close to home," he replied merrily. "California. My dear, where else would we have found such an expert soundstage? Ah, do not be too hard on yourself for not noticing your moon was no more than a secret room in a Hollywood backlot. They do good work, the CIA, do they not?" The other two men nodded, though one of them rolled his eyes. "Yes, the program began with us, but once your CIA got wind of what we were doing, they realized you might be more useful to them as an enemy than as a friend. And so they gave us a bit of help. Happens more frequently than you think."

Katherine lifted a paper cup of water, shakily, to her dry lips.

The man continued, "You might say your work has been a joint program for us, a tool of propaganda for both the KGB and your Central Intelligence officers. For us, you are heroine; for the U.S., antiheroine. The anger toward you is apparently so great in your country that your Congress is shoveling money into the American space program. Besides that, they have had record numbers of young people applying to work as astronauts. Especially girls." He had a twinkle in his eye, which disgusted her. "Think of what you have done for the American girls!"

"It's all based on a lie, though. What will they do if I expose the lie?"

"Ah, but is it? Whether or not you were really on the moon, my dear, you agreed to work for the Soviets! You defected!" His finger punctured the air righteously. "I would not say you are in a strong bargaining position, but, luckily for you, they are willing to bargain."

"Please," she said, weary now, "please just bring me my baby."

The man stood and adjusted his white coat. "I believe I hear him coming as we speak."

She burst into tears when the door to her room opened, and a young woman, unmistakably an American woman, with high-teased hair and a broad grin, came in holding a wailing bundle. She laid him across Katherine's chest with a flurry of well-meaning instructions that Katherine ignored, and with a warmed bottle that Katherine pushed aside. Instead, she opened her gown and pressed the baby's face to her waiting breast. He latched greedily, his tiny rosebud lips suckling against her, releasing a pressure valve that she hadn't realized needed to be opened. She sighed in relief.

"Oh, honey, you don't want to do that," said the nurse. "Here, let him have the formula, it's more balanced."

"Get out of my room," Katherine barked at her. The nurse's face fell, but Katherine refused to feel guilty. She was tired of being told what to do. Silently, the nurse tucked the blanket around the baby and under Katherine's forearm. Katherine gazed at him. His head was covered in soft, dark down; his eyebrows were barely perceptible. His cheeks were downy, too, and red. His little nose turned upward. He was the image of Sergey.

"I'll leave you with your visitors," the nurse said quietly. As she retreated, Katherine noticed the men. More men in suits, more strangers, coming toward her. These would be the Americans, though she could hardly tell the difference between them and the ones who'd just left her. These were the men who were supposed to protect her, and yet they'd used her just as badly as her supposed enemies had.

She did not cover her chest or the baby. She had already been exposed. Now she would choose when to expose herself.

As they came closer, the men in suits, she already knew what she would ask for. She would ask for an island home. Lord knew the United States had plenty of those in its collection, plenty of isolated spots where they could tuck someone away. She would ask them to send her somewhere warm and pleasant. Somewhere she could be alone, she and this little copy of the man she'd thought she loved. She'd go somewhere no one could find her, not even Sergey himself. And she would begin again.

27

Margot Mayer's office in Paramus, New Jersey, occupied the entire second story of a nondescript five-floor office building. I walked into an open space with books piled everywhere, lining the walls from ceiling to floor, stacked on desks and in heaps on the thin carpet. Her secretary was at lunch, her brother and partner, Cal Mayer, out at the printing plant to check on production. He'd left a striped tie draped across his chair, which was laden with comic books. And so it was only Margot and I who sat down, facing each other across the mounds of papers crowding her desk.

"Miss Leithauser. Darling. Let me begin by telling you a bit about what we do." Margot herself looked to be about sixty, with a Long Island accent that sounded as if it were being strained through a cigarette filter. She wore a jaguar-printed jacket with padded shoulders, and her hair in a frothy beehive. "We are not a prestige publisher. We do crap like this—this is one of my brother's titles," she said, holding up a copy of *Green Women from Outer Space Meet Earth's Wolfmen*, Vol. 7. "We'd do a mass-market run of your book for one month and see how it does. You wouldn't get any reviews, or anything like that. You're not going to win awards for anything we publish here."

"Awards aren't what I'm after."

Margot shrugged. "One-month print run, we see how it does. After that, the thing might be dead in the water."

I recrossed my legs. "Miss Mayer, with all due respect, I believe you're my only hope."

Three weeks had passed since I'd met with Joe, and in that time, I'd heard from none of the publishers Eli had promised to connect me with. Soon I'd be essentially penniless.

Margot stared at me a minute, tapping her cheek. "I've read your manuscript. It's good. It's also dangerous." She shuffled things around on her desk, shoving a great ream of paper to the floor and ignoring it. Somehow, she found my book. Mumbling to herself, she rummaged through this drawer and that, at last finding a pair of half-moon glasses on a gold chain and a nubby rubber fingertip, which she shoved onto her thumb. Then she leaned back in her squeaky chair and began turning pages.

I watched all of this expectantly. Despite the strangeness of this office, despite the green women and the wolfmen, I meant what I'd said: W. P. Fullerton Books felt like my last hope on Earth. I held my square black purse tight against my bouncing knees. I didn't know if I'd ever been so nervous to meet someone.

"Yep," she said after a while. "This might be the most dangerous book we ever publish." She unhooked her glasses from her ears and let them dangle against her chest. Then she smiled at me. "You realize what you're asking me to print, don't you? Katherine gives birth to a bastard; then she has the nerve not to insist Sergey marry her! She runs from him! Not to mention what you put in there about the CIA."

Margot's hand slapped her chest, mimicking a heart attack. "My dear, this could amount to treason."

"But it's all fictitious. There was no faked lunar landing. There is no CIA conspiracy."

"Isn't there?" She mashed her thin lips together thoughtfully. We looked at each other for a moment.

"Look, Miss Mayer."

"Oh, you can call me Margot. 'Miss' reminds me I haven't got a fella."

"Margot—this would only be a dime novel for girls. Would anyone be paying attention?"

"I think this would be a"—glasses back on, she consulted a chart on her desk—"thirty-five-cent novel. We'd do it in digest format. Make it an itty-bitty book." Her eyes gleamed. I had the sense that she was toying with me a little, that she was the kind of person who liked to keep her audience in suspense. "So itty-bitty no one would ever give it a second glance. No one who matters, that is."

I felt a faint glimmer of hope squeeze at my stomach. I hadn't eaten all day. "Will you publish it, then, Miss Mayer?"

"Margot. And don't get ahead of yourself, sweetie. There's the matter of the ending." She slapped my manuscript back on the desk, tossing it toward me.

I caught a few loose pages. "The ending? What's the matter with it?"

Margot's eyes got wide. Her lashes nearly touched her eyebrows. "What's the matter with it? It's sad, that's what! You've got Katherine living alone on the island, you've got Sergey—*what* a beefcake, by the way!—he's God knows where, probably in some labor camp in Siberia. Our readers won't stand for that kind of ending, Miss Leithauser; you're going to have to make it happy."

"It can't be happy," I said, indignant. "He betrayed her. He lied to her the entire time."

Margot waved a hand at me. "Did he, though? The man was a deserter, he needed the gig, they gave him orders not to say anything to her. It seemed to me as if he wanted to tell her everything. He loved her!"

I couldn't help smiling, hearing her speak about the characters, even argue with me about their motives, as if they were real. They'd become real to her. It was a thrill like I'd never imagined. "I'm not so sure he loved her, though. He could have been faking it. In any case, Katherine isn't sure."

"Then have him prove it." Margot put her glasses back on and began shuffling papers around again. It seemed the meeting was almost over. "You write me a better ending, we'll see about publishing this novel."

"Margot." I stood over her, my hands flat on her desk. "You're looking at a desperate woman. I need to know, before I go any further, how good are the chances you'll offer me a book contract."

Slowly, her eyes rolled upward. She was smiling out of one side of her mouth. Then she closed her eyes and shook her head. "I can't even let my brother read this one. But, yes, my dear, I'd like to publish this. It's rare that any of the dreck that comes across my desk sticks with me in any way, and Sergey and Katherine have kept me up at night. I'm very interested to see if our readers agree with me on that." She stood up so that we were eye to eye. Hers were gray and piercing. As she spoke the next words, a chill passed from my scalp to the bottoms of my feet.

"I think you and I can pass this one right by the censors, and—who knows?—we might just get a few girls out there thinking."

I exhaled. "We might, indeed."

She shook my hand, then pulled back and shook a finger at me. "But you have to write that ending. How many days do you need?"

I thought for a second. "Three?"

"Good. I'll look for it in the mail. Then I'll call and talk contracts."

"Thank you, thank you. I won't let you down." I grabbed my purse and the disheveled manuscript, anxious to get back to Ossining and begin writing.

"Oh, and Louise . . . ?"

I turned at the door. "Yes?"

"Add a few more words about Sergey's *build*, would you?"

I went home to my parents' house feeling buoyant, as if I'd found a little trapdoor to Wonderland. Thank goodness for Margot, thank goodness for the drugstores that carried her books, for the thousands of girls who read those books and to whom nobody else paid much attention. My novel would find its way into their hands, its flashy cover a Trojan horse concealing the message inside: *The government lies to us. Men lie to us.* I felt like a code talker. I felt powerful.

As I turned my mother's Packard up the hill toward her house, I noticed an unfamiliar car parked across the street. I slowed my approach till I was creeping up the hill, but they saw me coming and quickly started their ignition. As the car, a gray Chevy with whitewall tires, passed me, neither of the men inside looked at me. Both wore sunglasses, and it sure as hell seemed they didn't want me to see them waiting outside my parents' house.

I peeled into the driveway and ran up the wooden porch steps. My mother was inside, talking to someone on the phone with the cord stretched from the kitchen to the living room. She had Francie on a blanket on the floor, lying on her belly, her head bobbing up as she batted at a rubber ball.

"How long were those men waiting out there?" I picked up Francie and began bouncing her jerkily. She started to fuss.

My mother had muttered a quick goodbye and hung up the phone. "What are you talking about? Did you see what Francie can do now? She can hold up her own head!"

"I saw. The men in the silver Chevrolet—how long were they out there?"

"Oh, I don't know—twenty minutes? I thought they came to visit the MacPhersons."

I stared out through the torn window screen, rubbing Francie's back. "Or to keep tabs on me."

"Louise, what's going on? Are you in some kind of trouble?"

It took me a minute, but I assembled my face into an unworried smile and spun around. "No, Mother. I'm not, I'm just being silly."

"Good," she said, though her eyebrow was arched in skepticism. "Remember, it's bridge night for me. I'll have to go take a bath, wash the baby smell off."

"Certainly," I said in a hurry. "I'll take care of Francie tonight. You deserve a break."

She went upstairs, and I turned back toward the road, rocking Francie slowly, shifting my weight from side to side. I'd meant what I said about my mother needing a break, but that wasn't all. I needed practice taking care of Francie on my own. We couldn't stay here and put my parents in danger much longer.

That evening, I gave Francie her bottles and a long, cool bath in my mother's bathroom sink. She was a beautiful baby, with long eyelashes and skin like a fresh peach, and I enjoyed watching her blink and sigh as I dribbled water gently down her back with a wet sponge. She seemed the only thing that had gone right for me in a long time—a lovely, healthy baby with a gentle demeanor—and when she fell asleep on my shoulder in the rocking chair, I let her snore softly against the fine hairs of my neck for quite a while before I finally laid her, on her belly, in the crib. I pulled the soft pink blanket up to her shoulders, caressed her cheek with the back of my forefinger, and crept from the room.

The house was quiet. My mother's bridge game, the one place I suspected she could truly let her hair down, went late, and my father was God knows where. I went out to the porch, where I'd left my typewriter. I intended to begin crafting the ending Margot demanded, but what came out first was a letter.

Dear Joe,

I had some visitors outside my parents' house tonight. They didn't have time to come inside or even to introduce themselves, but I'm quite sure it was I whom they came to see. I don't even know why I ask, as I'm no longer certain I will ever get the truth, but I sure hope you weren't the one who sent them my way.

I have been thinking a great deal about endings. What sort of ending, for example, will be in store for you and me? They call it a "happy ending" when the prince wakes the princess at the end of a fairy tale. But that isn't really an ending, not for them, is it? It's a beginning. At the moment I cannot imagine us having any such beginning, only an ending. I don't know. Perhaps circumstances will shift in some unforeseen way, and the future will be different.

This brings me back to my first question, regarding truth. The only way I can imagine you and me having any sort of beginning is if we stop dealing in lies and half-truths, and tell each other only full truths. I am entitled to the truth about the visitors outside my family home, and the truth about Harry.

In the meantime, a girl can only dream about the beginning I wish could have been possible for you and me.

Francie continues to do well. She is starting to lift up her own head.

—L

I sealed the note into an envelope, wrote down Joe's address, didn't bother with a return. Chances were, Francie and I would be gone by the time he replied. I planned to instruct my mother to return all my mail to the senders. At least he'd know why we left; the letter would make that clear.

Something had to be said to Eli as well, but what? I went and got the cigarettes I'd been hiding and lit one, blowing the smoke out through the porch screen as I paced and smoked. My fingers shook when I thought about him sending the hounds after me. How long would it be until one of them approached me to make it abundantly clear I was to keep my mouth shut? I knew it wouldn't matter if we left this place, if we changed our names, if we moved out of state to someplace where we hoped they wouldn't find us. I'd never stop looking over my shoulder.

Finally, I sat back down at the typewriter, the butt of the cigarette dangling from my lips.

Dear Mr. Cohn,

Would you believe it, so much time has passed since our ~~dinner~~ *walk that I can't remember which of my stories I showed you. I've got two pans on the burner right now, you see. If it was the romance we discussed, what do you say we forget all about it, old chum? I doubt the editors would be interested in that one, anyway. I'm quite sure you'll agree.*

Now, the other project I've gotten my hands on, that's the real gem. You remember, right, from the funeral? It's a collaboration between Harry Billings and myself, a sort of Ernest Hemingway interview, part two. I'm not sure where I'd like to place it, but I think I'll hold on to it for now.

Thanks a heap for the offer of help in any case.

Sincerely,
Louise Leithauser

I paused for a moment, staring out at the spot where the gray Chevy had been parked, before adding a postscript.

P.S. It is a shame that we skipped dinner. It would've been nice to try the lobster.

28

THE LUNAR HOUSEWIFE

The Woman with the Plane

For a year, Katherine had lived in an achromatic world. There had been nothing but black sky and white stars and gray land. Now, even though it all came with a tinge of sadness, she had at last the green sea, the blue sky, the edges of the brown reef frothing the waves white, and, of course, her little yellow plane.

Every morning, Katherine paid Inina, the retired woman who lived in the house next door to her in the coastal village, to watch baby Demetrius while she flew. She took her plane out from the small airport that the Japanese had built, which the Americans had later destroyed and then repaired. She'd hoped to be given a task, something like the crop dusting she'd once done in Nebraska. But nobody on the island needed help from any pilot, male or female. She asked if she could patrol for sharks, which were easy to spot in the crystal-clear, sparkling water, and the authorities in the little town laughed and said they'd been leaving the sharks alone for ages—no harm in letting them swim as they were. There'd been some incidents of vandalism at the old Japanese sugar mill, thought to be the work of teenagers, and she'd offered to patrol for similar shenanigans. Again the adults had said no: the teenagers were simply releasing their frustrations. Let them be, as well.

And so Katherine just flew. The awareness that her son was waiting for her on land tugged at her—she could feel it in her bones, in her aching bosom—and so she never let herself go faster than a hundred knots, never climbed past twelve thousand feet, to be cautious. She preferred staying close to land, anyway, skimming over the reefs, surveying the island's knobby green cliffs and flat beaches, its two small towns. She loved how her bird's-eye view of the island allowed her to see all of the shallow turquoise water surrounding it, the sapphire blue of the rest of the ocean. She loved seeing nothing but ocean beyond the island, a reminder of just how far away she was from everyone else on Earth.

Rota was not exactly what she'd had in mind when she asked to be sent to a remote island in the Pacific. Naïvely, she'd imagined herself and Demetrius alone on a deserted island, living in a straw hut, as isolated as she and Sergey had been on the moon. Instead, she and the baby occupied a tiny ranch house in a long row of cozy homes along a strip of rocky shore. Their neighbors were unbelievably friendly; everyone on the island waved at her as if they'd known her forever, as if it wasn't strange for the United States Army to have dropped a white woman and her baby here and left. She wondered if she deserved their warm welcome. Based on the bit of Chamorro she'd been able to learn so far, she discovered she'd come to be known as "the woman with the plane."

Her plane was an old Cessna T-50, retired after the war, freshly painted butter yellow with dark-blue wings. It had a maximum range of just a little more than a thousand miles. She'd never come close to that. The longest trip she'd taken was still the initial flight from Guam, the one she'd insisted on taking alone.

After her stay in the hospital had ended, the Americans had whisked her and the baby by night to an airforce base north of Los Angeles. Then they'd traveled by military jet—no windows—through the night and all during the next day.

"Where are we headed?" she'd finally had the nerve to ask one of the stony officers escorting them. None of them had made eye contact with her throughout the multi-hour journey. Whereas the Russians poked fun, made insulting jokes, and laughed over her head, the Americans pretended she wasn't there.

"You're the one who made the demands, ma'am" was all the reply she'd gotten.

She refused to believe they'd actually met her demands until they landed in Guam, greasy-haired and bleary-eyed, and she'd at last seen the T-50 on the tarmac. She'd collapsed to her knees with Demetrius in her arms, weeping. The baby was dehydrated, and so was she. It would have been safest to allow one of the soldiers to escort her to Rota. But she couldn't go another inch with these men breathing down her neck. She couldn't trust them as far as she could throw them, of that she felt sure. And so she'd asked for the map, for directions. Rota was only a thirty-minute flight away. She'd secured the baby in a basket behind her seat in the cabin and had flown the rest of the way by herself, her eyes red, knuckles white. When, at last, she'd seen a bit of pale water and brown land appear on the horizon, she'd let go of the yoke for only a second to raise both fists in the air.

On her solo flights, she tried only to think of the shapes of the clouds and their shadows on the water, of the pods of dolphins she sometimes caught up with in the Philippine Sea. Inevitably, she'd stop noticing the terns and her thoughts would wander to Sergey. She longed to have had a proper goodbye with him. First, so that she could punch him in the chest and call him all manner of vulgar words for having lied to her. Second, so that she could ask him what had been true. Had he loved her? Had he been able to fake all of the tender moments that passed between them?

More important, a question for herself: would she know, even now, if he was lying?

One morning, as she found herself scanning the horizon for ships, for fellow aircraft—she would never stop looking over her shoulder, for the Americans or the Russians, who she feared might snatch this peaceful existence away at any second—she noticed an unusual shape in the water. It was large and dark, like a colossal torpedo, and at first she thought it could be a whale. She'd seen them before, breaching with their long, pointed heads, their spouts of white spray, but this hulking form dwarfed even those giant creatures.

Her heart jumped into her throat as her plane buzzed closer to the mysterious seacraft. It was long and pale gray, with a blunt nose and a tail that seemed to stretch hundreds of feet. It approached the northwest corner of Rota, and it cut along at a fast clip, barely creating a ripple on the surface. If she hadn't been above it, and if the tropical waters hadn't been so clear, she'd have had no idea the ship was there. But now she could see the two periscopes skimming the top of the water.

She yanked her yoke to the right, toward the airport.

It was a submarine.

The Russians. The Americans. Would it matter which had come? Her first thought was of Demetrius, at home with Inina. Would they take him? Would they kill Inina? Approaching the airport, Katherine backed off on the throttle, but not quite enough, and she came in way too fast. She lifted the nose, fearing she'd have to do a go-around, but, miraculously, she managed a long, bumpy landing. She took the runway too fast as well, and taxied to her usual spot, then leapt out of the cabin and ran for her jeep.

There was a commotion, down on the beach. The children playing there were running toward something in the waves. Katherine stopped with her hand on the jeep door and followed them, first at a walk, then at a run.

The children splashed toward a man in a black diving suit whose head had just surfaced. He swam, frog-like, bobbing his head in its goggles and mouthpiece, and then his feet caught sand and he began to walk. He stepped deliberately through the water, like a spaceman fighting low gravity on the surface of some rocky planet, and then, as the water grew shallower, he moved faster and faster.

Katherine stood with the children on the beach, watching. At last, the man came all the way out of the water and took off his goggles, took the tube from his mouth, set down his oxygen tanks, peeled back the cap covering his head, and shook out his wet hair. He squinted at the children, and at Katherine, and then he smiled. He stood a few yards away from her, water dripping off his skintight black diving suit.

It was Sergey.

The children burst into applause.

"Hello, Katya," he called to her.

She crossed her arms. He didn't seem the least bit surprised to find her waiting here, right here where the submarine had dropped him off, as though she were still his lunar housewife, ready to help him out of his suit and give him his dinner. She was glad she had on her flight jacket, which she'd found abandoned in a locker in the airport, and not a housedress.

"You smile," she said back to him, "as if you have nothing to explain."

The children began to amble away, the excitement over. Sergey's face turned serious, and he nodded. "I could tell you they had power over me, Katya." He took a step closer, his foot sinking into the sand. "I could tell you I was just as much a pawn as you were. But that would not be entirely true, would it? And we must now tell the truth."

She wanted to grab him by the shoulders and kiss him. She looked out at the horizon. "I assumed you were sent to Siberia."

"No." He hung his head a bit. The sun gleamed on his wet hair. "No, in Russia I am still a hero. You are, too. There was a parade, even. They still believe we were . . ." He exhaled, water dripping off his nose. "After all I went through after the war, I thought it would feel good. But it didn't, not without you. I did not want it, Katya. I wanted to be here, with you. Here I am."

Katherine took a deep breath. She wanted to let him stay. She wanted to open her new home to him, to let him hold Demetrius and toss him in the air on the beach in front of her house. What did he have to say in order for her to allow him in? She turned away, so that he wouldn't see her eyes brimming with tears, and began to walk up the beach.

"You'll have to have the sub circle around," she called over her shoulder. "So that they can take you back to your parades in Russia."

Sergey's shadow caught up to hers on the sand. "Katya, please." He reached for her hand. His felt clammy. "I have come all this way to see you. Please." He spun her around. Reluctantly, she looked up into his eyes. His eyelashes were still wet. "Please, Katya. I want nothing on Earth but to be with you."

"You lied to me," she said, wiping away tears. "We were all alone there for all that time. You even found a way to turn off that thing that was recording us. And, still, you would not tell me the truth."

"I know. I was afraid."

"You let me fear for my life, for the baby's life. I thought we were all alone up there. I thought I'd die."

She still spoke as if they'd truly been on the moon. She couldn't help it.

Sergey brought his hand to her cheek, and stroked softly. "I would never have let you die, Katya. Never. What I wanted was to give you a real life. Yet here you are, an outcast once again. Please." He tucked her hair behind her ear. "Can we not be outcasts together, once more?"

She turned away, toward the sea. The sun sparkled across its surface like a million diamonds. Two frigate birds, a mating pair, coasted over the waves together. "You even lied about the stars," she said quietly.

"Ah." Sergey stepped back and opened a little pouch she hadn't noticed, the strap wrapped crosswise over his chest. From inside he produced what looked to be a watertight envelope. "I swam all the way with this, see?" He handed her the envelope and let her open it with her dry hands.

Inside was a book: a guide to the stars. On the cover, Orion raised his bow.

"You see?" Sergey stepped a bit closer, cautiously this time. He reached out and placed his large hands, which felt warmer now, on her shoulders. Gently, he gave her a squeeze. He pulled her a bit closer to him.

"From now on, we tell each other only the truth. You, and me, and our baby."

She stared down at Orion gazing off into the distance. The book, a hardcover, was heavy. Sergey had swum all the way from the submarine with it strapped to his chest.

"We will learn about the constellations together," he said softly. "What do you see here in the Mariana Islands? Are the stars the same?"

"No," she replied. "We're fairly close to the equator. The stars are different."

At the word "different," she let herself look at him, at his smooth jaw, at his mouth. Water still dripped from his diving suit, through which she could see the outlines of his pectoral muscles, his biceps.

She put the book down in the sand. It would be all right. Different felt good. Things *could* be different here, without anyone telling them who they were or what they could do. She wrapped her arms around Sergey's neck, let her fingers sweep into his wet hair. A tear fell from the corner of his right eye, and he smiled. She guided his head down to hers. His lips, warm and familiar, tasted of salt water.

SPRING

1955

❖ ❖ ❖
❖ ❖
❖
❖

29

By the time the first box of books arrived at our little apartment, Francie could pull herself up onto her knees. She grasped the edge of the cardboard box as I tore the tape open carefully, my heart pounding. It seemed only fitting that we'd open it together.

"This is it, my love," I sang to her. "Mama's book is here."

The box burst open, and there they were, a dozen shiny iterations of Katherine with her arm across Sergey's chest. Margot and I had decided to put him in a spaceman's uniform, but without the Soviet insignia—let that be another of the book's hidden secrets. Katherine had her hair pulled back, an apron over her housedress. Behind them was a stylized version of the moon's pockmarked surface. *The Lunar Housewife* blazed in garish red across the top of the cover, and beneath it "by Sharon Lysander."

In the end I'd decided to go with a pen name. Francie and I had just settled in an apartment in Hoboken, where we could look across the Hudson at the city I'd once called home. I couldn't quite see Joe's building, but I knew where it was, and sometimes I stared for what felt like hours at that spot. I wondered if he knew where we were. I also wondered if Eli did, and if it was still possible for either of them to pull the plug on my novel. As Papa Hemingway would have put it, I was chickenshit. But at least it wasn't "Alfred King" or another man's name I'd have to hide behind. We'd even used an actual photo of me inside the back cover.

Francie pulled a book out first, and I let her gum along the edge of the pages. I reached for one as well and lifted it to my nose to sniff. It smelled better than anything I'd ever inhaled before, except perhaps Francie's neck just behind her earlobe. The cover felt flimsy, the pages prone to yellowing, but I didn't care. The book was just the right size to fit inside a pocketbook, or a nightstand drawer, or under a mattress.

Margot called me three weeks later to let me know that the first print run of ten thousand had sold out. "We're going into a second edition," she crowed. "Get out your champagne flutes!"

I collapsed onto the couch, shaking with relief. Champagne would have been nice. Paying our rent was more like it. I'd borrowed the money for our first few months' rent and security deposit from my mother, and I intended to pay it back.

A month later, Margot called with the news that the second and third print runs had also sold out. This time her voice was serious. "We're getting fan mail like you wouldn't believe. I don't even know what to do with all this. Can I have a truck take it over to you? Are you done with the next book yet?"

After that, I hired a nanny to take care of Francie while I wrote, four days a week. Most Fridays, my mother came to spend time with her, bringing lunch and just enough probing

questions about whether I'd ever marry to keep my gratitude for her help and my appreciation for our paid nanny in
balance.

When I needed a break from writing, I read fan mail. Most
of it was polite, complimentary—"I've read a good many
dime-store novels, but none kept me awake quite as many
hours as this one"—but occasionally there were notes from
disgruntled husbands, or shocked patriots, male and female.
"To even imagine the government could pull a stunt like this
on one of its citizens! You should be hanged as a traitor."

I put that one right in the dustbin. To even imagine,
indeed.

Most of the letters I couldn't keep. There simply wasn't
room. But a few stood out, and these I folded into a locked
wooden box I kept on the top shelf of my closet.

This one, for instance, which had been sent to the publisher's office with all the others:

Dear Miss Lysander,

*I hope you won't think I sound desperate when I tell you
I've been combing the shelves of women's romance titles for
months, looking for a book just like yours. I'll admit your
novel isn't normally my cup of tea, and I take issue with some
of the plot points you invent, especially the parts regarding the
U.S. government. But you have a beautiful imagination and
a keen wit. I should have given your work more of a chance
earlier, I see. I look forward to reading more from you in the
future.*

*I wanted in particular to commend the ending you gave to
Katherine and Sergey. It was gratifying—or, I should say,*

inspiring—to read his apology and then her acceptance. A heartwarming reconciliation. Their ending, which was truly a beginning, gave this humble reader hope that one day I might have such a beginning as well.

Yours,
Joe Martin

I read and reread his note a hundred times. The formal tone, the pretension that I was really a stranger named Sharon Lysander—was he being funny? Or did he think someone might be monitoring his mail? In any case, it seemed as if he wouldn't try to find me, at least not anytime soon; nor would he be alerting anyone else about my book. The letter felt like an apology, a peace offering. I could feel his longing, could read it in the sad slant of the script.

After I read it the first time, I wiped my face and went to the telephone. I wanted to call him and to let him see Francie. But then I remembered the way he'd destroyed the first version of this book he now claimed to respect. I remembered the way he'd refused to admit even the possibility that something sinister had happened to Harry. I remembered Bob, driving us home from the hospital. And I put the handset down.

In some ways—even though I could live on my own, and could afford to have someone else help with Francie—I found the author's life to be anticlimactic. My book may have been on the verge of becoming famous, or an underground version of famous, but I certainly wasn't. I walked around

Hoboken, and sometimes the city, staring at the faces of the girls I passed, wondering which of them had taken a peek inside my mind. Once I saw a beat-up copy of *The Lunar Housewife* forgotten on the counter in a women's restroom, beside the attendant's cluster of perfumes and soaps. The book's appearance there felt like a little sign: a reader had been there. But she and I were like ships passing in the night.

One day I boarded a train headed into the city at a little past eleven. I was on my way to meet Glenys for lunch, to try to patch up our friendship. We were meeting downtown, near the stock exchange, to avoid Joe.

The train's seats were mostly empty, but there was a girl sitting across from me in a belted pink dress. A bag of peanuts sat balanced in her lap, and she chewed them thoughtfully, one after another, as she read from a book perched high in her left hand.

It was *The Lunar Housewife*.

For a while, I watched her eyes dart over the pages, excitement coursing through my veins. Her copy had white creases on the spine. Was she rereading it? Had she gotten it from a friend? Margot said the book had been spreading by word of mouth, across a network of sly female readers. I wanted so badly to ask this girl what she thought of it, but every time I opened my mouth something seemed to happen: the lights in the train flickered off for a minute; a busker boarded and blasted a trumpet at us, its case open on the floor for tips, before hopping to the next car.

We were approaching the city. I cleared my throat.

"Excuse me, miss," I said. She didn't budge, so I reached over and tapped her knee with my gloved hand. "I'm sorry to disturb you, but—I wrote that book."

"Oh!" Her face lit up like a Christmas tree. She put the peanuts down on the seat beside her, then flipped to the last page of *The Lunar Housewife* so that she could see my picture. "Well I'll be! That *is* you!"

"It's me," I said, beaming. "What do you think of it?"

"Oh, gosh, I just love it. This is my second time reading, and I'm noticing so many things I didn't the first time around. The locked door—"

"What's this about?" The man beside her had appeared from behind his newspaper. I hadn't realized they were together, but I could tell now, by the way he reached over and plucked the book right out of her hand. "*The Lunar Housewife*, eh?" He chuckled. "You say you wrote this?"

"I did," I said, wishing he'd go away.

"What's it about?"

I clicked my tongue, ready to say something quick that would let me get back to talking to his girlfriend, but she beat me to it.

"It's a romance, dear. Silly stuff."

"Ah." He handed the book back to her. Quickly, she slid it into her purse. She reached for her peanuts. The train had arrived in the station now, to my disappointment; the announcer's voice blared over the loudspeaker. People were beginning to get up out of their seats.

The girl in pink caught my eye between two suits standing in the aisle. She perched on the edge of her seat, ready to stand, and she gave me a little smile, which I returned with a shrug. Just before her fellow took her by the arm to guide her out the doors, she looked back at me—and winked.

The Lunar Housewife is inspired by the true story of the CIA's use of American arts and letters as propaganda during the Cold War. The agency's mission was to convince foreign intellectuals that American culture had as much to offer as Soviet or Communist-leaning art did. Funneling government money through shadow organizations like the Congress for Cultural Freedom, the CIA provided funds, reprints in the agency's (secret) official publications, and overseas publicity for American artists, writers, and magazines from Ernest Hemingway to Jackson Pollock to *The Paris Review*. Some American artists had no idea they'd become bedfellows with the CIA, which they may have loathed. Yet others, like Peter Matthiessen of *The Paris Review*, were actually trained as spies, tasked with keeping tabs on their fellow writers.

In *The Lunar Housewife*, Joe's character is loosely based on Matthiessen; his partner, Harry, is a mash-up of Doc Humes and George Plimpton, also cofounders of *The Paris Review*. James Baldwin was edged out of an editorial role at the magazine; the confrontation between Joe and the fictional Baldwin in this book imagines why, in part, this might have happened. Plimpton, who spent years working on his Hemingway "Art of Fiction" interview, was rumored to have believed in a lost, unpublished Hemingway novel, which he searched for the rest of his life. This inspired the little trick Hemingway and Louise play on Joe at the end of this book.

Louise herself isn't based on any real-life figure in particular, though I did find inspiration for her lifestyle and ambitions in Anne Roiphe's memoir *Art and Madness*. Roiphe, an aspiring writer and single mother who lived on the Upper East Side of Manhattan, had an affair with Doc Humes in the early sixties. In her memoir, she mentions Humes's fear that the FBI had bugged his hotel suites, which she dismisses as paranoia, attributing this to his drug use. In actuality, Humes—who begged Plimpton in writing to come clean publicly about the magazine's connection to the CIA—may have been right.

ACKNOWLEDGMENTS

This book would never have come to fruition if it weren't for my agent, Shannon Hassan. Shannon, thank you for believing in me when I was ready to give up on myself. You have profoundly changed my life.

An enormous thank-you to my editor, Carolyn Williams, for your vision, kindness, good humor, and dynamite ideas. I'm so lucky to have found a friend and champion in you. Thank you also to the rest of my fabulous team at Doubleday: Rachel Molland, Lindsay Mandel, Kathleen Fridella, Mike Windsor, and Terry Zaroff-Evans.

Thank you to Andrea Kitamura, Lorie Kolak, Madeline Kotowicz, Lorel Meyer, and Steve Sanders for reading early drafts of this book and helping me bring Louise out of her shell. Thank you to my dad, Jim Woods, for your keen eyes.

My beloved Sheilas: Jordan Coriza, Joe Fazio, Kathleen Foster, Jill Maio, Jessica Ullian, Farley Urmston—thank you for helping me nurture this when it was only a baby book concept.

I have a lot of parents, and I owe them all a heap of gratitude for their love and support: Susan and Barry Niziolek, Jim Woods and Jane Crossan, and Julie and Jim Kerr. Special thanks to Mom, Barry, and Julie for stepping in to help me with the kids and saving me from a few more late nights while I wrote a book in a pandemic. It truly does take a village.

To my girls, Camille and Clare: thank you for going to bed on time when I was itching to write, and for being the best little friends a mommy could ask for. Camille, thank you for inspiring me to learn and write about the moon. Clare, I am so grateful you and I came through our scary introduction to each other safely, as Louise and Francie did. We are tough. I love you both so much.

Finally, thank you to Colin, the fella who still makes me go weak in the knees. You're the only one in the world I'd like to be cloistered on the moon with. Thank you for your unflagging belief in my writing career and your rock-solid dedication to our family. I love you.

Caroline Woods is the author of *Fräulein M*. She completed an M.F.A. in creative writing at Boston University, and has taught fiction writing at Loyola University Chicago, Boston University, and the Boston Conservatory. She lives near Chicago, Illinois, with her husband and two daughters.